Purr-colated Poison:
The Cozy Purrch Café Mysteries
Book 1

Erica J Whelton

Publisher: Sunseri Design Publishing
ISBN: 978-1-956069-49-5

Printed in the United States of America

To my cats Cash and June for all the inspiration

Table of Contents

Chapter One

The Tuesday morning light filtered through The Cozy Purrch's front windows, turning the dark wood floors honey-gold. I wiped down the counter for the third time, not because it needed it, but because my hands needed something to do. A year in Larkspur Valley and I still couldn't quite believe I'd stayed this long in one place.

"You're doing that thing again," Poppy said from her perch near the window, tail wrapped neatly around her paws. The calico's amber eyes tracked my movements with that unnerving intelligence that sometimes made me wonder if she knew more about me than I'd ever told anyone.

"What thing?" I tossed the rag into the small sink behind the counter.

"The nervous cleaning thing. It's Tuesday. Mabel will be here soon, same as every Tuesday, and she'll order the Lavender Dreams tea, same as every Tuesday, and you'll make it perfectly, same as every Tuesday."

"I don't know what you're talking about." But I stopped wiping and checked the pastry case instead. Flo had delivered fresh scones an hour ago: cranberry orange, blueberry lemon, and chocolate chip. The smell alone was enough to make my small café feel like home, or at least what I imagined home should smell like.

"You're a terrible liar," Gus grumbled from his cat bed near the fireplace. The elderly black and white cat cracked one eye open. "For a witch."

"Gus." I shot him a warning look, even though we were alone. Even though no one else could hear him. A year of relative safety hadn't quite erased the instinct to look over my shoulder.

"What? There's nobody here." He yawned, showing teeth that had seen better days. "And my joints hurt. This weather is murder on my arthritis."

"It's sixty-five degrees."

"Exactly. Too cold."

I smiled despite myself. Gus complained about everything: the temperature, the food, the other cats, the customers, the lack of customers. But he'd been the first one to curl up in my lap the day I'd opened the café, and sometimes I caught him watching me with something that looked almost like concern.

Rocky zoomed past, a streak of orange tabby chaos, and launched himself at one of the cat trees in the viewing room. The thud of his landing made me wince. Through the glass wall, I could see three other cats lounging on various perches: a gray and white long-hair grooming himself on a hammock, a sleek black cat watching birds through the window, and a tortoiseshell curled up on the highest platform.

"Does he have to do that?" Millie's voice was barely a whisper. The Siamese was tucked into her favorite hiding spot in the corner of the main café, behind a potted fern on a low bookshelf. Only her blue eyes were visible in the shadows. "It's so loud."

"He's young," I said, keeping my voice gentle. Millie had been with me for eight months, and she still startled at sudden movements. Whatever had happened to her before I'd found her shivering in that cardboard box had left scars I couldn't see. "He doesn't mean any harm."

"Nobody ever does," she murmured, and my chest tightened.

The bell above the door chimed, and I straightened automatically, smile in place, walls up. Then I saw who it was and felt something in me relax by a fraction.

"Good morning, dear." Hazel Blaine shuffled in, her cane tapping against the wooden floor. At seventy-eight, she moved slowly, but her dark eyes were sharp and kind. She wore a cardigan the color of spring lilacs over a floral dress, and her silver hair was pinned back in an old-fashioned style that somehow suited her perfectly.

"Morning, Hazel. The usual?" I was already reaching for the chamomile blend before she nodded.

"Please. And maybe one of those cranberry scones if you haven't sold out already."

I plated the scone and started the tea, watching as Poppy immediately hopped down from her perch and padded over to Hazel. The calico wound between Hazel's legs, purring loudly enough that I could hear it from behind the counter.

"Hello, sweet girl," Hazel murmured, bending carefully to stroke Poppy's head. Her fingers moved gently over the calico's ears, and Poppy leaned into the touch with obvious pleasure. After a long moment, Poppy gave Hazel's hand one more affectionate bump before returning to her window perch.

Hazel settled into her favorite table by the window, and I brought over her order. The chamomile blend was one of my most popular, but I'd made this one special, the way I always did for Hazel. A little extra lavender for calm, a touch of lemon balm for peace. My magic whispered through it without my quite meaning it to, responding to what I sensed she needed.

Hazel wrapped her hands around the cup and smiled. "You're looking thoughtful."

"Just thinking about how much has changed in a year." I set the teacup down carefully.

"Change can be good. You've built something wonderful here."

"I've built a cat café in a mountain town with a population of five thousand. Not exactly what anyone would call ambitious."

"Ambition isn't measured in numbers, dear." She took a sip and sighed contentedly. "It's measured in peace. And you seem more peaceful than when you first arrived."

I wanted to tell her she was wrong. I wanted to tell her I'd never be truly peaceful, that I was always waiting for the other shoe to drop, for the knock on the door in the middle of the night. Instead, I shrugged. "The cats help."

"I'm sure they do." Her eyes crinkled at the corners. "You have a gift with them."

Something in her tone made me look at her more closely, but her expression was serene as she broke off a piece of scone. If she suspected anything about me, she'd never said. And I'd never asked.

The bell chimed again, and Mabel Smalls walked in with the precision of someone who'd been keeping the same schedule for forty years. Eighty-three years old and sharp as the mountain peaks surrounding our town, she wore a navy pantsuit and sensible shoes.

"Tuesday," Poppy announced unnecessarily from her perch.

"Good morning, Mabel." I was already preparing her Lavender Dreams tea.

"Alexis." She nodded approvingly. "Punctual as always."

"Wouldn't have it any other way."

She settled at her usual table, two over from Hazel's, and pulled out a crossword puzzle book. The two women exchanged pleasantries about the weather and the upcoming Founder's Day celebration while I worked. This was my favorite part of the morning, when the café held just a handful of regulars and everything felt manageable, contained.

The next hour brought a steady trickle of customers. Felix Wren, the local artist, ordered a Ginger Spark and spent twenty minutes staring at the mountain view through the window, probably composing a landscape in his mind. Pearl Van brought her book club friends in, all of them cooing over the cats in the viewing room.

"That one's nervous," a quiet voice said from the viewing room. I glanced over to see the sleek black cat, Obsidian, watching Pearl's group intently. He was one of the newer rescues, only been with me three weeks, but he'd already proven himself observant in that unsettling way some cats had.

"Which one?" I asked quietly, knowing none of the customers could hear our conversation.

"The tall woman with the pearl necklace. She keeps looking at the door like she's expecting someone. Or afraid someone will walk in." His tail twitched. "Her heart's beating too fast. I can hear it from here."

I studied the woman he meant. Taller than the others, maybe late fifties, wearing what looked like expensive clothes that didn't quite match Larkspur Valley's casual mountain town aesthetic. Her fingers kept touching her necklace, a nervous gesture that Obsidian was right to notice.

"Probably just not used to cats," I said.

"Maybe." But Obsidian didn't sound convinced. "Or maybe she's got secrets. Humans with secrets always smell different. Sharp, like fear and something bitter."

I wanted to tell him he was being dramatic, but I knew better. Cats could sense things humans worked hard to hide. It was part of what made them such perfect companions for someone like me.

I made drinks, chatted just enough to seem friendly, and deflected every personal question with practiced ease. At exactly 8:15, Sheriff Iris Scott walked through the door.

"Black coffee," she said, not quite making it a question.

"Coming right up." I poured from the French press I'd started at 8:10, knowing her schedule as well as I knew my own. Iris was nothing if not predictable, which I'd learned was both a blessing and a complication. She noticed things. Remembered things. And she had absolutely no patience for anything she perceived as interference in her job.

She was younger than I'd expected when I first met her, probably mid-thirties, with dark hair pulled back in a practical ponytail and eyes that catalogued everything. Today she wore her crisp uniform and the kind of expression that said she'd already dealt with three problems before breakfast.

"Busy morning?" I asked, sliding the coffee across the counter.

"Cordelia Kelder's convinced someone's stealing yarn from her shop." Iris took a long sip and sighed. "It's been three balls of yarn over two months. I tried to explain that's not exactly a crime wave, but you know Cordelia."

"She does love to talk."

"That's one way to put it." Iris's lips twitched, almost smiling. Then her radio crackled and her expression shuttered back to professional. "Thanks for the coffee."

She was gone before I could respond, and I found myself oddly disappointed. In another life, maybe we could have been friends. But friends asked questions, and I couldn't afford answers.

"She likes you," Poppy observed.

"She tolerates me."

"Same thing for her."

The morning rush picked up after Iris left. Cordelia Kelder herself came in, still muttering about her yarn theft, and spent fifteen minutes describing her theories while I made her a Rosehip Radiance tea. According to her, it was either teenagers pulling pranks or a rival shop owner trying to sabotage her business. The fact that the rival shop was thirty miles away in Boulder didn't seem to factor into her logic.

"You should tell the sheriff to dust for fingerprints," Cordelia said seriously. "They do that on TV. Fingerprints and DNA."

"For three balls of yarn," I said, keeping my voice carefully neutral.

"Crime is crime, Alexis." She sniffed. "Today it's yarn, tomorrow it could be something worse. That's how these things escalate."

Atticus Monroe came in while Cordelia was still theorizing, and I caught the flicker of amusement in his eyes before he schooled his expression to polite interest. The park ranger was quiet most of the time, content to listen while others talked, which made him one of my favorite customers. He ordered his usual black coffee and claimed a corner table, pulling out a trail map he'd been updating.

"Morning, Atticus," Cordelia called over. "You should talk to Iris about increasing patrols. With all this theft happening."

"I'll mention it," he said diplomatically, though we both knew he wouldn't.

After Cordelia finally left, still convinced of an impending crime wave, I caught Atticus's eye, and he gave me a small smile. "You're patient with her."

"She means well."

"She does. Still exhausting, though." He took a sip of coffee and returned to his map, and I appreciated the comfortable silence that followed.

Jasper came back in around eight forty-five, having forgotten his travel mug on the counter. "Getting forgetful in my old age," he said with a self-deprecating laugh. He was only fifty-three, hardly old, but he'd been running the general store since his early twenties and sometimes moved like someone much older.

"Long hours catching up with you?" I asked, handing him the mug.

"Something like that. Inventory season. Never ends." He paused, then added, "You doing okay? You look tired."

The observation caught me off guard. I'd thought I was hiding it better. "Just didn't sleep well."

"Well, don't work yourself too hard. This place runs because of you." He tipped an imaginary hat and headed out, and I stood there feeling oddly seen in a way that made me want to hide.

Lionel came in at nine, same as always, and my traitorous heart did a small, stupid flutter. He was tall and lanky, with strawberry blonde hair that looked like he'd forgotten to comb it and freckles across his nose that made him look younger than his forty-six years.

Today he wore a graphic t-shirt with some superhero I didn't recognize and a smile that was entirely too warm.

"Morning, Alexis." He leaned against the counter with the easy comfort of someone who'd never learned to guard himself. "How's the best coffee in Larkspur Valley?"

"Flattery will get you a normal-sized portion," I said, already preparing his usual Dandelion Root Revival.

"Darn. I was hoping for extra large." His green eyes crinkled at the corners. "Hey, I'm doing a game night at the shop on Friday. Just some tabletop stuff, pretty casual. You should come."

I'd heard this invitation at least a dozen times in various forms. "I'm not really a game person."

"You don't have to play. You could just... hang out. Meet some people." He said it lightly, but I caught the concern underneath. Lionel worried about me, which would have been sweet if it wasn't so dangerous for both of us.

"I'll think about it," I lied, handing him his drink.

"I'll take that as progress." He grinned and dropped a generous tip in the jar. "Same time tomorrow?"

"Wouldn't miss it."

He waved at the cats in the viewing room, and I watched Rocky and even Gus perk up at his attention. Even Millie peeked out from behind her fern. The cats loved him, which should have told me something.

"You should say yes," Poppy said once he was gone.

"To what?"

"Don't play dumb. The game night. The man clearly adores you."

"He's a customer."

"He's a good human," Gus said from his bed. "Even if he does smell like old paper and ink. Not that I care. My opinion wasn't asked."

"I didn't ask," I agreed.

"See? No respect." But he settled back with a satisfied huff.

Flo bustled in around ten-thirty with another box of pastries, because apparently the first delivery hadn't been enough. "I made lemon bars," she announced. "Thought you might want some for the afternoon crowd."

"You didn't have to do that."

"Nonsense. We're neighbors." She set the box down and looked at me with that expression I'd come to recognize: the one that said she thought we were closer than we actually were. "You're coming to Sunday dinner, aren't you? The girls have been asking about you."

Eva and Ella, her granddaughters. Sweet kids who visited the café regularly to draw pictures of the cats. Ella had once told me I "sparkled happiness," which had made me deeply uncomfortable for reasons I couldn't explain to a six-year-old.

"I'm not sure I can make it," I said carefully.

"You said that last time." Flo's smile didn't quite waver, but something in her eyes did. "My door's always open, you know that."

"I know. I appreciate it." I did appreciate it, in theory. In practice, accepting meant letting her in, and I'd learned the hard way that letting people in meant eventually having to explain why you left.

She stayed for another ten minutes, chatting about her family and the diner and Cordelia's yarn conspiracy theory, and I listened and nodded and volunteered exactly nothing about myself. When she finally left, I felt the familiar mix of guilt and relief.

"You could have said yes," Hazel said quietly. She'd been so still at her table that I'd almost forgotten she was there. "Florence means well."

"I know she does."

"But you're not ready." It wasn't a question. Hazel gathered her things slowly, using the table for support as she stood. "That's all right, dear. Take your time. The good ones will wait."

Something in her voice made my throat tight. "Hazel..."

"Hmm?"

I wanted to say so many things. Thank you for being patient. Thank you for not pushing. Thank you for seeing me even when I'm trying to be invisible. Instead, I just said, "You're still coming for dinner tonight, right?"

Her face lit up. "Of course. Seven o'clock?"

"Perfect. I'll make that pasta dish you like."

"The one with the garlic and mushrooms?"

"That's the one."

She smiled, and it reached all the way to her eyes. "I'll bring wine. Something red."

I watched her make her way slowly out of the café, tapping her cane against the sidewalk as she headed toward her flower shop two doors down. We'd fallen into this routine over the past few months: dinner once a week, usually at my place since the stairs to her apartment above the flower shop were steeper than mine. It was the closest thing I had to family in Larkspur Valley, even if I kept most of my walls firmly in place.

"She knows," Poppy said softly.

"Knows what?"

"What you are. What you're running from. Maybe not the details, but she knows."

My hands stilled on the cup I was washing. "That's impossible."

"Is it?" Poppy's tail swished once. "She's never pushed you for answers. Never asked questions. Almost like she's waiting for you to be ready to tell her."

I wanted to argue, but something in me recognized the truth of it. Hazel had always been different. Patient in a way that suggested she understood more than she should.

The rest of the day passed in its usual rhythm. Customers came and went, the cats charmed and entertained, and I made drinks that did exactly what people needed them to do, even if they didn't know they needed it. By six o'clock, I flipped the sign to closed and started my end-of-day routine: wiping down tables, restocking for tomorrow, counting the register.

At six-thirty, I climbed the stairs to my apartment with Poppy, Gus, Rocky, and Millie trailing behind me. The space was modest but cozy: open concept with the kitchen, dining area, and living room flowing together, one bedroom off to the side, and plants scattered throughout. A small door in the living room led to a narrow balcony that overlooked the alley between my building and Hazel's flower shop.

I started dinner preparations, chopping garlic and mushrooms while the cats settled into their various favorite spots. Rocky immediately claimed the sunny patch on the living room floor. Gus arranged himself on the couch with a long-suffering sigh. Millie disappeared into the bedroom. And Poppy stationed herself on the back of the couch near the balcony door, where she could watch both me and the world outside.

At seven o'clock sharp, there was a knock at my door. I opened it to find Hazel holding a bottle of red wine and wearing a different cardigan, this one the color of autumn leaves.

"Right on time," I said, stepping aside to let her in.

"Old habits." She made her way to the small dining table, setting down the wine with a pleased sigh. "Something smells wonderful."

"It's almost ready. Make yourself comfortable."

We fell into easy conversation as I finished cooking, the kind of comfortable silence punctuated by small observations about the day. Hazel told me about a difficult customer at the flower shop who'd wanted roses but insisted they were the wrong shade of red. I told her about Cordelia's yarn theft conspiracy and Iris's exasperation. We carefully avoided anything too deep, too personal, but the warmth was real.

Over pasta and wine, Hazel asked about the café's anniversary coming up next month. "A year already. Time really does fly."

"Sometimes too fast," I said, twirling pasta on my fork. "Sometimes not fast enough."

She gave me one of those looks, the kind that saw straight through my deflections. "You're allowed to be happy here, you know. Whatever you're running from, you're allowed to stop and catch your breath."

My throat tightened. "Hazel..."

"You don't have to tell me." She reached across the table and squeezed my hand briefly. "I just want you to know that you're not as alone as you think you are. And this town, this life you've built, it's worth holding onto."

I blinked back the sudden sting in my eyes. "Thank you."

"Now." She pulled her hand back and picked up her wine glass with a smile. "Tell me about that young man who comes in every morning. The one who owns the comic shop."

"Lionel?" I felt my cheeks warm. "There's nothing to tell."

"Mm-hmm." Her eyes twinkled. "That's what I thought."

"He seems like a good man," Hazel continued, swirling her wine thoughtfully. "Patient. Kind. The type who'd wait for someone who needed time."

"You're reading too much into it."

"Am I?" She took another sip. "I've lived in this town for forty-eight years, dear. Seen a lot of people come and go. Some are just passing through, never really land anywhere. Others are running so hard they don't notice when they've found a place to stop."

My hand stilled on my wine glass. "And which one am I?"

"I think you're someone who's been running so long, you've forgotten what it feels like to stand still." Her voice was gentle, not accusatory. "But you're starting to remember. I see it in the way you talk to the cats, the way you arrange the flowers I bring you. The way you're letting Larkspur Valley become home even if you won't admit it yet."

I wanted to deny it, but something in my throat had closed up. "It's complicated."

"It always is." Hazel reached for another piece of bread, moving with the careful deliberation of someone whose body didn't always cooperate anymore. "I had a friend once. Wonderful woman. She showed up in Larkspur Valley about thirty years ago, middle of winter, with nothing but a suitcase and determination. Wouldn't talk about where she'd come from, what she was leaving behind. Just wanted a fresh start."

"What happened to her?"

"She stayed. Opened a bookshop. Made friends, slowly, on her own terms. Met a man who was patient enough to wait while she figured out she was allowed to be happy." Hazel's eyes were distant, caught in memory. "They had ten good years together before he passed. Heart attack, sudden thing. And she told me once that she'd almost left, right at the beginning. Almost ran before anyone could get close. Said she was glad she'd stayed."

"Is she still here?"

"Passed away five years ago. Cancer." Hazel's expression softened with old grief. "But she lived those thirty years fully. Let herself belong somewhere. That's not nothing."

I turned my wine glass, watching the liquid catch the light. "What if the past catches up? What if staying puts other people at risk?"

"Then you deal with it when it comes. But spending your whole life running from maybes and what-ifs?" She shook her head. "That's not living. That's just surviving. And you deserve better than that."

"I'm not sure I do."

"Well, I am." Her voice was firm. "And I'm old enough and stubborn enough that my opinion counts for something."

That startled a laugh out of me. "You're not that old."

"I'm seventy-eight, dear. That's plenty old." But she was smiling. "Old enough to recognize someone worth knowing when I see them. Old enough to be patient while they figure themselves out. And old enough to tell you that whatever you're afraid of, you're stronger than you think."

"You don't know what I'm afraid of."

"Don't I?" Something flickered in her expression, there and gone too quickly to read. "I may not know the details. But fear has a particular look, and I've seen it in you since the day we met. The kind of fear that comes from experience, not imagination."

My pulse kicked up. "Hazel..."

"You don't have to tell me," she said quickly. "I'm not asking for your secrets. I'm just saying that whatever they are, they don't make you less deserving of happiness. They don't make you less worthy of connection." She reached across the table again, her hand wrinkled and warm over mine. "And when you're ready to trust someone with the truth, I hope you'll know that you can."

I couldn't speak. Could only nod while something in my chest cracked open just slightly.

"Now," Hazel said briskly, pulling her hand back and picking up her wine glass. "Tell me about this anniversary celebration you're planning. Or not planning, knowing you."

I laughed, grateful for the subject change, and let her steer us toward safer waters. But something had shifted between us. Some acknowledgment that she saw more than I'd realized, understood more than I'd shown. And instead of terrifying me, it felt almost like relief.

We talked for another hour, and for once I let myself relax into it. Let myself imagine, just for a moment, that this could be enough. That I could have this small, simple life without the past catching up.

Hazel left around nine, insisting she could manage the stairs on her own despite my offer to walk her down. "I've been navigating those stairs for twenty years, dear. I think I can manage them one more night."

I watched from my doorway as she made her way carefully down the stairs and out onto Main Street. She waved once before disappearing around the corner toward her shop entrance.

I cleaned up the dinner dishes, changed into comfortable clothes, and settled onto the couch with a book I'd been meaning to read for weeks. The cats arranged themselves around me: Gus on the other end of the couch, Rocky sprawled on the floor, Millie appearing from the bedroom to curl up in the armchair. Poppy remained on the back of the couch by the balcony door, her usual evening post.

By eleven, my eyes were heavy and the words on the page had stopped making sense. I gave up, said goodnight to the cats, and headed to bed. Within minutes of my head hitting the pillow, I was asleep.

I don't know how long I'd been out when something landed on my chest, knocking the wind out of me.

"Wake up!" Rocky's voice was frantic. "Wake up now!"

I jolted awake, disoriented, my heart hammering. Rocky's face was inches from mine, his pupils blown wide. Behind him, I could see the other three cats crowded in my bedroom doorway.

"What? What's wrong?"

"The alley," Poppy said, and her voice had an edge I'd never heard before. "Hazel. Someone was with her. They were arguing."

I was already moving, throwing off the covers, my bare feet hitting the cold floor. "Where is she now?"

"She fell," Gus said quietly. "We saw her fall. The other person ran."

I grabbed my phone from the nightstand and ran, the cats streaming ahead of me. Down the stairs, through the dark café, out onto Main Street. The night air bit through my thin sleep shirt, but I barely felt it.

The alley was narrow, barely wide enough for a delivery truck, and shadowed by the buildings on either side. The single light above the back entrance to the flower shop cast everything in harsh relief.

I saw the shape on the ground before my eyes could fully make sense of it. Too still. Too crumpled.

"Hazel." Her name came out broken.

I dropped to my knees beside her, hands shaking as I reached for her neck, searching for a pulse I already knew I wouldn't find. Her skin was cool, her eyes closed. She looked like she'd fallen, one arm bent at an odd angle, her cane a few feet away. There was blood near her temple where her head had struck the pavement.

"Who?" My voice didn't sound like mine. "Who was she arguing with?"

"Couldn't see clearly," Poppy said, and I could hear the frustration in her voice. "Medium height, medium build. A woman, I think. They were standing close, angry voices."

"Hazel said something," Gus added quietly. "Said, 'You're making a terrible mistake.' Then she fell, and the person ran. Toward the back street, through the alley."

"I tried to see better," Rocky said, and he sounded smaller than I'd ever heard him. "But it was too dark. I'm sorry."

"We were on the balcony," Poppy said, her voice steadier than Rocky's but still shaken. "All four of us. It was late, maybe twenty minutes after you went to bed. We heard voices below. Loud voices."

"I thought it was teenagers at first," Gus added. "We get them sometimes, cutting through the alley. But then I recognized Hazel's voice. She sounded upset."

"The other person was angry," Millie whispered. "Scared angry, not just mad angry. Like cornered animal angry."

"What were they saying?" I asked, even though I knew every detail would matter, even though I wanted to not hear it.

"Couldn't make out most of it," Poppy said. "The words were too muffled, too fast. But Hazel said something like 'you don't understand' and the other person said 'I understand perfectly.' Then Hazel said the thing about the terrible mistake."

"And then she was falling," Rocky's voice cracked. "She was standing and then she wasn't. She hit the ground and the other person just stood there for a second. Just stood there looking at her."

"How long?" My throat was so tight it hurt.

"Three heartbeats," Gus said with the precision of someone who'd counted. "Three heartbeats and then they ran. Fast. Toward the back of the alley where it meets Willow Street."

"Did they take anything? Touch her? Anything else?"

"No," Poppy said. "Just stood there, three heartbeats, then ran. But..." She hesitated.

"What?"

"The person smelled like flowers. Strong flowers, artificial. Like the perfume some humans wear. I could smell it even from the balcony."

My mind catalogued that detail, filed it away. Perfume. A woman, probably. Medium build, medium height, artificial flower scent. It wasn't much. But it was all we had.

My phone was in my hand before I consciously decided to call. My fingers felt numb as I dialed.

"911, what's your emergency?"

"I need..." I swallowed hard, forcing the words out. "I need to report a death. Hazel Blaine. In the alley behind the flower shop on Main Street. I think... it looks like she fell."

But even as I said it, even as the dispatcher's calm voice asked me questions and told me to stay on the line, something in me knew it wasn't that simple. Hazel's words echoed in my head, relayed through my cats: You're making a terrible mistake.

I sat on the cold pavement, one hand hovering over Hazel's still form, and waited for the sirens.

The woman who'd welcomed me to Larkspur Valley was gone.

And the worst part was, I'd never gotten the chance to tell her the truth.

Chapter Two

The sirens came faster than I expected. Red and blue lights splashed across the alley walls, turning everything garish and unreal. I stayed where I was, kneeling on the cold pavement beside Hazel, one hand still hovering uselessly over her still form.

The cats had retreated to the shadows near my building's back door. Smart. The last thing I needed was questions about why four cats were loose in the alley in the middle of the night.

Sheriff Iris Scott was the first one through, her ponytail slightly askew like she'd been pulled from sleep. Behind her came a deputy I recognized from the café, a younger man with nervous energy, and finally someone carrying a medical bag.

"Alexis." Iris's voice was professionally neutral, but her eyes were sharp as they took in the scene. "Step back, please."

I moved on autopilot, my legs stiff from kneeling on pavement. The person with the medical bag, a woman with steel-gray hair and steady hands, knelt where I'd been moments before.

"Dr. Temperance Vex," Iris said, though whether it was for my benefit or just filling the silence, I wasn't sure. "County medical examiner."

Dr. Vex worked quickly and efficiently, checking for vital signs we all knew she wouldn't find, examining Hazel's head wound with gentle, practiced movements. I wrapped my arms around myself, suddenly aware that I was standing in an alley in the middle of October wearing only a sleep shirt and thin pajama pants.

"Dispatch said you called it in," Iris said, pulling out a small notebook. The deputy, whose name I thought might be Garrick, was already stringing yellow tape across the alley entrance. "What time did you find her?"

I pulled my phone from my pocket with shaking hands. "I called at 11:47. So maybe a minute or two before that?"

"And what brought you down here at that hour?"

This was it. The moment where I had to be careful. "The cats woke me. They were acting strange, agitated. I followed them to the balcony and saw..." I gestured helplessly toward Hazel. "I saw her lying here."

"The balcony." Iris's eyes flicked upward to where my small balcony overlooked the alley. "You saw her from up there?"

"Yes. I came down immediately and called 911."

"Did you see anyone else? Hear anything?"

I shook my head, hating the lie but knowing I had no choice. What could I say? My cats told me someone was arguing with her? My cats witnessed a murder? "Just Hazel. I didn't see anyone else."

"Head trauma consistent with a fall," Dr. Vex said, still examining Hazel. "Looks like she hit the pavement here." She gestured to the spot where blood had pooled. "But I'll know more after the autopsy."

Autopsy. The word made it all feel horribly final.

"When did you last see Mrs. Blaine?" Iris asked, her pen poised over her notebook.

"Tonight. She came over for dinner around seven. Left around nine." My voice sounded distant to my own ears. "She said she could manage the stairs to her apartment on her own."

"So, she lives above the flower shop." Iris made a note. "Was she in good spirits? Any health concerns you knew about?"

"She seemed fine. Happy." The memory of her smile, of her teasing me about Lionel, made my throat tight. "We talked about the café's anniversary coming up. She brought wine."

"Anyone have a problem with her that you know of? Arguments with neighbors, disputes at her shop?"

"No. Everyone loved Hazel." The words came out harder than I meant them to. "She was kind. She welcomed everyone."

Iris studied me for a long moment, and I forced myself to meet her gaze. I had nothing to hide. Except everything.

"Deputy Thorne," Iris said, turning to the younger man. "I want you to check the flower shop entrance, see if there's any sign of forced entry. And walk the alley, look for anything that seems out of place."

"Yes, ma'am." He hurried off, flashlight beam cutting through the darkness.

Dr. Vex stood, her knees cracking softly. "I'll need to transport the body. Given her age and the nature of the fall, this looks straightforward, but I'll run a full tox screen and workup."

"Appreciated." Iris finally looked away from me, giving Dr. Vex a nod. Then she turned back, and something in her expression had shifted. Not quite suspicion but not quite trust either. "Alexis, I'm going to need you to come down to the station tomorrow. Just to give a formal statement."

"Of course."

"And I'll need access to your apartment. To see the angle from your balcony, understand the sightlines."

My heart kicked, but I kept my face neutral. There was nothing incriminating in my apartment. Just plants and cat furniture and a carefully curated life that revealed absolutely nothing. "That's fine. Whenever you need."

Movement in the shadows caught my eye. Poppy had emerged slightly, just enough that I could see her amber eyes reflecting the harsh lights. She looked at me, and I knew what she was thinking. We saw who did this. We can help. But we can't.

"Sheriff?" Deputy Thorne called from the far end of the alley. "I've got something."

We all moved toward him, Dr. Vex staying with Hazel. Thorne was crouched near a dumpster, his flashlight aimed at something on the ground.

"Looks like someone was in a hurry." He stood, holding up an evidence bag. Inside was a button, dark colored, expensive looking. "Found it caught on the corner here. And there are scuff marks, like someone was running."

Iris took the bag, examining it in the light. "Bag it and tag it. And photograph those marks."

"Could just be from someone taking out trash," I said, then immediately regretted it. Iris's eyes cut to me.

"Could be," she agreed. "But right now, I'm collecting everything."

Deputy Thorne continued his methodical sweep of the alley, his flashlight beam moving slowly across the pavement. I watched from where Iris had positioned me, out of the way but still visible. Everything they did, every piece of evidence they collected, felt both desperately important and utterly useless. What good was a button when I knew things they'd never believe?

"Sheriff, there's more scuff marks here," Thorne called from near the back street entrance. "Fresh. Like someone came through fast, turned the corner hard."

Iris moved to examine them, her movements precise and professional. She crouched down, studying the marks without touching them. "Photograph these. And the trajectory. I want to know which direction they were heading."

"Toward Willow Street," Thorne said, already pulling out his camera. "Away from Main."

Away from witnesses. Away from the café. Toward the residential streets where someone could disappear into the night. My stomach twisted. The cats had said the same thing. Toward the back street. Running.

Dr. Vex approached Iris with a small evidence bag. "Found this near the body. Caught in her cardigan." She held it up to the light. A few strands of dark fiber, maybe from clothing. "Could be from her own clothes, or from whoever she was with."

"Bag it," Iris said. "We'll need to compare it to what she was wearing."

I wanted to tell them it wasn't from Hazel's clothes. Hazel had been wearing lilac and autumn leaves, spring colors and fall warmth. Those fibers looked dark, almost black. But how could I know that without revealing I'd been closer than I claimed?

"Alexis." Iris's voice made me jump. "You said she left around nine. Did you notice what she was wearing? The cardigan color?"

My heart hammered. This I could answer. "The autumn one. Rust colored, like leaves. She changed from the lilac one she'd worn earlier."

Iris made a note, glanced at the fibers Dr. Vex held. Something shifted in her expression. "Thank you. That's helpful."

Thorne had moved to the flower shop's back entrance, testing the door. "Locked. No signs of forced entry. And the security light is working." He gestured to the single bulb above the door. "She would have been visible to anyone passing by."

"Unless it happened fast," Iris said quietly. Almost to herself. "Unless whoever it was knew her. Knew her routines."

I watched her piece it together, watched her sharp mind work through the possibilities. She was good at this. Maybe good enough to figure it out without my help. But maybe not fast enough. The killer had hours, maybe days, to cover their tracks before Iris realized this wasn't an accident.

"There's no blood trail," Dr. Vex observed, moving around Hazel's body with careful steps. "No signs she tried to catch herself, no defensive wounds on her hands. Either it happened very quickly, or she was already disoriented when she fell."

Already disoriented. I filed that away. The cats had said Hazel sounded upset but not confused. Not sick. Upset like someone arguing, someone trying to reason with another person.

A van pulled up at the end of the alley, and two more people in medical examiner jackets got out. Dr. Vex directed them with calm efficiency, and I watched as they prepared to move Hazel.

"You should go inside," Iris said, and for the first time her voice held something that might have been kindness. "Get warm. I'll come by in the morning to look at that balcony."

"Okay." But I didn't move, couldn't seem to make my legs work. Hazel had been alive four hours ago. Laughing over pasta and wine. Telling me I was allowed to be happy.

"Alexis." Iris touched my arm briefly. "Go inside."

This time I listened. The cats materialized from the shadows and followed me back through the café and up the stairs. None of them spoke until we were safely in my apartment with the door closed.

"We should have seen more," Rocky said, his voice small and miserable. "I should have jumped down, chased whoever it was."

"You did everything right," I said, sinking onto the couch. My legs were shaking. "If you'd chased them, you could have been hurt."

"But we could have helped," Rocky insisted, his young voice breaking. "I could have gotten closer. I'm fast. I could have seen their face."

"And then what?" Poppy said, more sharply than usual. "You're a cat, Rocky. What would you have done? Attacked someone twice your size? You'd be dead too."

The words hung in the air, brutal and true. Rocky made a small, wounded sound and pressed himself flatter against the floor.

"Poppy," I said quietly.

"I'm sorry." She moved closer to Rocky, touching her nose to his head in apology. "I'm sorry. I'm scared too. I've never seen someone die before. Never seen anyone hurt like that."

"It was so fast," Millie whispered from behind the couch. I could barely see her, just the gleam of her blue eyes in the shadows. "One second Hazel was standing there, talking, and then she was on the ground, and everything was wrong. Everything smelled wrong."

"Wrong how?" I asked, trying to focus through my own grief.

"Like fear. Like pain. And that flower smell, so strong it made my nose hurt." Millie's voice wavered. "I wanted to help her. But I was too scared to move. I'm always too scared."

"That's not true," I said gently. "You ran to wake me up. You came downstairs with the others. That took courage."

"I hid behind the dumpster the whole time you were down there."

"You were smart. You stayed safe while still being there for her." I looked at all four of them, these cats who'd witnessed something horrible and were trying to process it with me. "You all did exactly what you should have done. You watched. You remembered details. You told me. That's everything."

"But it's not enough," Rocky said again, though quieter now.

"Maybe not yet," Gus said, finally speaking. He'd been silent since we came upstairs, unusual for him. "But it's what we have. We know it was a woman, medium build, medium height. We know she wore strong flower perfume. We know she argued with Hazel and then Hazel fell and the woman ran. That's more than the sheriff knows right now."

"We also know Hazel wasn't afraid at first," Poppy added slowly, as if working through it. "When we first heard voices, Hazel sounded upset but not scared. Like she knew the person. Like she was trying to reason with them."

"You don't reason with strangers in dark alleys," Gus agreed. "You run. Or scream. Hazel did neither. She knew whoever killed her."

The word 'killed' made it real in a new way. Not just death. Not just a fall. Someone had killed Hazel deliberately, and she'd known them well enough to try talking to them instead of running.

"Three suspects," I said, mostly to myself. "Medium height, medium build," I said, mostly to myself. "That describes a lot of people."

"But not just anyone," Gus said firmly. "Someone Hazel knew. Someone she trusted enough to meet in an alley at night. And someone who wore that perfume." He settled into a more comfortable position, wincing as his joints protested. "That perfume was strong enough that it'll be on her clothes, in her hair. Even if she washes, it'll take days to fade completely. Cats remember scents. It's what we do."

I looked at him, this grumpy old cat who complained about everything but had just offered me the closest thing I had to evidence. "You're sure?"

"I'm sure. Get me close enough to smell her, whoever she is, and I'll know. I'll know if she was in that alley." His old eyes met mine, steady and certain. "My nose might be old, but it's reliable."

"So we need to find her first," Poppy said slowly. "Figure out who Hazel knew, who might have wanted her dead. Then get Gus close enough to confirm it."

"And then what?" Millie asked. "Even if Gus knows, Alexis can't tell the sheriff. 'My cat identified the killer by smell' isn't evidence."

She was right. But it was a start. If I knew who did it, I could find other proof. Real proof. The kind that would hold up without revealing what I was.

"One step at a time," I said. "First, we figure out who might have done this. Then we find the evidence to prove it."

Gus limped over and settled next to Rocky, which was about as close to comfort as the old cat ever got. "The sheriff is good at her job. She'll figure it out eventually. We're just going to help her figure it out faster."

"Will she?" Millie whispered from her hiding spot behind the couch. "Without us being able to tell her what we saw?"

That was the question, wasn't it? I leaned my head back against the couch cushions and closed my eyes. Behind my eyelids, I kept seeing Hazel's face across the dinner table, warm and alive and real.

"I don't know," I admitted. "But we have to try."

"How?" Poppy asked. "You can't tell the sheriff that we witnessed it. She'll think you're crazy, or worse, she'll start asking questions about how you know."

"I'll figure something out." I had to. For Hazel.

The apartment felt too quiet, too empty. Even Hugh's television next door was silent, which was unusual. My eighty-year-old neighbor was an early riser, and by six a.m. most mornings, I could hear the muffled sound of his TV through the wall. He couldn't hear well, so the volume was always up. I'd grown used to it over the past year, even found it oddly comforting. But now, at almost five in the morning, with Hugh still asleep and the usual sounds of his presence absent, the silence was deafening.

Someone had argued with Hazel in that alley. Someone had made her fall, or pushed her, and then ran away. The cats had seen it happen, but I couldn't use their testimony. I couldn't tell Iris that I'd heard Hazel say "You're making a terrible mistake" because I hadn't heard it myself.

I was going to have to solve this the hard way. Without magic. Without revealing what I was.

"We'll help," Poppy said, reading my thoughts the way she so often did. "We'll listen. We'll watch. We'll find out who did this."

"It's too dangerous."

"So was coming to Larkspur Valley in the first place." She held my gaze. "So was opening a café. So was letting Hazel become your friend. You've been hiding for so long, but Hazel was worth the risk. And finding her killer is worth it too."

My throat was too tight to answer, so I just nodded.

We stayed up until dawn, the five of us, watching the sky slowly lighten over the mountains. Somewhere out there was someone who'd taken Hazel from this world. Someone who thought they'd gotten away with it.

They were wrong.

I might not be able to use magic. I might not be able to tell anyone what my cats had witnessed. But I was going to find out the truth.

For Hazel. For the woman who'd welcomed me to Larkspur Valley without asking for anything in return. The woman who'd known

I was hiding something and had never pushed. The woman who'd told me I deserved to be happy just hours before someone killed her.

At seven-thirty, there was a knock at my door. I wasn't surprised to find Iris standing there, looking like she hadn't slept either.

"Ready?" she asked.

"Let me grab my keys."

She followed me through the apartment to the balcony door. I opened it and we stepped out into the cool morning air. The alley below was empty now, the yellow tape the only evidence that anything had happened.

Iris leaned over the railing, studying the sightlines. "You can see the whole alley from here."

"Yes."

"And last night, you said you saw Hazel but no one else."

"That's right." The lie tasted bitter.

She was quiet for a long moment, her eyes scanning the alley, the buildings, calculating distances and angles. Finally, she turned to me. "Must have been terrible. Seeing your friend like that."

"It was."

"You were close?"

"As close as I let anyone get." The honesty surprised me, but maybe I owed Hazel that much truth.

Something shifted in Iris's expression, though I couldn't quite read it. "I'm sorry for your loss. Hazel was a good person."

"Thank you."

We stood there in silence, two women looking down at the place where another woman had died. Iris didn't know what I knew. Didn't know that Hazel had been murdered. Didn't know that somewhere in Larkspur Valley was a killer who thought they'd committed the perfect crime.

But I knew. And somehow, I was going to prove it.

Even if it meant risking everything I'd spent the last year trying to protect.

Chapter Three

I unlocked the front door of The Cozy Purrch at eight o'clock exactly, muscle memory overriding the fog in my brain. I'd already fed the cats, cleaned litter boxes, prepped the tea and coffee stations, restocked creamers and sugars. All the usual morning tasks completed on autopilot while my mind kept circling back to the alley, to Hazel's still form, to the weight of secrets I couldn't share.

"You don't have to open today," Poppy said from her perch near the window. "No one would blame you."

"I have to do something." I flipped the sign from Closed to Open and stepped back, staring at the empty café. "If I sit upstairs thinking about it, I'll go crazy."

"Fair point," Gus muttered from his bed by the fireplace. "Though I question the wisdom of being around people when you're this upset. You're liable to accidentally hex someone's coffee."

"I would never—"

"I didn't say on purpose."

He had a point. My magic responded to emotion, and right now my emotions were a tangled mess of grief and anger and guilt. I took a deep breath, centering myself the way I'd been taught years ago. Control. Always control.

The first customers trickled in around eight-fifteen, and I could see it in their faces before they even spoke. The news had already spread. In a town of five thousand, tragedy traveled faster than any form of transportation.

Jasper Sharpe, who ran the general store, was first through the door. His weathered face was somber as he approached the counter. "Alexis. I heard about Hazel. I'm so sorry."

"Thank you." I kept my hands busy wiping down the already-clean counter. "Black coffee?"

"Please." He hesitated, then added, "I know how close you two were. If there's anything you need..."

How close we were. The phrase made my chest ache. We'd been close but not close enough. Not honest enough. "I appreciate it."

He took his coffee and settled at a corner table, and within minutes, more people arrived. Mabel Smalls came in and simply squeezed my hand before ordering her usual Lavender Dreams tea.

Felix Wren mumbled condolences while staring at his shoes. Pearl Van brought her entire book club, all of them wearing expressions of sympathy that made me want to crawl out of my skin.

I made drinks and accepted condolences and kept my walls firmly in place, even as something inside me wanted to scream.

Cordelia Kelder arrived mid-morning, her usual chatter subdued but not silenced. "I saw the sheriff this morning," she said, gripping her Rosehip Radiance tea like a lifeline. "She was at the flower shop. Yellow tape everywhere. Alexis, do you think..." She lowered her voice conspiratorially. "Do you think it wasn't an accident?"

"I don't know what to think," I said honestly.

"Well, I told Iris she should check for fingerprints. And security cameras. Hazel's shop has a camera, doesn't it? Over the back door?" She didn't wait for an answer. "This is exactly what I've been saying. Crime is escalating. First my yarn, now this. Where does it end?"

I wanted to point out that three balls of yarn and a woman's death weren't exactly a crime wave, but I bit my tongue. Cordelia meant well, in her way.

Atticus came in shortly after, his quiet presence a relief after Cordelia's theories. He ordered his black coffee and lingered at the counter, his weathered hands wrapped around the cup. "Hazel was good people," he said simply. "Used to make special arrangements for the ranger station every spring. Said we needed beauty in our lives, not just trees and trails."

"She did say that," I managed, throat tight.

"You doing okay?" His eyes were kind, the sort of kindness that came from someone who'd seen enough of life to know when to ask and when to just listen.

"Not really. But I'm here."

He nodded. "That's something. Don't let people push you to be fine before you're ready. Grief takes its own time." He took his coffee to a corner table, and I was grateful he didn't say anything else.

Hugh Leland shuffled in around nine-thirty, moving slower than usual. My eighty-year-old neighbor lived in the apartment next to mine, and I'd grown used to the sound of his television through the walls. This morning, he looked every one of his years, his face gray with exhaustion.

"Didn't sleep much," he said when I asked if he wanted his usual Earl Grey. "Kept thinking about Hazel. Saw her just yesterday, you know. At the post office. She asked about my hip, told me about some tea you'd made that helped with inflammation." His hands shook slightly as he accepted the cup. "Hard to believe she's gone."

"It is," I agreed.

"You found her, didn't you? I heard the sirens last night. Saw the lights from my window." He studied my face with the careful attention of someone who'd lived long enough to recognize trauma. "That's a hard thing to carry. You need someone to talk to, my door's open. I know what it's like to see things you can't unsee."

The kindness in his gravelly voice nearly undid me. "Thank you, Hugh."

"Mean it. We're neighbors. That means something." He took his tea and made his way slowly to a table by the window, and I had to turn away to hide the tears threatening to spill.

Around nine, a woman I didn't recognize walked in. She was in her late forties, with Hazel's dark eyes and sharp cheekbones, though her expression held none of Hazel's warmth. She wore a black pantsuit that looked expensive and carried herself with the kind of rigid posture that suggested she was holding something tightly controlled.

"You must be Alexis," she said, approaching the counter. "I'm Carla Lynch. Hazel's niece."

"I'm sorry for your loss." The words were becoming automatic, but I meant them. Hazel had mentioned Carla occasionally, though never with much warmth.

"Thank you." Carla's eyes scanned the café, cataloguing everything with an intensity that made me uncomfortable. "I heard you were the last one to see her alive. Before... before it happened."

"We had dinner together." I kept my voice steady. "She seemed fine. Happy, even."

"That's some comfort, I suppose." Carla's shoulders relaxed slightly. "I'm glad she wasn't alone. That she had someone who cared about her in her final hours."

There was something genuine in her voice that caught me off guard. Whatever complicated relationship Carla and Hazel had shared, the grief seemed real.

"Can I get you something? Coffee? Tea?" I gestured to the menu board.

"Just black coffee, thank you." She pulled out her wallet. "I'm in town to... well, to oversee her affairs. The flower shop, her apartment, all of it. It's what she would have wanted. Family taking care of family."

"Watch this one," Gus said quietly from his bed. "She's already counting her inheritance."

I shot him a warning look, but he just yawned and closed his eyes.

"Hazel loved that shop," I said carefully, handing Carla her coffee.

"She did. And I intend to honor that. I'll be taking it over, of course. Keeping it in the family." Carla took a sip and nodded approvingly. "Good coffee. Hazel mentioned your place a few times. Said you had a gift."

The word "gift" made my skin prickle, but Carla's expression remained neutral. Just small talk. Nothing suspicious.

"That's kind of her to say."

"Well." Carla set down her cup. "I should get going. I have a meeting with her lawyer this afternoon, and I need to go through her apartment first. See what needs to be sorted."

She left, and I watched her walk past the front window toward the flower shop. Poppy hopped down from her perch and padded over to the counter.

"She's not grieving," Poppy said flatly. "She's calculating."

"People grieve differently."

"That wasn't grief. That was a woman doing math in her head about property values."

Before I could respond, the bell chimed again. This time it was a woman in her early fifties with over-styled hair and a smile that didn't reach her eyes. She wore too much perfume and a bright floral dress that seemed aggressively cheerful given the circumstances.

"Hello!" She approached the counter with the kind of forced enthusiasm that immediately put me on edge. "You must be Alexis. I'm Trish Lawrence. I own Petals and Prose, the flower shop over on Birch Street?"

"Nice to meet you." It wasn't, but manners were automatic.

"I heard about poor Hazel. Just tragic." Trish leaned against the counter conspiratorially. "We were in the same business, you know. Friendly competitors. I always admired her work."

"I'll bet," Gus muttered.

"I was actually hoping," Trish continued, lowering her voice slightly, "that you might know who's handling her estate? I'd like to make an offer on the shop. Before things get complicated with family and lawyers and all that mess. Sometimes it's better to move quickly, you know?"

I stared at her. "Hazel died less than twelve hours ago."

"Oh, I know, I know. It seems crass." Trish had the grace to look slightly embarrassed. "But business is business, and I'd hate to see that prime location go to waste. I could really do something with it. Expand my inventory, maybe offer both locations. It would be a fitting tribute to Hazel, really."

"A tribute." I kept my voice flat.

"Exactly! Keeping the flower business alive in Larkspur Valley. I'm sure Hazel would approve."

"I don't think Hazel would approve at all," I said, my control slipping slightly. "And I don't know anything about her estate. You'd need to speak with her family."

"Right, of course. That niece of hers." Trish's nose wrinkled slightly. "Carla, is it? I'll have to track her down. Well, if you do hear anything..."

"I won't."

She finally picked up on my tone and stepped back. "Of course. My condolences, naturally. I can see you're upset. We all are. Such a loss for the community."

She left without ordering anything, and the moment the door closed behind her, Rocky made a retching sound from the cat room.

"She's the worst," he announced. "Absolutely the worst. Did you smell that perfume? It's like she bathed in flowers. Fake flowers. Dead flowers."

"Rocky," I said, but my heart wasn't in the reprimand. He was right. Trish Lawrence had shown her true colors, and they weren't pretty.

"That perfume is giving me a headache," Gus grumbled, rising stiffly from his bed. "I'm going upstairs. My old nose can't take it."

"Want me to come with you?" I asked.

"I'm not an invalid. I can manage stairs." He limped toward the back, tail swishing with irritation. "Just need some peace and quiet away from all these people and their terrible smells."

I watched him disappear through the door that led to my apartment stairs, then turned my attention back to the café. The morning continued in fits and starts. More customers came in, more condolences, more weighted looks and careful questions. Everyone wanted to know what I'd seen, what Hazel had said, how she'd seemed. I deflected and redirected and kept my answers vague, all while making drinks and trying not to think about the truth sitting heavy in my chest.

At ten-thirty, another woman walked in. She was around fifty, medium height and build, with graying brown hair pulled back in a practical bun. She wore simple clothes: jeans, a cardigan, and comfortable shoes. Nothing remarkable. Nothing memorable.

Except that Poppy's ears went back slightly, and Rocky stopped his usual bouncing around.

"Good morning," the woman said with a pleasant smile. "I'm on my way to Cordelia's Yarn Haven, just wanted to grab a quick coffee before my shift."

"Of course." I forced my attention away from the cats, who were watching her with an unusual intensity. "What can I get you?"

"Just a plain latte, please. Nothing fancy." She glanced around the café with what seemed like genuine interest. "This is lovely. I keep meaning to stop in, but mornings are always so rushed."

"You work at the yarn shop?" I started steaming milk, keeping my movements casual even as I noticed Millie had retreated further into her hiding spot.

"Yes, I'm Orla Weston. I've been at Cordelia's for about a year now." She pulled out her wallet. "Terrible news about Hazel Blaine. I didn't know her well, but she always seemed so kind."

"She was."

"Were you close?" Orla's voice was sympathetic, her expression concerned. Nothing about her seemed threatening. Nothing obvious.

But something about her made my skin prickle. An instinct I'd learned to trust over years of running and hiding.

"We were friends," I managed.

"That must be so hard." Orla accepted her latte with a grateful smile. "Finding her like that. I can't imagine."

How did she know I'd found her? It hadn't been in the news yet, and while gossip traveled fast in Larkspur Valley, that particular detail felt too specific, too soon.

"Yes," I said carefully. "It was difficult."

"Well, I hope they figure out what happened. Such a tragedy." Orla took a sip and nodded approvingly. "This is excellent. I'll have to come by more often."

She left, and the moment the door closed, Poppy and Rocky came to attention.

"Something's wrong with her," Rocky said, his tail puffed out slightly. "I don't like her."

"You don't like a lot of people," I pointed out, though my own instincts were screaming the same thing.

"No, he's right," Poppy said slowly. "There's something... off. Did you notice how she knew you found Hazel? How would she know that?"

"Small town. Word travels." But even as I said it, I wasn't convinced.

"Maybe," Poppy said, but her tail was swishing with agitation. "I wish Gus had been down here. He would know if she smells like the person from last night."

My stomach dropped. "You think it could be her?"

"I think she's the right size and build. And there's something about her that feels wrong." Poppy looked up at me with those unnervingly intelligent amber eyes. "But without Gus's nose, we can't be sure. It could have been her. Or it could have been Carla. Or even Trish, though she's a bit taller."

"So, we still don't know."

"No," Poppy admitted. "We don't."

"What do we do?" Millie asked from her hiding spot, her voice trembling slightly.

I looked out the window, watching Orla Weston walk down Main Street toward the yarn shop. She looked completely normal. Completely harmless. But so had Carla. So had Trish, underneath all that aggressive friendliness.

Any one of them could have been in that alley. Any one of them could have argued with Hazel. Any one of them could be a murderer.

"We pay attention," I said finally. "We watch. We listen. And we figure out which one of them did this."

"How?" Rocky asked.

That was the question, wasn't it? How did you catch a killer when you couldn't use the one piece of evidence that mattered? When telling the truth meant exposing yourself as something this town would never understand?

I didn't have an answer yet. But I had to find one.

For Hazel.

The bell above the door chimed again, and I looked up to see Lionel walking in, his usual smile replaced by an expression of such genuine concern that something in my chest cracked slightly.

"Hey," he said softly, approaching the counter. "I heard about Hazel. Are you okay?"

No. I wasn't okay. I was the furthest thing from okay. But I couldn't tell him that. Couldn't tell anyone that.

"I'm managing," I said, and started making his Dandelion Root Revival without being asked.

He didn't push, didn't ask questions, just stood there with his quiet presence while I worked. After a moment, he said, "I closed the shop for the morning. Didn't feel right, opening like normal when..." He trailed off, then started again. "Hazel used to come in sometimes. Looking for comics for her granddaughters, she said. Though I always suspected she read some of them herself."

That startled a small, broken laugh out of me. "She did?"

"She had good taste. Loved the ones about ordinary people discovering they were extraordinary. Said it gave her hope." He accepted his drink but didn't move away from the counter. "I remember the last time she came in. About two weeks ago. She bought this series about a woman who could talk to animals but had to hide it from everyone around her. Said it reminded her of someone she knew."

My hands stilled on the cloth I'd been using to wipe down the espresso machine. Hazel had known. Or suspected. Or at least understood enough to leave that message.

"She was a good person," I managed.

"She was. And she cared about you. Anyone could see that." Lionel's green eyes were gentle, understanding without needing explanations. "When my ex-wife left, three years ago, everyone in town had an opinion about it. Everyone wanted to tell me how to feel, what to do, how to move on. But Hazel just brought me flowers. Different ones each week. Never said a word about the divorce, just left them at the shop with a note that said 'these ones are for hope' or 'these are for new beginnings.' She understood that sometimes people just need to grieve in their own way."

"I didn't know you'd been married," I said, then immediately worried that it was too personal.

But he just smiled, sad and a little wry. "High school sweethearts. Thought we'd figured out forever. Turns out forever is a lot more complicated when you're actually living it day by day." He took a sip of his drink. "She wanted kids, travel, a big life in a big city. I wanted a comic shop in a small town and quiet mornings. We spent five years trying to compromise ourselves into people we weren't. Finally admitted it wasn't working and went our separate ways. She's in Denver now. Happy, I think. I hope."

"I'm sorry."

"Don't be. It hurt at the time, but it was the right thing." He leaned against the counter, comfortable in a way I envied. "The point is, Hazel got it. Didn't try to fix me or rush me or tell me everything happens for a reason. She just showed up with flowers and kindness and let me figure it out."

I wanted to tell him that Hazel had done the same for me. That she'd welcomed me without questions, befriended me without demanding explanations, and somehow known exactly what I needed even when I didn't know myself.

"She was good at that," I said instead. "Seeing people."

"She was." Lionel straightened, seemed to realize he'd been taking up space at the counter for a while. "Anyway. I just wanted to check on you. And to say... I know we don't know each other that well. But if you need someone to just sit with you, no talking required, I'm around. Sometimes that's all you need. Someone who'll just be there."

"Thank you." The words felt inadequate, but they were all I had.

He started toward the door, then paused and turned back. "One more thing. That woman who came in earlier, the one with all the perfume? Trish Lawrence?"

"What about her?"

"She's been by the shop three times in the last week. Always with some excuse to stop in, always asking about the building, the rent, the landlord. I thought she was just being nosy, but now..." He shrugged. "Might be nothing. But after what happened to Hazel, it felt weird. Like maybe she was planning something."

My pulse kicked. "Planning what?"

"I don't know. But Hazel's flower shop is two doors down from you, and my shop is on the other side. We're in a row. Prime Main Street location. If someone wanted to expand their business..." He trailed off. "Like I said, might be nothing. But it seemed worth mentioning."

"Thank you," I said, meaning it more than he could know. "That's helpful."

He nodded and left, and I stood there processing. Trish hadn't just been watching from the outside. She'd been talking to neighboring businesses, asking questions, and laying groundwork.

"You could trust him," Poppy said quietly from her perch.

"I can't trust anyone." The words came out harsher than I meant them. "Not with this. Not with what we know."

"He's not asking for your secrets," Poppy pointed out. "He's just offering to be there. That's not the same thing."

"It's how it starts," I said. "You let someone in a little, and then they want more, and then they find out what you really are, and everything falls apart." I'd seen it happen. Lived it. Lost everything because I'd trusted the wrong person.

"Or," Rocky suggested carefully, "sometimes people just want to help because they're good people."

I wanted to believe that. But years of running had taught me that wanting something didn't make it true.

"Then we do it alone," Poppy said, her voice sad but accepting. "Like always."

Like always. The story of my life. Running alone, hiding alone, keeping secrets alone.

But this time, the stakes were higher. This time, someone I cared about was dead.

And this time, I wasn't going to run.

Chapter Four

The afternoon had stretched endlessly. After Lionel left, more customers had come and gone, each one bringing their own version of sympathy that I had to accept gracefully. My face ached from holding neutral expressions, and my hands moved through the familiar motions of making drinks on pure muscle memory.

Around two-thirty, there was finally a lull. The café sat empty except for Hugh at his usual table by the window, quietly working on a crossword puzzle. The silence felt both like a relief and a weight.

I couldn't stop thinking about Hazel's shop sitting empty two doors down. The flowers in her cooler would be dying. The business she'd spent decades building, just sitting there dark and closed.

"I need some air," I said to no one in particular. "I'll be right back."

I stepped outside into the October afternoon, the crisp air a shock after the warmth of the café. The walk to Larkspur Blooms was short, just past the insurance office next door. I stopped in front of the shop, Hazel's hand-painted sign swaying slightly in the breeze.

Through the window, I could see the darkened interior: the counter where she'd arranged bouquets, the cooler full of flowers that would need attention soon, the small table where she'd kept her coffee mug and reading glasses.

My throat tightened. Yesterday morning, she'd been here. Had opened this door, had helped customers, had lived her life.

"Can I help you?" A sharp voice made me turn. Trish Lawrence stood a few feet away, arms crossed, her perfume reaching me even at this distance. "Shop's closed, obviously."

"I know. I was just..." I gestured helplessly at the window.

"Paying respects?" Trish's tone softened slightly, though her eyes remained calculating. "She was a good businesswoman. Knew her flowers. It's a shame to see the place sit empty like this. Such a waste of prime location."

"She just died yesterday."

"I know, I know." Trish held up her hands. "I'm just saying, from a practical standpoint, someone will need to take over eventually. These flowers in there? They'll die if someone doesn't tend to them. The business will lose value. It's almost irresponsible not to plan ahead."

I stared at her. "You're unbelievable."

"I'm realistic." She sniffed. "But I can see you're upset. I'll leave you to your mourning."

She walked away, heels clicking on the sidewalk, and I stood there a moment longer before heading back to the café. The encounter had left me feeling like I needed another shower.

"That woman has no shame," Poppy observed from her perch when I returned.

"No," I agreed. "She doesn't."

I was restocking tea canisters behind the counter when the bell chimed again. A woman I vaguely recognized from the post office rushed in, slightly out of breath and cradling something against her chest.

"Are you the cat lady?" she asked without preamble.

"I... run a cat café, yes."

"Thank God." She approached the counter, and I could see now that she was holding a tiny kitten wrapped in what looked like someone's jacket. "I found this baby crying behind the Mountain Market about twenty minutes ago. Everyone I asked said you'd know what to do."

My heart clenched. The kitten was tiny, maybe six weeks old, gray with white paws and the biggest green eyes I'd ever seen. It was making pitiful mewing sounds, clearly distressed.

"Let me see." I came around the counter, automatically falling into the familiar routine. Over the past year, people had brought me strays, surrenders, and rescues regularly. Larkspur Valley didn't have an animal shelter, so somehow I'd become the de facto cat rescue.

The woman handed over the kitten carefully. "I would have taken it home, but I've got three dogs and a husband who's allergic. I couldn't just leave it there crying."

The moment the kitten was in my hands, I could feel how frighteningly light it was. Too light. Its tiny body trembled against my palms, and when I looked closer, I could see its ribs pressing against thin fur. The kitten's eyes were slightly sunken, a sign of dehydration, and its cry was hoarse, like it had been calling for help for a long time.

"You did the right thing bringing it here." I examined the kitten more carefully, my hands gentle but thorough. Thin, but not quite emaciated. Scared, definitely. Dirty, the gray fur matted and dull. But no obvious injuries that I could see, no blood or wounds. "Has it been eating or drinking?"

"I tried to give it some water from my bottle, but it wouldn't take much."

"Okay." I looked around at my nearly empty café, grateful no customers other than Hugh were here to see me turn it into a makeshift vet clinic. Hugh, bless him, was focused entirely on his crossword and wouldn't notice if the building caught fire. "I'm going to need to get it cleaned up and checked over. Do you have a few minutes to give me your contact information? In case it has an owner looking for it?"

"Of course." She pulled out her phone. "Though honestly, the way it was crying, I think someone dumped it. People do that sometimes, drop off animals they don't want, thinking someone else will deal with it."

My jaw tightened. I'd seen it before, the casual cruelty of people who treated living creatures like inconveniences to be discarded. This kitten couldn't be more than six or seven weeks old at most. Far too young to be away from its mother, let alone abandoned behind a grocery store.

After getting her information and thanking her for bringing the kitten in, I held the tiny creature close to my chest and headed for the stairs. The kitten's cries had quieted slightly, but I could feel its rapid heartbeat against my palm, frantic and terrified.

"Another one?" Gus asked as I reached the top of the stairs, though his tone was more resigned than annoyed.

"What was I supposed to do, leave it?" I was already moving toward the bathroom, the cats following close behind. I'd done this enough times to have a routine, a system. New rescues needed to be isolated until I could confirm they were healthy. "This one's in bad shape."

I set the kitten down gently on the bathroom counter while I prepared the quarantine area. Clean towels layered in the corner, creating a soft nest. A heating pad set on low, wrapped in a fleece blanket. A shallow litter box with non-clumping litter, safe for kittens.

The baby gate I kept stored behind the door, ready to install across the bathroom entrance.

The kitten mewed pitifully from the counter, and my chest ached.

"Poor baby," Millie whispered from the doorway. "It's so scared."

"I know." I picked up the kitten again, cradling it close. Up close, I could see it was even more desperate than I'd first thought. Its tiny pink nose was dry, another sign of dehydration. Its fur was clumped and dirty, and there were small bits of what looked like leaves and debris stuck in the matted patches. The white-tipped paws were gray with grime.

This kitten had been on its own for at least a day, maybe longer.

I set up the quarantine nest, placing the heating pad at one end so the kitten could choose whether to be on the warmth or move away from it if needed. Then I filled a shallow dish with water and another with a bit of wet food I kept on hand for exactly these situations. Kitten formula would be better, but I'd need to get to the store for that. For now, high-quality wet food mixed with a little warm water would have to do.

The kitten sat where I'd placed it on the towels, too frightened to move. It stared at me with those huge green eyes, mewing softly, a sound that broke my heart.

"It's okay," I murmured, sitting down on the bathroom floor, making myself small and non-threatening. "You're safe now. I know you don't believe that yet, but you are."

I moved the food dish closer, letting the kitten smell it without forcing the issue. Slowly, so slowly, the tiny nose twitched. One small paw reached out, testing, then pulled back.

"Take your time," I said softly. "It's right here when you're ready."

The other cats had arranged themselves around the bathroom doorway, watching with varying expressions of concern. Rocky pressed his face against the baby gate I'd installed, eyes wide. Poppy sat with her tail wrapped around her paws, calm but attentive. Gus had settled on the hall floor with a grumble, and Millie peeked around the doorframe.

"It's too small to be alone," Poppy said quietly. "Far too young."

"I know." My throat felt tight. "Someone dumped it. Just... left it to die."

The kitten finally crept toward the food dish, moving with the careful uncertainty of an animal that had learned the world wasn't safe. It took a tentative bite, then another. Then suddenly it was eating with desperate urgency, tiny face buried in the food.

"Slow down," I worried aloud, watching the kitten inhale the food. "You'll make yourself sick."

But I understood that hunger, that panic-driven need to eat while food was available. After a minute, I gently pulled the dish back.

"I know you want more," I told the protesting kitten. "But your stomach's been empty too long. Too much too fast will make you throw up. We'll try again in an hour."

The kitten mewed unhappily but didn't have the strength to do more than protest. I moved the water dish closer instead, and the kitten drank gratefully, tiny pink tongue lapping at the water.

"What will you call this one?" Rocky asked, his voice uncharacteristically quiet.

I studied the gray kitten with its white-tipped paws, now licking water from its whiskers. Something about the gray coloring reminded me of the kitchen spice I used regularly, the one that meant healing and protection in the old traditions. "Sage," I decided. "We'll call her Sage."

"Good name," Poppy approved. "Healing and cleansing. Appropriate."

The kitten, Sage, finished drinking and looked around with slightly more alertness. Her eyes were still frightened, but the edge of panic had faded now that she had food and water in her belly.

"Let's get you cleaned up," I said softly, reaching for her. "I know you won't like this, but you'll feel better after."

I filled the sink with a few inches of warm water, testing it carefully with my elbow the way I'd learned long ago. Not too hot, not too cold. Body temperature. Then I lowered Sage into the water, keeping a firm but gentle grip as she immediately began to squirm and cry.

"I know, I know," I soothed, using a soft washcloth to work through the matted fur. "But look at all this dirt. You'll feel so much better when you're clean."

The water turned gray almost immediately as I worked. Sage protested, her tiny claws scrabbling against the porcelain, but she was too weak and exhausted to put up much of a fight. Once the warm water started working through her fur, she quieted somewhat, as if realizing I was trying to help rather than hurt.

I worked carefully, checking her over as I cleaned. No fleas that I could see, which was a small mercy. No wounds or injuries, no signs of abuse. Just a scared, hungry kitten who'd been abandoned and left to fend for herself. Her fur, once clean, was actually quite lovely, a soft silver-gray with those distinctive white paws.

"You're going to be beautiful once you put some weight on," I told her.

Drying took longer than bathing. Sage was so small that even the gentlest towel felt rough against her delicate skin. I patted her carefully, getting most of the water out, then wrapped her in a clean, dry towel and held her close to my chest, letting my body heat and the towel's warmth soak in.

"You'll be okay," I whispered to her. "I know it doesn't feel like it right now, but you will."

Was I talking to the kitten or myself? I wasn't sure anymore.

When Sage was mostly dry, I set her back on the heated pad, making sure she was directly on the warm spot. She curled up immediately, exhausted from the ordeal. Within seconds, she was asleep, her tiny chest rising and falling with rapid kitten breaths.

I sat there on my bathroom floor for a long moment, watching this small creature that had been abandoned and rescued all in the span of a few hours. Tomorrow I'd take her to Dr. Dover for a proper check-up, make sure there wasn't anything I'd missed, get kitten formula and any medication she might need. Today, she just needed to sleep and heal.

"You did good," Gus said from the hallway. "Even if your timing is terrible and you're barely holding yourself together."

"Thanks for the vote of confidence."

"Just stating facts." But his tone was gentler than his words. "That kitten needed you. Sometimes that's enough reason to keep going."

He was right. Life didn't stop because I was grieving. Animals still needed help. The café still needed to run. And somewhere out there, Hazel's killer was still free.

I stood up, joints creaking from sitting on the tile floor. My legs had fallen asleep, pins and needles shooting through them as I moved. "Keep an eye on her?"

"Of course," Poppy said. "We'll take shifts."

I headed back downstairs, feeling fractionally more centered than I had before. Saving one small life didn't make up for losing Hazel. But it was something. A reminder that not everything was loss and death and grief.

Sometimes, there was rescue. Sometimes, there was hope.

Even on the hardest days.

By five-thirty, I was running on fumes. The day had been a blur of sympathetic faces and careful conversations, of making drinks while my mind spun in circles trying to figure out how to catch a killer without revealing what I knew. My hands ached from gripping the counter too tightly, and my face hurt from maintaining a neutral expression for hours.

"You should close early," Poppy said from her perch. The café had finally emptied out, the last customer leaving ten minutes ago.

"It's almost six." I glanced at the clock. "May as well finish out the day."

But my heart wasn't in it. I moved through the closing routine mechanically: wiping down tables, cleaning the espresso machine, putting away the pastries that hadn't sold. My mind kept drifting upstairs, wondering if Sage was okay, if she'd woken up yet, if she needed another small meal.

I was counting the till when the bell chimed.

Carla Lynch stood in the doorway, holding a cardboard box. She'd changed since this morning, now wearing a black dress that looked expensive but didn't quite fit right, like she'd bought it specifically for mourning and hadn't had time to get it tailored. Her eyes were red, but her jaw was set in a hard line.

"I need to give you something," she said without preamble.

I set down the stack of bills I'd been counting. "Carla. I'm so sorry about---"

"Don't." She cut me off. "I can't hear another 'sorry for your loss' today. I'll scream."

I nodded, understanding more than she knew. "What can I do for you?"

She crossed to the counter and set the box down with more force than necessary. It was about the size of a shoebox, sealed with packing tape. My name was written across the top in Hazel's distinctive handwriting: *For Alexis Belrose.*

My breath caught.

"This was in Aunt Hazel's instructions," Carla said, her voice tight. "Her lawyer gave it to me today with explicit directions to deliver it to you within twenty-four hours of her death. Apparently, she made arrangements months ago."

Months ago. Hazel had prepared this months ago.

"I don't understand," I managed.

"Neither do I." Carla's laugh was bitter. "Apparently, my aunt thought you were more important than her actual family. The lawyer wouldn't tell me what's in it. Said it was sealed and private. But there's probably a letter or something explaining why she left the flower shop to some stranger instead of me."

"She left the shop to you?" That didn't match what the cats had overheard.

"No." The word came out sharp. "She left everything in some complicated trust. I can't touch anything for six months while they 'determine the best course of action.'" Carla made air quotes around the phrase. "And there's some clause about her lawyer having final say. Six months before I even know if I'll inherit it."

I looked up from the box. "Her lawyer?"

"Some clause about maintaining the integrity of the business or some legal nonsense. He gets to decide whether to sell it, run it, give it away." Carla's laugh was sharp and humorless. "I'm going to fight this. Contest the will. She wasn't in her right mind at the end, clearly."

"Hazel seemed perfectly lucid to me." The words came out harder than I meant them.

"Of course you'd say that. You got your mystery box." Carla grabbed her purse from where she'd set it on a chair. "Just know that if there's anything of value in there, anything that should rightfully belong to family, I'll be coming for it."

She was gone before I could respond, the bell chiming harshly in her wake.

I stood there for a long moment, staring at the door Carla had just walked through. Then I moved quickly, almost frantically, crossing to the entrance. I turned the deadbolt with shaking hands, flipped the sign from Open to Closed, and reached for the light switches. The overhead lights went dark, leaving only the dim glow from the small lamp I kept on the counter overnight.

The box felt heavier now as I picked it up again, my name on top seeming to glow in the dimness. I carried it toward the back, past the counter, toward the stairs.

But first, I needed to check on Sage.

In the bathroom, the tiny kitten was just waking up, stretching in that boneless way kittens have. Her eyes were clearer now, less sunken, and when she saw me, she mewed softly.

"Hey, little one." I set the box on the hallway floor and knelt by the baby gate. "Feeling better?"

Rocky was on guard duty, lying just outside the bathroom with his eyes fixed on Sage. "She woke up about ten minutes ago," he reported. "Made some small noises but didn't cry."

"That's good." I unlatched the gate and moved into the bathroom, offering Sage another small portion of food mixed with water. She ate more slowly this time, with less desperation, which eased something in my chest. After she'd eaten and used the litter box, stumbling a bit on uncertain legs, I held her for a moment, feeling her tiny heartbeat against my palm.

She was so small. So fragile. How could anyone have abandoned her?

"You'll need to feed her again in a few hours," Poppy said from the hallway. "Kittens this young need frequent small meals."

"I know." I set Sage back on the heating pad, watching her curl up immediately. "I'll set an alarm."

"Are you going to open it?" Rocky asked, having materialized beside the box I'd left in the hall.

"Not here." My voice sounded strange, distant. "Not now."

"But it might have answers," Poppy pressed. "About what happened. About who?"

"I can't." My voice cracked, and I had to stop, clutching the box to my chest. "I can't look at it right now. I can't... I can't see whatever she wanted me to know. Not yet."

The cats followed me in silence as I walked to my bedroom. Everything felt distant and muffled, like I was moving underwater.

I opened the closet door and set the box on the floor in the back corner, behind my winter boots and the suitcase I'd arrived with a year ago. The suitcase that was always packed, always ready for the next escape. Ready for the night I'd inevitably need to run again.

But the box. The box was different.

I knelt there on the closet floor, my name staring up at me in Hazel's handwriting. The packing tape was professionally sealed, the lawyer's sticker stark and official. Inside could be anything. Everything. Answers I wasn't ready for.

What had Hazel known? What had she wanted me to understand?

My hand hovered over the box, fingers trembling. I could open it now. Could tear through the tape and face whatever truths Hazel had left for me. But my chest was too tight, my eyes already burning with tears I'd barely held back in front of Carla.

What if it was a letter explaining that she'd known what I was all along? What if it was proof that I'd put her in danger just by being near her? What if she'd written down things that could expose me, that could bring my past crashing down on this small life I'd built?

Or worse, what if it was just her way of saying goodbye? A message left behind because she'd somehow known she wouldn't be here to say the words herself?

I couldn't. Not now. Not when I was barely holding myself together. Not when opening this box might break me completely.

I pulled my hand back and stood up, my knees protesting. The box would keep. Whatever secrets it held, whatever Hazel had wanted me to know, it would still be there tomorrow. Next week. Whenever I found the strength to face it.

I closed the closet door and sat down on my bed, but I could still feel it there. A presence. A weight. Hazel's final message, waiting patiently in the dark.

The apartment was quiet. Even Hugh's television next door was just a low murmur, barely audible through the wall. The cats had dispersed to their usual evening spots, giving me space in a way that meant they understood.

Except Rocky, who'd stationed himself outside the bathroom again, keeping watch over Sage.

For the first time since I'd found Hazel in that alley, I let myself stop. Let myself feel it.

The grief hit like a physical blow.

Hazel was gone. The woman who'd welcomed me without questions, who'd been patient when I kept my walls up, who'd shared wine and pasta and conversation just last night. The woman who'd known, somehow, that she might die. Who'd prepared a box for me, sealed it, left instructions.

What was in it? What had she wanted me to know?

But I couldn't open it. Not now. Not when my hands were still shaking and my throat was tight, and my eyes burned with tears I'd been holding back all day.

I lay down on top of the covers, still fully dressed, and finally let myself cry.

It started quietly, just tears sliding down my temples into my hair. Then my breath hitched, and suddenly I was sobbing, pressing my face into my pillow to muffle the sound. Not because anyone could hear, but because I'd spent so long being silent, being controlled, being careful.

Hazel had been my friend. My only real friend in Larkspur Valley. Maybe my only real friend in years. And I'd never told her the truth. Never trusted her with who I really was, even though some part of me had known she'd understand.

"She knew anyway," Poppy said softly. I hadn't heard her jump up onto the bed, but now she was curled against my side, a warm weight. "She knew, and she loved you anyway."

That made me cry harder.

One by one, the other cats joined us. Gus settled near my feet with a grumbling sigh. Millie crept up and tucked herself into the curve of my knees. Even Rocky left his post at the bathroom long enough to press against my stomach, purring so loudly I could feel it vibrating through the mattress.

They didn't tell me it would be okay. Didn't try to fix it or make it better. They just stayed, solid and real and present.

I cried until I had nothing left, until my eyes were swollen and my throat was raw, and exhaustion pulled me under like a tide. The last thing I was aware of was the weight of four cats surrounding me, keeping watch.

And in my closet, hidden in the dark, sat a box labeled with my name in Hazel's handwriting.

Whatever secrets it held, whatever truths Hazel had wanted me to know, they would have to wait.

Tonight, I just needed to grieve.

I woke sometime in the middle of the night, disoriented and still dressed. The apartment was dark except for the faint glow of streetlights through the curtains. My face felt tight and swollen from crying, and my mouth was dry.

The cats were still with me, though they'd shifted positions. Poppy was now on the pillow beside my head. Gus snored softly at my feet. Millie was still curled at my knees. Rocky had returned to his post outside the bathroom.

Then I heard it. A small, pitiful mew from down the hall.

Sage.

I dragged myself out of bed, my body protesting every movement. The clock read 2:47 AM. I'd been asleep for hours, which meant Sage hadn't eaten since before six.

In the bathroom, the tiny kitten was awake and crying softly, that heartbreaking sound of a baby who needs help. I prepared another small meal, mixing the wet food with warm water to make it easier for her to eat. She ate eagerly, then drank water, then used the litter box.

"Good girl," I murmured, checking her over. She felt warmer than before, which was good. The heating pad was doing its job. And she had more energy now, actually trying to play with my finger when I offered it.

After she'd eaten and settled, I sat on the bathroom floor for a few minutes, watching her curl back up on the warm pad. Her tiny chest rose and fell steadily, and some of the tension in my own chest eased.

This kitten would live. Would grow. Would eventually become strong enough to join the others, to maybe find a forever home or stay here with me. Despite everything, despite Hazel's death and the box in my closet and the killer still out there, this tiny creature would survive.

I returned to bed, where the cats had maintained their vigil. As I settled back under their watchful eyes, I let myself acknowledge what I'd been avoiding all day.

Someone had killed Hazel. Someone had argued with her in that alley and caused her to fall, or pushed her, and then run away. The cats had witnessed it, but I couldn't tell anyone what they'd seen without revealing what I was.

And now I had three suspects: Carla, who'd expected to inherit and gotten nothing. Trish, who'd shown up barely twelve hours after the death trying to buy the business. And Orla, who'd known details she shouldn't have known and made the cats uneasy.

One of them was a murderer. And I was going to prove it.

But first, eventually, I was going to have to open that box.

Not tonight, though. Tonight I was too raw, too broken, too tired. And tonight I had a tiny kitten who needed me to check on her every few hours, who depended on me to keep her alive.

I closed my eyes and let sleep pull me back under, surrounded by cats and grief and secrets I couldn't share.

Tomorrow, I'd start looking for answers.

Tomorrow, I'd figure out how to catch a killer.

Tonight, I just needed to survive. And keep Sage alive too.

That would have to be enough.

Chapter Five

Wednesday morning arrived too early and too bright. I woke to find myself still fully dressed from the night before, my face stiff from dried tears, and four cats staring at me with varying expressions of concern.

"You need to get up," Poppy said gently. "It's almost six."

I wanted to argue. Wanted to pull the covers over my head and pretend the world didn't exist. But I'd already been up twice in the night to feed Sage, and the tiny kitten would need another meal soon. The café wouldn't run itself, and lying in bed wouldn't bring Hazel back or catch her killer.

So I got up.

The first thing I did was check on Sage. She was curled up on the heating pad, still asleep, but when I knelt by the baby gate, she stirred and blinked those huge green eyes at me.

"Good morning, little one." I unlatched the gate and moved into the bathroom. "Let's get you fed."

Sage was stronger than she'd been yesterday afternoon. She stood on wobbly legs and mewed at me, actually coming toward the food dish instead of waiting for me to bring it to her. Small progress, but progress nonetheless.

While she ate her small meal, I called Dr. Dover's clinic. Meredith, his receptionist, answered on the second ring with her usual cheerful efficiency.

"Larkspur Valley Veterinary Clinic, this is Meredith."

"Hi Meredith, it's Alexis. From the café."

"Oh, Alexis." Her voice immediately softened. "I heard about Hazel. I'm so sorry."

I closed my eyes against the wave of grief. "Thank you. I, um, I actually need to bring in a kitten. Rescue. She was found yesterday, and she's in pretty rough shape. Young, maybe six or seven weeks, dehydrated and underweight."

"Oh no, poor baby. Let me check the schedule." I heard papers rustling. "Dr. Dover has an opening at nine-thirty if you can make that work?"

I glanced at the clock. Six-fifteen. "That's perfect. Thank you."

"Of course. Bring the little one in, and we'll get her checked out. And Alexis?" She paused. "I'm really sorry about Hazel. She was special."

"She was," I managed. "See you at nine-thirty."

After ending the call, I sat on the bathroom floor and watched Sage eat. She was taking her time now, no longer inhaling food with desperate panic. That was good. Her eyes were brighter too, less sunken. The water and food were helping.

"You're going to the vet today," I told her. "Dr. Dover is nice. You'll like him."

Sage looked up at me and mewed, a tiny sound that said she had opinions about being taken anywhere.

"I know. But we need to make sure you're healthy. That you don't have anything we can't see."

After Sage finished eating and used the litter box, I gave her a quick check. Her fur was still dull but cleaner than yesterday. Her ribs still showed, but that would take time to fix. No discharge from eyes or nose, which was a good sign. No sneezing or coughing. Just a very small, very thin kitten who'd been abandoned and was slowly learning to trust again.

I left her to nap on the heating pad while I took the fastest shower of my life, then threw on clean clothes. Black jeans, a soft gray sweater that had seen better days, my hair pulled back in a ponytail. Foundation to hide the evidence of last night's breakdown. By seven, I looked almost normal in the mirror, if you didn't look too closely at my eyes.

The morning routine was the same as always: feed the four adult cats plus the six adoptable ones scattered between my apartment and the viewing room downstairs, clean what felt like endless litter boxes, head downstairs to prep the café. Butterscotch, the long-haired orange cat, wound between my legs as I worked, and Cinnamon watched from her favorite perch with those knowing eyes. Coffee stations, tea selections, pastries from yesterday that would have to do since I'd texted Flo late last night asking her to skip today's delivery.

I couldn't face her maternal concern right now. Couldn't handle her trying to mother me while I was barely holding myself together.

I unlocked the door and flipped the sign to Open at exactly eight o'clock, even though part of me wanted to stay closed. Wanted to hide. But routine was all I had right now, and routine meant opening on time.

The first hour was a blur of sympathetic faces and awkward condolences. Everyone in town had heard about Hazel. Everyone had something to say, some comfort to offer, some memory to share. I smiled and nodded and made their drinks and counted the minutes until I could escape.

By nine-fifteen, I'd had enough. I flipped the sign to Closed with a note: "Back at 11 AM." Let them think what they wanted. I had a kitten to take to the vet.

Upstairs, Sage was awake and mewing softly. I'd found a small cat carrier in the storage closet, one I kept for exactly these situations. I lined it with a soft towel and gently placed Sage inside. She protested, crying pitifully, and my heart ached.

"I know," I told her. "But it's just for a little while. I promise."

"She'll be okay," Poppy said from the hallway. "Dr. Dover is good with the scared ones."

He was. In the year I'd been running the café, I'd brought him at least a dozen rescues, and he'd treated each one with patience and kindness. He'd never once made me feel like I was wasting his time, even when I'd shown up with a cat that turned out to be perfectly healthy but terrified.

The walk to the clinic took ten minutes, Sage crying in her carrier the entire time. The October air was crisp and cool, the mountains surrounding Larkspur Valley painted in fall colors. Under different circumstances, it would have been beautiful.

The clinic sat at the end of Pine Street, a converted house with a cheerful blue door and a hand-painted sign that read "Larkspur Valley Veterinary Clinic." Wind chimes made from old spoons hung by the entrance, tinkling softly in the breeze.

Meredith looked up from the reception desk when I entered, her round face creasing with concern. She was in her fifties, with gray-streaked brown hair and the kind of warm energy that put nervous pet owners at ease.

"Oh, Alexis." She came around the desk immediately. "And who do we have here?"

"This is Sage. Found behind the Mountain Market yesterday."

Meredith peered into the carrier, where Sage was pressed into the corner, eyes huge with fear. "Poor little thing. She's tiny. Let me get you checked in, and Dr. Dover will be right with you."

I signed the necessary forms while Meredith made soft cooing sounds at the carrier. The waiting room was empty except for a woman with a corgi sitting calmly by her feet, and a teenager with a guinea pig in a cage on his lap. The walls were covered in photos of happy pets and their owners, and the air smelled like antiseptic and the lavender diffuser on the reception desk.

I couldn't bear to leave Sage crying in the carrier. I opened the door and carefully scooped out the tiny kitten, cradling her against my chest with one hand supporting her bottom. She was trembling, her little heart racing against my palm.

"Shh," I murmured, bringing her close to my face. "It's okay. I've got you."

I used one finger to stroke gently along the bridge of her nose, up to the top of her head, over and over in a slow rhythm. It was how mother cats cleaned their babies, and I'd found it worked wonders with frightened kittens. Sage's crying quieted to small mews, then to silence as she leaned into the gentle touch. Her eyes started to drift closed.

"That's better," I whispered. "See? You're safe."

The corgi's owner smiled at me from across the waiting room. "You're so good with her."

I just nodded, continuing the gentle stroking motion. Sage's trembling gradually eased, and she tucked her tiny gray head under my chin with a soft sigh.

"Exam room two," Meredith said, handing me back my paperwork. "You know the way."

I did. Exam room two was the smallest, the one Dr. Dover used for the really frightened animals because it was quieter, further from the main waiting area.

I stood by the exam table, still holding Sage close, continuing the gentle one-finger strokes along her nose and forehead. She'd relaxed completely in my arms, trusting me to keep her safe.

"It's okay," I murmured. "Dr. Dover is nice. He helped Gus with his arthritis, and he treated Rocky when he ate that plant he wasn't supposed to."

A soft knock on the door, then Dr. Colton Dover stepped in with a gentle smile. He was in his mid-thirties, tall and lean with sandy brown hair that always looked slightly disheveled and kind hazel eyes behind wire-rimmed glasses. He wore his usual blue scrubs, a stethoscope draped around his neck.

"Alexis." His smile faltered slightly. "I heard about Hazel. I'm so sorry."

"Thank you." The words came automatically. I'd said them so many times in the past day that they'd lost all meaning.

"Is this the little one Meredith mentioned?" He approached slowly, keeping his movements calm and unthreatening. "May I?"

I transferred Sage to the exam table, keeping one hand on her tiny body so she wouldn't feel abandoned. She immediately started trembling again, her eyes huge as she stared at this new person.

Colton moved with practiced care, his hands gentle as he examined her. He checked her eyes, her ears, her mouth. Listened to her heart and lungs. Palpated her tiny belly. Throughout it all, he spoke in a low, soothing voice, telling Sage what a brave girl she was, how well she was doing.

"Approximately seven weeks old," he said finally. "Severely underweight, dehydrated, but no signs of respiratory infection or parasites. Her heart sounds strong. She's a fighter."

"Will she be okay?"

"With proper care, absolutely. She needs frequent small meals, warmth, and lots of rest. I'll send you home with some high-calorie kitten food and a vitamin supplement." He paused, his eyes meeting mine. "Are you keeping her? Or is she going up for adoption?"

The question hit me harder than I expected. Sage looked up at me with those huge green eyes, trembling on the exam table, completely dependent on my answer.

"Keeping her," I said before I'd made the conscious decision. "She's mine."

Colton's smile warmed. "Good. She's lucky to have found you." He paused, then added more quietly, "How are you doing? Really?"

The genuine concern in his voice made my throat tight. "I'm managing."

"That's not what I asked."

No, it wasn't. But managing was all I could offer right now. Anything more would crack the walls I'd so carefully built, and if they came down, I wasn't sure I could put them back up.

"I'm taking it one day at a time," I said, which was at least partly true.

He nodded, not pushing. "Well, if you need anything, you know where to find me. And I don't just mean for the cats."

There was something in his voice, something gentle and hopeful, and for just a moment, I let myself see it. See him. Dr. Colton Dover, who never made me feel like I was bothering him, who treated every frightened animal like they mattered, who was looking at me right now like I was someone worth noticing.

Part of me wanted to lean into that warmth. To let someone care about me the way his eyes suggested he might.

But I couldn't. Couldn't risk letting anyone too close. Couldn't take the chance that he'd see too much, understand too much, ask questions I couldn't answer.

So I just nodded and reached for Sage. "Thank you, Dr. Dover. Really."

"Colton," he said softly. "You can call me Colton. You've been bringing me cats for a year now. I think we're past 'Dr. Dover.'"

"Colton," I repeated, testing the name. It felt strange on my tongue, too personal. "Thank you."

He smiled again, that warm genuine smile, and helped me settle Sage back into her carrier. His fingers brushed mine as he handed me the bag of supplies, and the brief contact made my pulse jump in a way I didn't want to examine too closely.

"Take care of yourself too," he said as I headed for the door. "I know you're worried about the kitten, but you matter too. Make sure you're eating, sleeping. Letting yourself grieve."

The unexpected kindness made my throat tight. I nodded, not trusting my voice, and left before I could do something stupid like cry in front of him.

The walk back to the café was quieter. Sage had stopped crying and was curled up in the carrier, exhausted from the exam. The morning was warming up, the sun bright overhead, and I could hear the distant sound of the creek that ran through the center of town.

Dr. Dover, Colton, was nice. A really nice man. Kind, patient, good at his job. The kind of man who would probably be a good partner to someone. Someone who wasn't carrying the weight of a murdered mentor and a secret that could destroy her.

I pushed the thought away and focused on the kitten in the carrier. Sage needed me. That was what mattered right now.

Back at the café, I carried Sage upstairs and set the carrier on the bathroom floor. The other cats immediately gathered, curious about where we'd been.

"How'd it go?" Poppy asked.

"She looks good." I unlatched the carrier door. "Dr. Dover says with proper care, she'll make a full recovery."

"Good." Gus settled on the hallway floor with a grunt. "I'm getting too old to get attached to kittens who don't make it."

"Gus," Millie scolded softly.

"What? I'm just being honest."

I mixed up some of the high-quality kitten food with warm water, making it into a soft mush like Colton had instructed. I also poured a small amount of the formula into a separate dish as a supplement. Sage ate the food eagerly, then lapped at the formula, her tiny pink tongue working quickly.

"That's it," I encouraged her. "Get your strength back."

After she'd eaten and used the litter box, I held her for a moment, feeling her tiny heartbeat against my palm. She was so small, so fragile, but she was alive. She was going to make it.

I'd officially decided to keep her. Had said it out loud at the clinic, made it real. Five cats instead of four. One more heartbeat in my life, one more creature depending on me.

I should have felt overwhelmed. Should have felt like I was taking on too much. But instead, I felt... settled. Like this tiny kitten was supposed to be here, supposed to be mine.

I set Sage back on the heating pad and watched her curl up, ready to nap again. The morning exam had exhausted her, but she looked better. Stronger. Like she understood, finally, that she was safe.

"You're going to be okay," I told her softly. "You're part of the family now. These four grumpy cats and me. We're your people now."

Sage opened one eye, looked at me for a long moment, then closed it again with a small sigh.

And then I heard it.

A tiny voice, barely more than a whisper in my mind.

"Thank you for saving me."

My breath caught. My hand froze where it had been reaching for the baby gate.

Sage was too young. Kittens didn't develop the ability to communicate with me until they were older, until their magic matured enough to bridge the gap. Usually not until they were at least three or four months old.

But Sage was speaking. This tiny, fragile kitten who'd been abandoned behind a grocery store, who'd almost died, who was barely seven weeks old.

She was speaking to me.

"Sage?" I whispered.

"Warm," she said, her mental voice small and sleepy. "Safe. Thank you."

Tears blurred my vision. I knelt there by the baby gate, one hand pressed to my mouth, while this impossibly young kitten told me she was grateful.

"You don't have to thank me," I managed. "You're safe now. I promise."

"Know." Another tiny sigh. "Feel safe. First time... feel safe."

She drifted off to sleep then, her consciousness fading into dreams, but I stayed kneeling there for a long moment.

Poppy came to sit beside me, pressing her warm body against my leg. "She's special," the calico said softly. "To speak so young. She must have powerful magic."

"Or trauma made her mature faster," Gus added, his tone unusually gentle. "Sometimes survival forces us to grow up before we're ready."

I knew something about that.

"She's ours now," Rocky declared, his tail swishing. "One of us. The pack protects her."

"Always," Millie agreed quietly.

I wiped my eyes and stood up, my legs protesting after kneeling so long. Sage was asleep on the heating pad, unaware of the emotional bomb she'd just dropped. She'd spoken. This tiny, barely-alive kitten had reached out to me with magic she shouldn't possess yet.

Maybe it was trauma. Maybe it was survival. Maybe Sage was just special, gifted in ways I didn't understand yet.

Or maybe, like me, she'd been forced to grow up too fast because the world wasn't kind to the small and vulnerable.

Either way, she was mine now. Five cats instead of four. Five voices in my head, five creatures depending on me, five heartbeats sharing my life.

I'd told Dr. Dover, Colton, that I wanted to keep her. Had made it official. But I'd known the moment I'd held her yesterday, felt her tiny body trembling in my hands, that I wasn't going to let her go.

Sage needed me.

And maybe, just maybe, I needed her too.

Downstairs, the café was waiting. Customers would be wondering why I'd closed mid-morning. Life was waiting to continue, to demand things of me, to keep moving forward whether I was ready or not.

But first, I sat on my bathroom floor for a few more minutes and watched a tiny gray kitten sleep peacefully, safe and warm and loved.

"Thank you for saving me," she'd said.

But the truth was, she might be saving me too.

One tiny heartbeat at a time.

Chapter Six

I flipped the sign back to Open at eleven o'clock, right on schedule. The note I'd left said "Back at 11 AM" and I was determined to keep at least that one promise today. The morning had already been too much: waking up still dressed from crying myself to sleep, feeding Sage multiple times, the vet visit, and then that impossible moment when she'd spoken to me.

"Thank you for saving me."

A kitten that young shouldn't be able to communicate yet. But Sage had, and now she was upstairs sleeping peacefully on her heating pad, her tiny body finally starting to heal.

The box in my closet still whispered at the edge of my awareness, but I shoved the thought away. Not yet. Not today.

I'd barely had time to brew a fresh pot of coffee when the bell chimed. Sheriff Iris Scott walked through the door at 11:15, three hours later than her usual 8:15 morning visit but with the same purposeful stride.

"Black coffee," she said, and for a moment everything felt almost normal. Almost like Hazel hadn't died just yesterday morning. Almost like the world made sense.

"Coming right up." I poured from the French press, grateful for something routine to hold onto. "You're later than usual."

"Had some things to take care of this morning." Iris accepted the cup, her expression neutral but watchful.

With the investigation. With processing the scene. With doing her job while I sat here making coffee and pretending I didn't know more than I should.

I slid the cup across the counter and took a breath. "Have you found anything? About what happened to Hazel?"

Iris's expression shuttered immediately, going from almost-friendly to completely professional. "I can't discuss an ongoing investigation."

"But was anyone else around? That time of night, the alley is usually empty, but sometimes people cut through from Willow Street. Maybe someone saw something?"

Iris set her coffee down slowly, studying me. "That's interesting."

"What is?"

"Most people, when someone they care about dies suddenly, they ask if the person suffered. If it was quick. If they were in pain." Her gaze sharpened. "You're asking about witnesses and who might have been around. Those are investigative questions, Alexis. Why is that?"

My pulse spiked. She was right. I hadn't asked the normal questions because I already knew the answers from the cats. "I just want to understand what happened."

"Then let me do my job." She leaned slightly against the counter. "I do need to ask you something, though. When you looked down from your balcony that night, did you see anyone else? Anyone leaving the scene, walking away?"

"No." The answer came easily because it was the truth. I hadn't seen anyone. "It was dark. I was focused on Hazel."

Iris studied me for a long moment. "If you remember anything else, anything at all, you'll let me know?"

"Of course."

"Good." She picked up her coffee and headed for the door, then paused. "And Alexis? Don't go asking questions around town. Don't try to investigate this yourself. I know you cared about her, but let me do my job."

She left before I could respond, and I watched her go with frustration burning in my chest, but also with a cold seed of worry. Iris suspected something. Maybe not the truth, but something. And that made everything more complicated.

"That went well," Gus observed drily from his bed by the fireplace.

"She's not going to tell us anything," Poppy said from her perch. "She's too good at her job."

"So what do we do?" Rocky asked, appearing beside the counter. "We know things she doesn't know. We saw it happen."

"But we can't tell her what we saw." I wiped down the counter harder than necessary. "Which means we have to figure this out ourselves."

"How?" Millie's voice was barely a whisper from behind her fern.

That was the question. How did you investigate a murder when you couldn't use your only evidence? When you couldn't tell the sheriff that your cats had witnessed it? When you couldn't reveal that you were a witch running from your past?

The lunch hour brought a scattering of customers. The morning had been slow because I'd been closed, so people were just now getting their coffee fix. Mabel came in looking confused, having missed her morning routine entirely.

"Everything feels wrong," she said quietly. "Like the whole town is off balance."

"I know what you mean." I handed her the Lavender Dreams tea she'd been craving.

Felix Wren came in and couldn't meet my eyes. Pearl from the library came in and hugged me without asking, her eyes wet with tears. Jasper brought me a bag of Hazel's favorite tea from his store. "Thought you might want it," he said gruffly. "For yourself."

I thanked them all and made their drinks and kept my walls firmly in place.

The café settled into a quieter rhythm after the initial rush. Around twelve-thirty, I went upstairs to feed Sage again. She was awake and mewing, stronger than this morning. I gave her another small meal, supplemented with a bit of the formula Colton had sent home, and watched her eat with growing confidence.

"You're doing so well," I told her. "Dr. Dover would be proud."

After she finished eating, I set her back on the heating pad and headed downstairs. Rocky was still on guard duty in the hallway, watching the bathroom door with those intense orange-cat eyes.

I'd barely made it back behind the counter when I heard it. A tiny, triumphant mew from upstairs, followed by Rocky's surprised voice.

"Uh, Alexis? You might want to come back up here."

I took the stairs two at a time and stopped short at what I saw.

Sage had somehow climbed over the baby gate.

The tiny gray kitten sat on the hallway floor on the wrong side of the barrier, looking immensely pleased with herself. She wobbled slightly on unsteady legs, but her green eyes were bright with mischief and accomplishment.

"How did you..." I stared at the gate, which was easily three times her height. "You're supposed to be resting."

"Feel better," Sage's small voice said in my mind. "Want play."

"She's been trying for the last five minutes," Rocky reported, sounding half-impressed and half-concerned. "Kept climbing and falling back down. Finally made it over on the fourth try."

"Sage, you're supposed to be taking it easy." But I couldn't help smiling as I knelt down. The kitten immediately wobbled toward me, tail held high despite her unsteady gait.

"Play?" she asked hopefully, bumping her tiny head against my hand.

Rocky crept closer, keeping his body low and his movements slow. "I could play with her. Carefully. I know how to be gentle with the little ones."

I looked at Rocky, the orange cat who usually had exactly one brain cell and all the chaos that came with it, and saw something different in his eyes. Concern. Protectiveness. The same way he'd been watching over Sage since she'd arrived.

"Very carefully," I warned. "She's still recovering. No rough play, no jumping on her, no orange cat chaos."

"I can be calm," Rocky protested. "I can be responsible."

Gus snorted from down the hall. "This I have to see."

I moved the baby gate aside completely, opening up the hallway. "All right. But I'm watching."

What followed was possibly the sweetest thing I'd seen in weeks. Rocky, who usually zoomed around the apartment like his tail was on fire, moved with exaggerated slowness around Sage. When the tiny kitten pounced at his tail with wobbly determination, he swished it gently just out of reach, letting her "catch" it every few attempts.

"Got you!" Sage's tiny voice was filled with pride each time she managed to grab the orange tail.

"Oh no, you got me," Rocky played along, flopping dramatically on his side. "I'm defeated."

Sage climbed over his paw, which was bigger than her entire body, and Rocky stayed perfectly still, letting her explore. When she started to wobble too much, getting tired, he gently nosed her upright.

"Okay, that's enough excitement for now," I said after about ten minutes. Sage was starting to sway on her feet, exhausted from her great adventure. "Back to the warm bed."

"Aww," Rocky complained, but he didn't argue when I scooped Sage up.

"You did good," I told him quietly. "You were very gentle with her."

"She's little," Rocky said, as if this explained everything. "Pack takes care of the little ones."

I settled Sage back on her heating pad, but this time I left the baby gate open. She'd proven she could climb over it anyway, and maybe being able to see the others, to feel less isolated, would be good for her.

"Sleep now," I told her, stroking her head with one finger. "You can play more later."

"Rocky nice," Sage murmured, already drifting off. "Pack."

My throat tightened. Yes. Pack.

When I came back downstairs, Poppy was waiting with that knowing look in her amber eyes.

"What?" I asked.

"Dr. Dover," she repeated with emphasis. "You called him by his first name in your head."

"Colton," I corrected automatically, then realized my mistake. "He asked me to call him that."

"Did he now?" Poppy's tail swished. "And did you notice the way he looked at you? The way he offered to be there for more than just cat emergencies?"

"He's nice. That's all."

"He's interested. There's a difference."

"It doesn't matter." I turned away to straighten the pastry case that didn't need straightening. "I can't let anyone get close. You know that."

"What I know is that you're using fear as an excuse to stay lonely." Poppy's voice was unusually sharp. "But if you want to hide behind your walls forever, that's your choice."

I didn't have an answer for that.

Around one o'clock, Lionel walked in. He didn't smile, just came straight to the counter with those concerned green eyes.

"How are you holding up?" he asked quietly.

"I'm here." It wasn't really an answer, but it was all I had.

"That's something." He paused, then added, "The offer still stands. For game night, or coffee, or just... if you need someone to sit with you. No talking required."

Something in my chest squeezed. He was so genuine, so kind, and I couldn't let him in. Couldn't risk it. "Thank you. I'll keep that in mind."

He nodded like he'd expected that answer and didn't push. "Dandelion Root Revival?"

"Coming up."

I made his drink in silence, hyperaware of him watching me. Not in a creepy way, just in the way someone watches a person they're worried about. Like he was afraid I might break.

He wasn't wrong to worry.

As I handed him his cup, he hesitated, then said, "You know that woman from the yarn shop? Orla Weston?"

My attention sharpened. "What about her?"

"She walks past my shop every single day at exactly 10:15 in the morning. Coming from Willow Street, heading toward Main. I only noticed because I'm usually doing my register count right then." He shrugged. "Been happening for months. Same time every day, like clockwork."

"That's... very precise."

"Right? I thought it was odd. Most people vary by a few minutes, but not her. 10:15 exactly, every single day." He took a sip of his drink. "Probably nothing. But after what happened to Hazel, it seemed worth mentioning. Like maybe she was checking on something. Or watching something."

My pulse kicked. "Did you tell the sheriff?"

"Not yet. Wasn't sure if it mattered." He studied my face. "But you think it might."

"I don't know. But thank you for telling me."

"Alexis," he said, his voice gentle. "I know you probably won't take me up on this, but I'm going to say it anyway. You don't have to carry everything alone."

I wanted to tell him he was wrong. Wanted to explain that I did have to carry it alone, that I'd been carrying it alone for years, that it was the only way to keep people safe. Instead I just said, "I appreciate that."

He left, and Poppy made a disgusted sound from her perch.

"What?" I asked.

"First Dr. Dover, now Lionel." She swished her tail irritably. "Two perfectly good men who care about you, and you push them both away."

"Poppy—"

"You should let someone in. Someone to make you happy." Her amber eyes held mine. "But I suppose you'll keep hiding behind your walls and calling it protection."

I didn't have an answer for that.

Around two o'clock, I went upstairs to check on Sage. What I found made my heart melt.

She was curled up on her heating pad, fast asleep, and Rocky was curled around her, his larger orange body forming a protective semicircle. The tiny gray kitten was tucked against his belly, safe and warm, and Rocky's tail was draped gently over her.

"She tried to play again about half an hour ago," Rocky said quietly, not moving. "Batted at my tail a few times. Got tired fast. I laid down to rest too, and she just... snuggled right in."

"That's the sweetest thing I've ever seen," I whispered.

"She's one of us now," Rocky said simply, his eyes soft. "Pack takes care of pack."

Something warm bloomed in my chest. Despite everything, despite the grief and fear and uncertainty, I had this. I had them. Five cats now instead of four, and they were all mine.

When I returned downstairs, Trish Lawrence was walking past the window. She didn't come in, just slowed down to peer through the glass at me with that calculating expression. When she saw me looking back, she smiled brightly and waved before continuing on her way.

"That woman gives me the creeps," Rocky announced, having followed me back downstairs.

"She's definitely up to something," Poppy agreed. "Probably still plotting how to get that flower shop."

"Could she have killed Hazel for it?" I asked quietly, making sure no customers were close enough to overhear.

"Wrong motive," Gus said from his bed. "If she wanted the shop, she'd want Hazel alive to sell it to her. Dead, it goes to lawyers and family. More complicated."

He had a point. But that didn't mean Trish was innocent. Just that her motive was less obvious.

Around two-thirty, Orla Weston walked past on the other side of the street. She didn't look at the café, didn't wave, just kept walking toward the yarn shop with her head down. But something about seeing her made my skin prickle.

"That one walks past twice a day," a voice said from the viewing room. I looked over to see Cinnamon, the tortoiseshell, watching from her perch on the highest platform. She'd been with me for three months, a surrender from an elderly woman who'd moved into assisted living. Observant, particular, with a memory for patterns that sometimes seemed almost uncanny.

"Twice?" I asked quietly.

"Morning and afternoon. The afternoon one is always at 2:00 exactly. I've watched her for weeks now." Cinnamon's tail twitched. "Same pace, same route, same time. That's not normal. That's checking on something."

My mind raced. Lionel had said 10:15 AM. Now Cinnamon was saying 2:00 PM. "You're sure about the time?"

"I'm sure. The sun hits my platform a certain way at 2:00. I use it to know when to move to the shadier spot." She tilted her head. "The comic shop human mentioned a morning walk. But she comes past here in the afternoon too. Two precise times every day. That's not a commute. That's surveillance."

My breath caught. "And yesterday? The day Hazel died?"

"She walked past at 2:00 like always. But then she came back at 2:30. And again at 3:00. Three times in one hour instead of her usual once." Cinnamon's ears flattened slightly. "The pattern changed. And when patterns change, something's wrong. That night, Hazel died."

Three times. Orla had broken her precise routine the day of the murder, checking on something multiple times. Whatever she'd been watching for, she'd been watching more carefully that day.

That was not a coincidence.

The bell chimed, and I looked up to see Flo bustling in with two boxes of pastries.

"I know, I know," she said before I could say anything. "You texted me not to come today. But I had to." Her eyes were red-rimmed. "Sitting at home just made it worse. I needed to do something normal."

"I'm glad you did." And I meant it. Seeing her familiar face, even tear-stained, was a comfort.

"I brought extras," she said, setting down the boxes. "Couldn't face the thought of you running out and not having anything to serve. Hazel would have hated that." Her voice cracked on Hazel's name.

"She would have," I agreed softly.

Flo wiped her eyes. "We're having a memorial service on Friday. At the community center. I hope you'll come. I know she'd want you there."

Friday. Two days away. A memorial service meant suspects in one place. Opportunities to observe, to listen, to learn.

"I'll be there," I promised.

After Flo left, Poppy came to sit beside me.

"You're really doing this," she said quietly.

"I'm really doing this."

"Then we're with you." She looked at the other cats, and they all nodded, even Millie. "We saw what happened. We'll help however we can."

Upstairs, tiny Sage was sleeping peacefully, the newest member of our strange family. And down here, I had four adult cats ready to help me find justice for Hazel.

I wasn't completely alone.

And somehow, together, we were going to figure this out.

Chapter Seven

Friday morning arrived with gray skies that matched my mood perfectly. I stood in front of my closet, staring at the limited selection of dark clothing I owned, and tried not to look at the box still sitting in the back corner.

Four days since Hazel died. Four days of making coffee and smiling at customers and pretending I was fine. Four days of watching Carla, Trish, and Orla, looking for signs of guilt that I couldn't quite find.

And now, a memorial service.

"I wish we could come," Poppy said from her perch on my bed. The other cats were arranged around the room, all watching me with worried eyes. Gus on his usual spot by the pillow, Millie tucked behind my reading chair, Rocky sprawled across the foot of the bed. And tiny Sage, curled up in the warm indent I'd left in the blankets, so much stronger than she'd been just days ago.

"Me too." I pulled out a dark gray sweater and black pants. "But a memorial service full of people and five cats would be... complicated."

"We'll be here when you get back," Gus said. "Try not to do anything stupid."

"Like what?"

"Like accusing someone of murder in the middle of a memorial service."

I almost smiled. "I'll try to restrain myself."

By one-thirty, I was dressed and as ready as I'd ever be. I'd spent the morning at the café, which had been unusually quiet. Most of the town would be at the memorial. Hazel had touched more lives than I'd realized.

I was locking the café door when I heard footsteps behind me.

"Alexis, wait up!" Flo hurried down the sidewalk, slightly out of breath. She wore a black dress and cardigan, her usually cheerful face somber. "I thought we could walk over together. If that's all right?"

Something in my chest loosened slightly. "That would be nice. Thank you."

We fell into step together, heading toward the community center three blocks away. Flo filled the silence with gentle chatter about the weather, about her granddaughters, about anything except the reason we were walking to a memorial service on a Friday afternoon.

"Eva wanted to come," Flo said as we turned the corner. "But I told her she was too young. Ella asked if Hazel was going to be a star now. I didn't know how to answer that."

"What did you say?"

"That Hazel would always be watching over us. That she'd want us to take care of her flowers and remember her kindness." Flo's voice wavered. "I don't know if that was the right thing to say."

"I think it was perfect."

The community center came into view, and my steps slowed. The parking lot was packed, cars lining the street in both directions. People were streaming through the front doors, more than I'd expected.

"Everyone loved Hazel," Flo said softly, echoing my thoughts. "She'd been a pillar of this community for decades. Always the first to volunteer, first to help, first to welcome newcomers." She glanced at me. "Like she welcomed you."

My throat tightened. "Yeah. Like she welcomed me."

Inside, the community center had been transformed. Flowers covered every surface, arrangements in purples and whites and soft pinks. Photos of Hazel lined the walls: young Hazel with dark hair, middle-aged Hazel in her flower shop, older Hazel laughing at some community event. A life lived fully, documented in images.

The main room was filled with chairs, easily over a hundred, and almost all of them were taken. People stood along the walls, clustered in small groups, speaking in hushed voices. I recognized faces from the café mixed with people I'd never seen before. A significant portion of the community had turned out to honor Hazel.

"There must be two hundred people here," I murmured.

"At least." Flo spotted someone across the room and waved. "Come on, there are a couple of seats together."

I followed her to the middle section, right on the aisle. As I sat down, I scanned the crowd, looking for familiar faces. Looking for suspects.

Carla Lynch sat in the front row, her black pantsuit pristine, her posture rigid. She was alone, staring straight ahead at the podium where someone had placed a large photo of Hazel surrounded by sunflowers.

Trish Lawrence sat three rows back on the opposite side, wearing a dress that was slightly too colorful for a memorial service. She kept checking her phone, barely glancing at the photos on the walls.

But Orla Weston was nowhere to be seen.

"Have you seen that woman from Cordelia's yarn shop?" someone asked nearby, and I turned to see two older women I didn't recognize talking in hushed tones.

"Orla? No, I haven't. That's odd, isn't it?"

"Very odd. Cordelia was saying just yesterday how fond Hazel was of Orla, always stopping in to chat when she came by for yarn. You'd think she'd be here."

"Maybe she's working. Someone has to mind the shop."

"On a Friday afternoon when the whole town is at a memorial? I don't think so. Cordelia closed for this. Everyone did."

They moved away before I could hear more, but my mind was racing. According to Cordelia, Hazel had been fond of Orla, stopped in regularly to chat. But I'd never heard Hazel mention her. Never seen them together. And now Orla wasn't here when, according to those women, everyone had closed their businesses to attend.

That absence felt deliberate. Calculated.

Flo leaned over. "Looking for someone?"

"Just... taking it all in." I forced my attention back to the front of the room, where Jasper Sharpe was approaching the podium.

The service started with Jasper welcoming everyone and thanking them for coming. His weathered face was solemn as he gripped the podium.

"Hazel Blaine was the kind of person who made Larkspur Valley feel like home," he began, his voice carrying across the packed room. "She came to this town forty-eight years ago, bought that little flower shop on Main Street when it was barely more than a closet, and turned it into something beautiful. Just like she did with everything she touched."

He paused, collecting himself. "Hazel believed that flowers weren't just decoration. They were conversation. Comfort. Connection. She knew exactly which arrangement to send when someone was grieving, which bouquet meant congratulations, which single stem said 'I'm thinking of you.' She remembered every customer's preferences, every story they told her, every important date in their lives. That wasn't business sense, though she had plenty of that. That was love."

The room was silent except for scattered sniffles.

"I remember when my mother was dying, twenty years ago," Jasper continued, his voice rougher now. "Hazel showed up at the hospital every single day for three weeks with fresh flowers. Different ones each time. She'd sit with me for ten minutes, never asking questions, never offering platitudes. Just sitting. And when my mother finally passed, the first thing I saw when I came home was an arrangement on my doorstep with a note that said, 'These are for hope.' I still have that note."

He stepped back from the podium, and for a moment no one moved. Then Pearl Van stood, smoothing her skirt as she made her way to the front.

"Hazel donated flowers to the library every single month for thirty years," Pearl said, her librarian's voice clear and steady despite her red eyes. "But it wasn't just about making the building pretty. She'd choose books from our new arrivals and create arrangements that matched them. A mystery novel got dark purples and deep reds. Romance got soft pinks and whites. Children's books got bright, cheerful wildflowers. She said books and flowers both told stories, and they should complement each other."

Pearl pulled a tissue from her pocket, dabbed at her eyes. "Last month, she brought in a sunflower arrangement for our autumn display. She told me sunflowers were her favorite because they always turned toward the light, even on cloudy days. I think that's who Hazel was. Always turning toward the light, always helping others find it too."

Felix Wren went next, surprisingly articulate for someone who usually mumbled at his shoes. He described how Hazel had been the first person to buy one of his paintings, how she'd encouraged him to enter the county art show, how she'd told him that creating beauty was never a waste of time even when practical people called it foolish.

"She hung that painting in her shop," Felix said, his voice thick with emotion. "Right behind the counter where she could see it every day. When I tried to thank her, she said she was the one who should be grateful. Said looking at it reminded her why she did what she did. Made beauty for people who needed it. I never forgot that."

Mabel Smalls spoke about Hazel's sharp wit and sharper business sense, about how Hazel had mentored her when Mabel opened her own shop decades ago. "She taught me that being kind in business wasn't weakness, it was strength. That customers remembered how you made them feel more than they remembered your prices. She was right about that. She was right about most things."

Atticus, the park ranger, stood next. He was a man of few words normally, but he spoke slowly and carefully about how Hazel had created special arrangements for the ranger station every spring. "She said we spent too much time with trees and not enough time with flowers. Said we needed reminders that the world was beautiful, not just functional. Every spring for fifteen years, she'd show up with those arrangements and refuse payment. Said it was her contribution to keeping the parks beautiful."

Cordelia Kelder went to the podium, and I braced myself for a rambling speech. But she surprised me, speaking briefly and with genuine emotion. "Hazel was patient with me, even when I was being difficult. And I know I can be difficult." A ripple of gentle laughter went through the room. "She never made me feel like a nuisance, even when I probably was one. That's a rare gift."

One by one, people shared their stories. The pattern that emerged was unmistakable: Hazel had touched every corner of this community, had seen people, had remembered them, had made them feel valued. She'd built relationships one flower at a time, one conversation at a time, one act of kindness at a time.

And now she was gone, leaving a hole that two hundred people couldn't quite fill.

Each story painted a picture of a woman who'd given more than she'd taken, who'd built relationships across every part of this community, who'd been beloved by almost everyone who knew her.

Almost everyone.

I watched Carla's face during the testimonials. It remained blank, polite, giving nothing away. But her hands were clenched in her lap, knuckles white.

Trish looked bored, checking her phone again before someone nearby shot her a disapproving look.

"Would anyone else like to share?" Jasper asked.

The room fell quiet. People looked at each other, waiting. Then Flo squeezed my hand.

"You should say something," she whispered. "About your friendship."

Panic flared in my chest. "I can't—"

"You can. You were close to her. She'd want you to."

But I couldn't. Couldn't stand up there and talk about Hazel without my voice breaking, without revealing how much I'd kept from her, without admitting that I'd never been honest with the one person in Larkspur Valley who might have understood.

I shook my head, and Flo squeezed my hand again before letting go.

The service continued. More stories, more flowers, more reminders of everything Hazel had been and everything I'd lost. By the time Jasper wrapped up and invited everyone to the reception in the adjoining hall, I felt scraped raw.

"I need a minute," I told Flo.

"Of course. I'll be in the other room when you're ready."

She left with the crowd, and I stayed in my seat, staring at Hazel's photo surrounded by sunflowers. A shining light, someone had called her. That was exactly right. She'd been warm and bright and steady, and now that light was gone.

"Alexis."

I looked up to find Carla standing in the aisle, her expression unreadable.

"Carla. I'm sorry for your loss."

"Are you?" She sat down in the chair Flo had vacated, turning to face me fully. "Because it seems like everyone in this town was closer to my aunt than I was. Twenty years of being her only living relative, and I might as well have been a stranger."

"I'm sure that's not true—"

"Don't." Carla's voice was sharp. "Don't patronize me. I heard all those stories. All those people talking about how generous she was, how kind, how welcoming. But where was that generosity when it came to her own family? Where was that kindness when she was writing her will?"

"Maybe she had her reasons."

"Maybe she was a selfish old woman who wanted to control everything even after death." Carla's face was flushed now, anger breaking through her composure. "That lawyer, that pompous man who gets to decide the fate of my family's business? He came to my hotel yesterday. Do you know what he told me?"

I shook my head.

"He told me Hazel left explicit instructions. The shop is to be preserved exactly as it is for six months before any decisions are made about its future. Six months of paying rent and utilities and insurance on a business that's not making money because there's no one to run it. Six months of watching it gather dust while that lawyer 'assesses options.'"

"Why six months?"

"Who knows? One last manipulation from beyond the grave." Carla stood abruptly. "And that box she left you. I want to know what's in it."

My spine stiffened. "That's private."

"Private." She laughed bitterly. "My aunt leaves her entire business to a lawyer, leaves mysterious sealed boxes to near-strangers, and I'm supposed to accept that it's all private? I don't think so."

"I haven't even opened it yet."

Something flickered in Carla's expression. Surprise, maybe. Or suspicion. "Still? Why not?"

"Because it's too painful." The truth slipped out before I could stop it. "Because opening it makes it real. Makes her death final."

Carla stared at me for a long moment, and some of the anger seemed to drain out of her. "When you do open it," she said finally, her voice tired, "if there's anything in there about the shop, about her wishes, I'd appreciate knowing. That's all I'm asking."

She walked away before I could respond, leaving me alone in the now-empty room.

I took a deep breath and forced myself to stand. The reception. I needed to get through the reception, needed to observe, needed to look for clues that might help me understand who had killed Hazel and why.

The adjoining hall was crowded with people holding paper plates of cookies and small sandwiches, cups of punch or coffee, all of them talking in that peculiar hushed tone reserved for funeral receptions. I accepted a cup of punch I didn't want and positioned myself near the wall where I could watch.

Carla stood alone near the windows, looking out at the gray sky. No one approached her. Either they didn't know who she was, or they were giving her space.

Near the coffee table, I overheard two men discussing Hazel's business.

"Twenty-eight years she ran that shop," one said. "Started with nothing but a loan and a dream, according to what I heard."

"Built it into the best flower shop in three counties. Could have expanded, franchised, but she said she liked it small. Liked knowing every customer." The other man shook his head. "Can't imagine anyone else running it the same way."

"That niece of hers doesn't seem too broken up about it."

"Noticed that too. Barely shed a tear during the service."

I moved on, ears open, collecting information like puzzle pieces I couldn't quite fit together yet.

Hugh was sitting in a chair near the wall, his cane resting beside him. I hadn't seen him at the service, but here he was, looking exhausted but determined.

"Didn't think you'd make it," I said, approaching him.

"Wouldn't miss it. Hazel brought me flowers every time I was laid up with my hip. Never asked for anything, just wanted to brighten my day." He gestured to the room. "Quite a turnout."

"Over two hundred people, I think."

"She touched a lot of lives. That's how you know someone mattered, isn't it? By who shows up to say goodbye." He paused, then added quietly, "That yarn shop woman didn't show up, though. The one who's been working for Cordelia."

"Orla?"

"That's the one. Cordelia mentioned it to me, said she gave Orla the afternoon off to come, but Orla said she had personal business. On the day of Hazel's memorial." Hugh's expression was troubled. "Seemed strange to me. Everyone else made time."

I filed that away. More evidence that Orla's absence was noticed, was unusual, was wrong.

Across the room, I caught sight of Maeve watching me with those too-perceptive eyes. She raised her coffee cup in a small salute, acknowledging something neither of us had said aloud. Then she turned back to her conversation, and I wondered what she saw when she looked at me. What she suspected.

I moved closer to Trish, pretending to study the cookie table while I listened.

"...such a shame about the business," Trish was saying. "Prime location, beautiful storefront. It would be perfect for expansion."

"It's a memorial service," the other person said, sounding uncomfortable.

"I know, I know. But business doesn't stop just because someone dies. Someone needs to think practically about these things." Trish lowered her voice slightly, but not enough. "I heard the niece is contesting the will. If she wins, I might have a chance to buy it from her. Carla has no interest in flowers. She'll want the cash."

I felt my jaw clench. Less than an hour after a memorial service, and Trish was already plotting her acquisition strategy.

"She's disgusting," someone said behind me, and I turned to find Maeve Atwater, the bookshop owner. She was short and round with wild curly hair and eyes that seemed to see too much. "Trish Lawrence has been circling that flower shop like a vulture since the day Hazel died."

"You heard that?"

"Hard not to. The woman has no volume control." Maeve selected a cookie and bit into it with more force than necessary. "I knew Hazel for thirty years. She couldn't stand Trish. Called her a snake in floral print."

Despite everything, I almost smiled. "That sounds like Hazel."

"She talked about you sometimes," Maeve said, studying me with those perceptive eyes. "Said you reminded her of herself when she was younger. Guarded, but with a good heart."

My throat tightened. "I wish I'd known her better."

"She knew you as well as you'd let her. That was enough for Hazel. She was patient." Maeve finished her cookie and brushed crumbs from her hands. "She left you something, didn't she? A box?"

Word traveled fast in Larkspur Valley. "How did you—"

"Small town. The lawyer's secretary mentioned it to someone who told someone who told me." She smiled gently. "Whatever's in that box, Hazel wanted you to have it. Don't let Carla's bitterness make you feel guilty about that."

She drifted away before I could respond, leaving me standing alone by the cookie table.

I spent another thirty minutes circulating through the reception, listening to conversations, watching interactions, looking for anything that might be useful. But mostly I just heard stories about Hazel: her kindness, her generosity, her love of flowers and people and this town.

Orla Weston never appeared. Her absence felt significant, but I couldn't figure out why. Maybe she simply hadn't known Hazel well enough to come. Maybe she was working. Maybe it meant nothing.

Or maybe it meant everything.

By three-thirty, people were starting to leave. Flo found me near the door, her eyes red from crying.

"Ready to go?" she asked.

"More than ready."

We walked back in silence, the gray sky finally releasing a light drizzle. By the time we reached Main Street, I was cold and exhausted and no closer to answers than I'd been before the service.

"Thank you for walking with me," I said when we reached my café.

"Of course, honey. That's what neighbors do." Flo hesitated, then added, "If you need anything, anything at all, you let me know. Okay?"

"Okay."

I watched her hurry next door to her diner, then let myself into the café. The cats were waiting, all five of them lined up like a welcoming committee. Sage was at the end of the line, her tiny gray body dwarfed by the others, but her tail was held high with confidence.

"How was it?" Poppy asked.

"Sad. Crowded. Over two hundred people, easily." I locked the door behind me and leaned against it. "Carla is bitter about the will. Trish is already plotting to buy the shop. And Orla didn't show up at all."

"Didn't show up?" Gus's ears perked forward. "That's interesting."

"Is it? Maybe she just didn't know Hazel well."

"Or maybe," Poppy said slowly, "she didn't want to be there. Didn't want to face what she'd done."

I thought about that as I climbed the stairs to my apartment, the cats trailing behind me. Sage took the stairs carefully, still a bit wobbly but determined to keep up with her pack. A memorial service for someone you'd killed. Would you go? Would you risk being seen, being remembered, being connected?

Or would you stay away?

In my apartment, I changed out of my memorial clothes and into comfortable pants and an oversized sweater. The box in my closet called to me, but I still wasn't ready. Not yet.

Instead, I made tea and settled on the couch with a blanket and five cats. Outside, the drizzle turned to steady rain, and the sky grew darker even though it was barely four o'clock.

Sage had claimed a spot on my lap, purring so loudly I could feel it vibrating through my legs. Just this morning, I'd watched her get the zoomies for the first time, that sudden burst of kitten energy that sent her careening around the apartment like a tiny gray rocket. Rocky had chased after her, playing along, while the others watched with amused tolerance.

It had been the first moment of pure joy I'd felt since finding Hazel in that alley. Watching this tiny creature who'd been abandoned and near death now full of life and mischief.

"What now?" Rocky asked, curled against my other leg.

"Now," I said quietly, stroking Sage's soft head with one finger, "I figure out why Orla Weston didn't come to Hazel's memorial. And whether that means she's guilty, or just doesn't care."

"How?" Millie whispered.

I didn't have an answer yet. But I was going to find one.

For Hazel. For justice. For the truth that had died with her in that alley.

The rain fell harder, drumming against the windows, and I sat surrounded by cats and questions and the weight of secrets I couldn't share.

Tomorrow, I'd keep investigating. Tomorrow, I'd get closer to the truth.

Tonight, I just needed to survive another day without the one person in Larkspur Valley who'd made me feel like I might belong.

Chapter Eight

Sunday morning arrived with weak autumn sunlight filtering through my bedroom curtains. I lay in bed longer than I should have, staring at the ceiling while the cats moved around the apartment in their usual morning routines. Another day. Another stretch of hours to fill while pretending everything was normal.

Saturday had been unbearable. The café had been quiet, almost funeral in its silence. The customers who did come in spoke in hushed tones and left quickly. I'd made drinks mechanically, cleaned surfaces that didn't need cleaning, and watched the clock drag its way through the hours. By closing time, I'd been ready to crawl out of my own skin.

I'd spent Saturday evening on the couch, trying to read, trying to watch something mindless on my laptop, trying to do anything except think about the box in my closet or the fact that Hazel's killer was still walking free. The cats had tried to distract me with their usual antics, but even Rocky's chaos couldn't quite break through the fog. Though watching him teach Sage to pounce on his tail had been a brief bright spot.

Now it was Sunday, and I had to do it all over again.

"You can't keep going like this," Poppy said from her spot on my pillow. "You're going to make yourself sick."

"I'm fine."

"You're not fine. You barely ate yesterday. You didn't sleep well. And you keep staring at that closet door like it's going to open itself."

She wasn't wrong. The box sat in there, sealed and waiting, and every time I walked past the closet I felt its pull. But I couldn't open it. Not yet. Maybe not ever.

I forced myself out of bed and went through the motions of my morning routine. Feed the cats. Sage was eating regular kitten food without any trouble, getting stronger every day. Shower. Get dressed. Make coffee that I wouldn't drink.

By ten o'clock, I was standing in my living room with nothing to do and nowhere to go. The café was closed on Sundays. I had no errands, no obligations, no excuses to leave the apartment. Just me and the cats and a box I couldn't face and memories I couldn't escape.

My phone buzzed. A text from Flo.

Family dinner today at 2. Standing invitation still stands if you want to join us. No pressure, but we'd love to have you.

I stared at the message for a long moment. Every instinct screamed at me to decline, to make some excuse, to stay safely alone in my apartment where I couldn't let anyone too close.

But the thought of spending another day in this apartment, alone with my thoughts and that box, was suddenly unbearable.

Before I could talk myself out of it, I typed back: *I'd love to come. Thank you.*

The response came almost immediately: *Wonderful! 2pm, you know where. Casual dress. Can't wait!*

"You said yes," Poppy observed.

"I said yes."

"Good." She settled onto the back of the couch, looking satisfied. "You need this."

Maybe I did. Or maybe I was just too tired to keep all my walls up. Either way, I'd committed now.

The next few hours dragged by. I changed clothes three times, unable to decide what "casual" meant for family dinner. Finally settled on dark jeans and a soft blue sweater that Hazel had once complimented. The thought made my chest ache, but I kept it on anyway.

At 1:55, I stood outside Flo's house, stomach twisting with nerves. The historic home sat on a tree-lined street near the center of town, a beautiful Victorian with wraparound porch and detailed woodwork. Flo's family had founded Larkspur Valley, and this house had been in her family for generations. It looked warm and inviting and absolutely terrifying.

I forced myself up the porch steps and knocked.

The door flew open almost immediately, and Ella's face appeared at hip height.

"You came!" She grabbed my hand and pulled me inside with surprising strength for a six-year-old. "Grandma said you might come and I drew you a picture just in case!"

"Ella, let her breathe," Flo called from somewhere deeper in the house. She appeared in the hallway, wiping her hands on a dish towel and smiling warmly. "I'm so glad you're here. Come in, come in."

The house smelled like roasted chicken and herbs and something sweet baking. Voices and laughter floated from what I assumed was the dining room. My instinct was to turn around and run, but Ella still had my hand in a death grip.

"This is for you," she announced, thrusting a piece of paper at me with her free hand. "It's you and Poppy and Gus and Rocky and Millie and Sage. Grandma told me you got a new baby kitten! See? I remembered all their names."

The drawing showed a stick figure version of me surrounded by five cats of varying colors and sizes. A tiny gray one sat near my feet. Hearts floated around us, and at the top, in careful letters, she'd written "Alexis and her cat friends."

Something in my chest cracked. "This is beautiful, Ella. Thank you."

"You can keep it. I made Grandma one too." She finally released my hand and skipped ahead. "Come meet everyone!"

I followed Flo and Ella into a large dining room where a massive wooden table was set for eight. A woman who looked like a younger version of Flo was setting down a basket of rolls, and a man was helping an older girl fold napkins. Another younger man was adjusting chairs.

"Everyone, you remember Alexis," Flo announced. "Alexis, this is my daughter Piper, her husband Lee, and you've met Eva and Ella. And this is my son Henry."

Piper smiled warmly. "We've met a few times at the café. It's nice to have you here."

Lee nodded in greeting. He was tall and quiet, with kind eyes and the patient demeanor of someone used to being around energetic children.

Henry, who looked to be in his mid-twenties with Flo's dark hair and easy smile, stuck out his hand. "Good to finally meet you properly. Mom talks about you all the time."

"Henry," Flo chided.

"What? You do." He grinned at me. "Apparently you make the best coffee in three counties."

"I don't know about that," I managed, shaking his hand.

"And Maeve should be here any minute," Flo continued. "She's bringing dessert."

As if on cue, the doorbell rang, and Maeve Atwater bustled in carrying a pie that smelled like apples and cinnamon.

"Sorry I'm late," she said cheerfully. "Had to close up the bookshop. Sunday browsers never know when to leave." She spotted me and her face lit up. "Alexis! So glad you decided to come."

"Here, sit, sit." Flo directed me to a chair between Maeve and Eva. "We're just about ready."

The next few minutes were a flurry of activity as dishes made their way to the table: roasted chicken, mashed potatoes, green beans, those rolls, a salad, and what looked like homemade gravy. It was more food than I'd seen in one place in months.

"Grandma always makes too much," Eva said, noticing my expression. "But that's okay because leftovers."

"Best part," Henry agreed, already reaching for the chicken.

"Grace first," Flo said firmly, and everyone bowed their heads while she said a quick blessing. Then chaos erupted as food was passed and plates were filled and conversations overlapped.

It was overwhelming and warm and completely foreign to someone who'd eaten alone for the better part of a year. I took small portions and tried to look like I belonged here, at this table full of people who knew each other's rhythms and inside jokes.

I'd eaten like this once, in another life. Communal meals with the coven, everyone gathered around a table, sharing food and conversation and fellowship. I'd had that warmth, that connection. And I'd walked away from it. From all of them, but especially from Lily, my best friend who'd never understand why I left without saying goodbye.

This felt like that, but different. Safer, maybe, because these people didn't know what I was. Or more dangerous, because I was starting to care what they thought.

"How are you holding up?" Piper asked quietly, passing me the potatoes. "With everything that happened?"

"I'm managing." The automatic response.

"It must be so hard. I know you and Hazel were close."

Were we? I'd thought so, but close would have meant being honest with her. Close would have meant opening that box she'd left me.

"She was a good friend," I said instead.

"The best," Flo agreed. "I still can't believe she's gone. Every time I look down the street at her shop, I expect to see her in the window arranging flowers."

"Has anyone decided what's happening with the shop?" Lee asked, helping Eva cut her chicken.

"That awful niece is trying to contest the will," Maeve said, her tone disapproving. "Can you imagine? Not even a week yet and she's already got lawyers involved."

"I heard she's claiming Hazel wasn't of sound mind," Henry added. "Which is ridiculous. Hazel was sharp as a tack right up until..."

He trailed off, glancing at Eva and Ella, who were absorbed in their mashed potatoes.

"Well, anyway," Flo said, changing the subject smoothly. "The lawyer is following Hazel's instructions. Six months before any decisions are made."

"Six months seems oddly specific," Maeve mused. "I wonder why she chose that timeframe."

I wondered too. What happened in six months? What had Hazel been waiting for?

"And then there's Trish Lawrence," Piper said, lowering her voice. "Did you hear she approached the lawyer about buying the shop? Before Hazel was even buried."

"That woman has no shame," Flo said firmly. "Never has. She's been trying to put Hazel out of business for years."

"Really?" I leaned forward slightly, though I'd heard hints of this before. "How bad was it between them?"

"Oh, honey, it was more than just competition." Flo passed the gravy boat. "Hazel never said much about it, but I could tell it bothered her. Nobody likes being undermined in their own town."

"Bothered her enough to..." I caught myself, glancing at the girls. "To be really upset?"

"Hazel didn't let people like Trish get to her," Maeve said. "She just kept being her wonderful self and let her work speak for itself. That's what drove Trish crazy. She couldn't compete with genuine talent and kindness."

"I heard someone say the sheriff is still investigating," Lee said carefully. "That they're not sure it was just an accident."

The table went quiet for a moment, everyone's attention suddenly focused on their plates.

"Lee," Piper said with a warning tone.

"What? I'm just saying what everyone's thinking." He glanced at me apologetically. "Sorry, Alexis. I didn't mean to bring it up so directly."

"No, it's okay." My heart was pounding. "What do you mean they're not sure?"

"Well, it's just gossip," he said carefully. "But I ran into Deputy Thorne at the hardware store yesterday. He mentioned they'd found something that didn't quite add up. Wouldn't say what, just that the investigation wasn't closed yet."

"That button they found," Henry said. "The one in the alley. I heard it was expensive. Like, designer expensive. Not the kind of thing Hazel would wear."

"How do you know about the button?" Flo asked, surprised.

Henry shrugged. "Small town, Mom. Word gets around. Thorne was asking Jasper if he recognized it, since Jasper sells some clothing at the general store. He said it looked like it came from a high-end coat or jacket."

Carla's black pantsuit had looked expensive. So had Trish's flashy clothes. I didn't know what Orla typically wore well enough to judge.

"And there's the timing," Maeve added quietly. "Hazel was in perfect health. Went to her doctor just two weeks ago for her annual checkup. Clean bill of health for a seventy-eight-year-old woman. Then suddenly she falls in an alley she'd walked through thousands of times?"

"People fall," Piper said, though she didn't sound convinced. "Especially at night."

"In front of her own shop? When the security light was working?" Maeve shook her head. "I don't buy it."

"What are you suggesting?" Lee asked.

"I'm not suggesting anything. I'm just observing that it doesn't make sense." Maeve took a sip of her wine. "And apparently Dr. Vex agrees, because she's been very thorough with the autopsy. More thorough than a simple fall would require."

My throat was tight. "What did she find?"

"No one knows exactly. She's being very quiet about it. But she did mention to someone at the hospital that there were 'inconsistencies' that needed further investigation." Maeve paused. "And she sent samples to a lab in Denver. For toxicology."

"Toxicology?" Flo looked alarmed. "You think someone poisoned Hazel?"

"I think Dr. Vex thinks it's worth checking." Maeve's eyes met mine across the table. "Which means this might not be over. Which means whoever did this might still be out there."

The words hung in the air, heavy and ominous.

"Can we talk about something else?" Piper asked, nodding toward Eva, who was now paying attention. "Little ears."

"Right, sorry." Lee smiled at his daughter. "Eva, tell Alexis about your school project."

Eva launched into an enthusiastic description of something involving volcanoes and baking soda, and the conversation shifted to safer topics. But my mind was racing. Toxicology. Dr. Vex had found something worth testing for poison.

"You're a million miles away," Maeve said quietly beside me.

"Sorry. Just thinking."

"About Hazel?" Her perceptive eyes studied me. "Or about who might have wanted to hurt her?"

I nearly dropped my fork. "What?"

"Don't look so shocked. I've been running a bookshop for thirty years. I know a mystery when I see one." She took a bite of chicken, chewing thoughtfully. "Hazel's death was too convenient for too many people. That niece who wanted the business. That rival who wanted the location. Even that new woman at Cordelia's yarn shop."

"Orla?" I kept my voice low. "Why would she have anything to do with it?"

"Probably nothing. But she's been asking a lot of questions about Hazel since it happened. About her routine, her family, her business. Cordelia mentioned it to me. Said it seemed odd."

Before I could press for more information, Ella tugged on my sleeve.

"Are your cats sad without you?" she asked, her face concerned.

"I think they're okay for a few hours."

"Do they miss Hazel too? She used to visit them sometimes, right?"

The innocent question hit harder than it should have. "Yes. They miss her very much."

"Me too." Ella leaned against my arm. "Grandma says Hazel is watching over us now. Like an angel. Do you think angels can talk to cats?"

"Of course they can," Eva said matter-of-factly. "Angels can do anything. And Hazel loved cats. She told me once that cats could see things people couldn't."

My hand stilled on my fork. "She said that?"

"Uh-huh. Last time we visited her shop, there was a black cat outside and Hazel said it was watching something invisible. She said cats see the world differently than we do. They notice things." Eva took a bite of her chicken. "I think she was right. Your cats always seem like they're paying attention to everything."

"They are," I said carefully. "Cats are very observant."

"Even baby Sage?" Ella asked. "She's so tiny. Can she see things too?"

"Especially Sage," I said softly, thinking of that impossibly young kitten speaking to me. "Sometimes the smallest ones see the most."

"That yarn lady doesn't like cats," Ella announced suddenly. "The one who works for Mrs. Kelder."

Everyone looked at her.

"Ella, where did you get that idea?" Flo asked.

"From her face. When we walked past your café with Mommy last week, the yarn lady was going in and she saw Rocky in the window. She made a mean face. Like this." Ella scrunched up her face in an exaggerated grimace. "Mommy said I shouldn't make faces, but the yarn lady did it first."

"You mean Orla?" I tried to keep my voice neutral.

"I guess. The one with brown hair who's always walking by herself." Ella leaned closer to me, lowering her voice. "I don't like her. She feels... wrong."

"Ella," Piper said more firmly. "That's not a nice thing to say about someone."

"But it's true!" Ella's eyes were wide and earnest. "She feels cold. Like when you open the freezer and the air comes out. That's what she feels like."

An uncomfortable silence fell over the table. Adults exchanged glances, unsure how to respond to a six-year-old's unsettling observation.

"Some people are just quiet, sweetie," Flo said gently. "That doesn't mean they're bad."

"I didn't say bad. I said cold." Ella picked up her fork again, apparently satisfied that she'd made her point. "There's a difference."

Maeve was watching Ella with that same intensity she'd turned on me earlier. Then she looked at me, and something passed between us. Understanding, maybe. Or recognition.

"Out of the mouths of babes," she murmured, so quietly only I could hear.

The rest of the meal passed in a blur of conversation and laughter and the warm chaos of family. I contributed where I could, deflected personal questions with practiced ease, and tried not to think about how much I'd been missing. How much I'd denied myself in the name of safety.

After dinner, Flo wouldn't let anyone help clean up. "You're guests," she insisted. "Go sit in the living room. I'll bring coffee and pie in a minute."

The living room was as warm and welcoming as the rest of the house, with overstuffed furniture and family photos covering every surface. Eva and Ella immediately claimed spots on either side of me on the couch.

"Can we come visit the cats tomorrow?" Eva asked.

"If it's okay with your mom."

"It's fine with me," Piper said, settling into an armchair. "As long as you're not too busy."

"Never too busy for these two."

Henry and Lee had drifted off to discuss something about trucks, leaving me with Piper, Maeve, and the girls. Maeve was studying the family photos with the same intensity she probably brought to organizing her bookshop.

"This house has good energy," she said suddenly. "Strong foundations, both literal and figurative. The kind of place that protects what matters."

"That's an interesting way of putting it," Piper said, amused.

"I'm right though, aren't I?" Maeve turned to face us. "I've lived in this town long enough to know the history. This house has been in your family since the founding. It's weathered storms and protected your family through everything. Some places are like that. They have a quality that goes beyond just wood and stone."

"Like the café!" Ella announced. "The Cozy Purrch has good energy too. That's why the cats are so happy there."

"You're absolutely right," Maeve agreed. "Very perceptive of you."

Ella looked pleased, and I felt that familiar prickle of unease. These casual observations that hit too close to truth. Maeve's talk of energy and places that protected. Ella's insistence that I "sparkled happiness" and that the café had good energy.

Could they sense something? Or was I just paranoid?

Flo returned with coffee and generous slices of pie, and the conversation shifted to lighter topics. But I couldn't quite shake the feeling that Maeve was watching me with those knowing eyes, seeing more than I wanted her to see.

By four o'clock, I was starting to feel the weight of social interaction. As much as I'd needed this, needed the distraction and the warmth, I was reaching my limit.

"I should probably get going," I said, standing carefully so as not to disturb Ella, who'd fallen asleep against my side.

"Already?" Flo looked disappointed. "Well, I'm glad you came. You're welcome anytime, you know that."

"Thank you. For everything. The meal was wonderful."

Maeve walked me to the door. "Alexis," she said quietly, where the others couldn't hear. "Whatever you're looking for, whatever questions you're asking yourself about Hazel, be careful. Some answers are dangerous."

My heart stuttered. "I don't know what you mean."

"Don't you?" She smiled gently. "I think you do. Just... be careful. And if you need help, ask. You don't have to do everything alone."

She went back inside before I could respond, leaving me standing on the porch with my drawing from Ella and a head full of questions.

The walk back to my apartment felt longer than usual. The afternoon had been exactly what I'd needed and exactly what I'd feared: a glimpse of what connection could look like. Of what I'd been denying myself.

But it had also given me information. Dr. Vex had found something unusual. Toxicology. Orla had been asking questions about Hazel. And Maeve somehow knew I was investigating, even though I'd been careful.

The cats were waiting when I climbed the stairs to my apartment. My core four lined up at the door, with tiny Sage at the end, looking so much stronger than when she'd first arrived.

"How was it?" Poppy asked immediately.

"Good. Strange. Overwhelming." I set Ella's drawing on my kitchen counter, where I could see the five cats she'd carefully drawn, including tiny Sage at the bottom. "And possibly useful."

I filled them in on everything I'd learned while I made myself actual dinner for the first time in days. The cats listened intently, interrupting occasionally with questions or observations.

"So Orla's been asking about Hazel," Gus said thoughtfully. "That's suspicious."

"Or just curious," I countered. "People talk after someone dies."

"Not like that. Not detailed questions about routine and family." Poppy's tail swished. "That sounds like someone trying to piece something together. Or trying to figure out if anyone suspects them."

She had a point.

"And the autopsy found something," Rocky added. "Toxicology. That means poison, right?"

"Maybe. Or maybe they're just being thorough." But I didn't believe that. If Dr. Vex had sent samples to Denver for testing, she suspected something.

I scooped up Sage from where she was curled on the couch, needing the comfort of her tiny, warm body against my chest. She purred immediately, that rumbling sound too big for such a small creature.

"Safe," she murmured sleepily. "Warm."

"Yes, baby. You're safe." I held her close for a moment.

I needed to talk to Iris. Needed to find out what the autopsy revealed. But how could I ask without seeming suspicious? Without revealing that I knew more than I should?

My gaze drifted to the closet door. The box was in there, sealed and waiting. Maybe it had answers. Maybe Hazel had left me something that would help.

But I still couldn't bring myself to open it.

"One thing at a time," I said, settling Sage back on the couch with the others. "Tomorrow, I'll figure out how to get more information from Iris. And I'll watch Orla more carefully. See if she does anything suspicious."

"And the box?" Millie asked softly.

"Not yet." I couldn't explain why, couldn't put into words the fear that sat heavy in my chest every time I thought about opening it. "Soon. But not yet."

The cats didn't push, just settled around me as I finished eating and cleaned up. Sage curled up in my lap, purring contentedly. Outside, the sun was setting, turning the sky orange and pink. Another day survived. Another step closer to truth, maybe.

Or another step closer to danger.

But I'd made my choice. I wasn't running this time. I was staying, investigating, risking everything for justice.

For Hazel, who'd believed I deserved to be happy here.

For myself, who was starting to believe maybe she'd been right.

Chapter Nine

Monday morning came with crystalline blue skies and temperatures that hinted at the winter to come. I was up before dawn, unable to sleep, my mind racing with everything I'd learned at Flo's dinner.

Dr. Vex had found something unusual. Orla had been asking questions. And I needed to figure out what Iris knew before another day passed with Hazel's killer walking free.

By six-thirty, I'd completed all my usual morning tasks. The café gleamed in the early light, pastries were arranged just so in the display case, and I'd wiped down the counter three times already. Upstairs, I could hear the soft sounds of the cats beginning their day. Five cats now, I reminded myself. Five, not four.

I climbed the stairs to check on Sage before opening.

The tiny gray kitten was curled in her heated bed in my room, a small ball of fluff that rose and fell with steady breathing. Five days since the Mountain Market employee had brought her to me, and she'd already gained weight. The haunted look in her eyes had eased somewhat, though she still startled at sudden movements.

"How's our patient?" Poppy asked from the doorway.

"Sleeping. Finally eating well." I crouched down to stroke Sage's soft fur, marveling at how something so small could have survived alone. "Dr. Dover said another week and she'll be strong enough to explore more."

"Rocky's taken his protector duties very seriously," Poppy said with amusement. "He follows her everywhere now that she's getting around."

I smiled despite my anxiety. Rocky, my chaotic orange tabby, had surprised everyone by appointing himself Sage's mentor. He spent hours shadowing the little kitten as she explored, ready to intervene if she got into trouble or tried to venture somewhere she shouldn't.

Downstairs, I heard the familiar scratch of cats at the door between the apartment and café.

"Breakfast time," Gus announced, his elderly voice carrying up the stairs. "Some of us have been waiting patiently."

"Some of us," Poppy corrected, following me down. "You've been complaining for ten minutes."

The morning feeding routine took longer now with five core cats plus the six adoptables currently rotating between the café viewing room and the apartment. I measured food carefully, distributed medications to those who needed them, refreshed water bowls. The familiar tasks should have been soothing.

Instead, my hands shook as I worked.

"You're doing that thing again," Poppy observed, settling into her perch near the window as I unlocked the café door.

"What thing?"

"The nervous cleaning thing. You've wiped that counter enough times to remove the finish."

"I'm not nervous." But I tossed the rag aside and busied myself checking tea canisters instead. Chamomile, lavender, peppermint, all stocked and ready. Everything in its place, everything controlled, everything safe.

Except nothing felt safe anymore. Hazel was dead, her killer walked free, and I was playing detective with skills I'd learned from years of paranoia rather than any actual investigative training.

The morning rush started at seven-thirty with the usual regulars seeking their caffeine fixes. I made lattes and cappuccinos and pour-overs, smiled and chatted and deflected questions about Hazel's case with practiced ease. By nine o'clock, the rush had ebbed to a manageable trickle.

That's when Lionel walked in.

He approached the counter with an easy smile, running one hand through dark hair that always looked slightly disheveled. "Morning, Alexis. Slow morning?"

"Relatively. The usual?" He typically ordered a simple medium roast, black, nothing fancy.

"Actually, I was hoping for a recommendation." He leaned against the counter, and his jacket shifted open to reveal a shirt featuring some kind of dragon. Most of his wardrobe seemed to involve mythical creatures or comic book characters. "Something that might help with focus? I've got inventory to organize and my brain's already trying to distract itself with anything else."

I considered the options. "Citrus green tea might work. The green tea provides steady energy without the coffee jitters, and the citrus helps with mental clarity. I could add a bit of ginger for an extra boost."

"That sounds perfect." His smile widened. "You really know your stuff."

"It's literally my job."

He laughed, the sound warm and genuine. "Fair point. Though you make it seem like art rather than just work."

I felt a small flush of pleasure at the compliment anyway. I turned to prepare his tea, grateful for something to do with my hands. The familiar motions of measuring leaves, heating water to the precise temperature, timing the steep helped ground me.

Behind me, I heard Millie's voice drift down from the cat room. "He's watching you."

I didn't respond. Didn't turn around. Just focused on the tea, on keeping my hands steady, on not acknowledging the warmth creeping up my neck.

When I handed Lionel his cup, our fingers brushed briefly. His hand was warm, slightly callused. I pulled back quickly, professionally.

"Thanks." He wrapped both hands around the cup, inhaling the steam. "So, how are you holding up?"

The question caught me off guard. Most people had stopped asking, or asked in that performative way that expected reassurance rather than honesty. Lionel sounded genuinely concerned.

"I'm managing," I said carefully. "Keeping busy helps."

"If you ever need to talk, or just want company while you work, I'm usually around." He gestured vaguely toward his shop. "We could grab dinner sometime. Nothing fancy, just two business owners commiserating about small-town life."

There it was. The gentle invitation I'd been half-expecting, half-dreading. Lionel had been circling around asking me out for months, always careful, always giving me space to decline.

And I wanted to say yes.

That was the terrifying part. I actually wanted to say yes, to sit across from him at Mountain Brew or Flo's and talk about normal things. To pretend I was a normal person living a normal life, not a witch in hiding investigating a murder while trying not to expose her magic to the world.

I missed having a shared meal with someone who mattered. And now, with Hazel gone, I didn't even have that small comfort anymore.

In the coven, we'd eaten together every night. Long communal tables filled with food and laughter and fellowship. Lily always sat next to me, our shoulders touching, sharing whispered jokes while Elder Miriam said the blessing. The warmth of being surrounded by people who knew exactly what I was and loved me anyway.

I'd given that up. Traded it for safety, for secrecy, for this carefully constructed life where no one knew me at all.

"That's really kind," I said slowly. "But I'm pretty swamped with the café and everything going on. Maybe some other time?"

Something flickered across his face. Disappointment, quickly masked. "Of course. The offer stands whenever you're ready."

He took his tea with a friendly wave and headed for the door. I watched him leave, noticed the slight stiffness in his shoulders that suggested I'd hurt him more than he wanted to show.

"That was painful to witness," Rocky said from somewhere near my feet.

"What was?" I busied myself wiping down the espresso machine.

"You, running away from a perfectly nice human who clearly likes you." Rocky hopped onto a stool, his orange tail swishing. "He asked you to dinner. Humans do that when they're interested."

"I know what dinner invitations mean."

"Then why did you say no?"

Because saying yes meant letting someone get close. It meant risking them asking questions I couldn't answer, noticing inconsistencies in my carefully constructed cover story, wondering why I sometimes smelled like herbs when I shouldn't or why I always knew when a storm was coming before the weather report confirmed it.

It meant risking everything I'd built here.

"I'm not interested in dating right now," I said firmly.

"Liar." But Rocky dropped it, probably sensing my tone meant the conversation was over.

The morning continued quietly. A few more customers came and went, and I found myself glancing toward The Gilded Dragon more often than I wanted to admit. At eleven-thirty, during the pre-lunch lull, I finally allowed myself to check on Sage again. She was awake now, stretching in her little bed with that particular kitten elasticity that made them seem boneless.

"Good morning, sweetheart." I sat on the floor beside her.

Sage blinked up at me with enormous gray eyes. She'd been speaking more lately, her voice growing stronger along with her body. That first whispered "Thank you for saving me" on the day of the visit to Dr. Dover which had been followed by small observations, questions, the occasional comment. Each word a little clearer, a little more confident. Magic didn't care about developmental timelines, apparently.

I stroked her soft head with one finger, and she leaned into the touch, purring. The sound was barely audible, a tiny motor struggling to life, but it meant she was healing. Physically, at least.

"Rocky wants to show you the café when you're stronger," I told her. "He's very excited about it. He's planned an entire tour, including the best sleeping spots and where the sun hits at different times of day. He's taking his mentor duties very seriously."

Sage's purr intensified slightly. I sat with her for a few more minutes, letting the simple act of comforting a scared kitten settle my own jangled nerves. This, at least, was straightforward. Sage needed care, I provided it. No mysteries, no lies, no performances.

Just kindness offered freely to something small and helpless.

When I returned downstairs, I found Poppy sitting in the window with an expression that suggested she'd been waiting to deliver important information.

"Well?" I asked.

"Lionel brought you a gift." She gestured with her tail toward the counter.

A small wrapped package sat next to the register, topped with a simple note in neat handwriting: *Thought you might enjoy this. Thanks for the tea recommendation. - L*

I opened it carefully. Inside was a graphic novel, something called *The Sandman*. The cover showed a pale figure with wild dark hair and eyes that seemed to see through reality.

The note inside read: *You mentioned once that you liked mythology and stories about magic. This series is incredible. If you like it, I've got the rest of the volumes at the shop.*

I stared at the book, feeling something complicated and warm unfurl in my chest. He'd listened. Remembered a casual comment I'd made months ago about reading habits. Chosen something specifically for me.

In the coven, we'd given each other gifts constantly. Small tokens of affection, herbs gathered specifically for a friend's needs, books we thought someone would love. Lily had been the worst offender, always leaving little surprises in my room. A perfect seashell she'd found on a beach walk. A bookmark with a quote she knew would make me laugh. A jar of honey from bees she'd helped a local keeper manage.

And here was Lionel, offering the same kind of attention, the same thoughtfulness. Only I knew his gesture was meant to mean more than friendship.

"You could go thank him," Poppy suggested gently. "It's just a few doors down. The lunch rush hasn't started yet."

"I'll thank him next time he comes in."

"Or you could be brave." Poppy's amber eyes held mine. "You could let yourself have one nice thing. One person who wants to know you, even if they can't know everything."

"It's not that simple."

"It never is. But that doesn't mean it's not worth trying."

I looked down at the graphic novel, at the figure on the cover who seemed to exist between worlds. Maybe Poppy had a point. Maybe keeping everyone at a distance forever wasn't sustainable. Maybe there was a way to let someone in without risking everything.

Maybe.

But not today. Today I had a murder to solve, a secret to protect, and a tiny kitten upstairs who needed me to stay focused and safe.

I tucked the book under the counter to read later and turned my attention back to preparing for the lunch rush. Outside, Larkspur

Valley went about its Monday business, oblivious to the investigation happening in its midst. Oblivious to the witch running a café, the killer walking its streets, the small acts of kindness and connection that happened every day between people just trying to survive.

The lunch rush hit at noon with the usual force, and I lost myself in the comfortable rhythm of making sandwiches and brewing tea and chatting with customers who knew nothing about me except that I made good coffee and kept clean tables.

It wasn't the coven. It wasn't communal meals with people who loved me. It wasn't Lily's laugh or Elder Miriam's blessings or the feeling of belonging somewhere completely.

But it was mine. My café, my cats, my carefully constructed life in this small mountain town.

And somewhere in that life, there might be room for a comic shop owner with a gentle smile and a talent for choosing perfect gifts.

Maybe.

Someday.

When it was safe.

Small things. Good things. Worth protecting.

I returned to work with renewed focus, determined to solve Hazel's murder so I could get back to the business of living instead of just surviving. Determined to find a way to have both safety and connection, secrets and community, magic and normalcy.

It shouldn't be impossible.

Chapter Ten

Tuesday morning brought clouds and the threat of rain. I opened the café at eight as usual, went through the familiar motions of serving customers and making drinks, and watched the clock creep toward ten.

The morning rush was steady but manageable. Mabel came in for her usual Lavender Dreams tea, adjusting her Tuesday routine to Wednesday after yesterday's confusion. Felix Wren ordered his Ginger Spark and wandered to a corner table with his notebook, already lost in whatever story he was crafting. The regulars came and went, their patterns as predictable as the sunrise.

Upstairs, Sage would be waking soon. She'd progressed from wobbly steps to confident exploration over the past week, though Rocky still followed her everywhere like an overprotective guardian. This morning before opening, I'd watched them play, Sage pouncing on a toy mouse while Rocky pretended to be surprised every single time.

The bell chimed at nine o'clock, and I looked up to find Dr. Colton Dover standing in the doorway, slightly damp from the misty rain that had started falling.

"Morning," he said with an easy smile, approaching the counter. His jacket was speckled with water droplets, and he brushed a hand through dark hair that stuck up in places from the moisture. "Quiet morning?"

"So far." I reached for a cup automatically. "Your usual?"

"Actually, I was hoping for a recommendation." He leaned against the counter, his expression casual but his eyes attentive. "Something warming. The clinic's been freezing all morning."

"Spiced chai might work. Or I could do a honey lavender latte if you want something sweeter."

"The chai sounds perfect."

I turned to prepare it, aware of his gaze following my movements. The silence stretched, comfortable but weighted with something unspoken.

"So," he said finally, "how's Sage doing?"

There it was. The real reason for the visit wrapped in professional concern.

"She's doing great. Gaining weight every day, getting stronger. Rocky's appointed himself her personal bodyguard." I smiled despite myself, thinking of the orange tabby's devotion. "He takes his duties very seriously."

"That's good to hear. And her energy levels? Any concerns about lethargy or appetite issues?"

"None. She eats like she's making up for lost time, and she's been exploring more. Just yesterday she figured out how to climb onto the couch." I handed him the chai, our fingers not quite touching this time. "You don't need to worry. She's thriving."

"Good. That's really good." He wrapped both hands around the cup, inhaling the spiced steam. A pause, then, "And the other cats? Everyone adjusting well to having a kitten in the house?"

"Surprisingly well. Millie's still cautious, but Poppy's been motherly. Gus tolerates her. And Rocky, well, he's obsessed." I wiped down the counter, giving my hands something to do. "They've all accepted her as part of the family."

"Family's important." He took a sip, his eyes never leaving mine. "For cats and humans alike."

The weight behind those words hung between us. An invitation, maybe. Or just observation.

"It is," I agreed carefully.

Another pause. The café was empty except for us and Felix in the corner, too absorbed in his writing to notice anything.

"Listen," Colton said, setting down his cup. "I know things have been difficult lately. With Hazel and everything. If you ever need to talk, or just want company that isn't feline, I'm around. No pressure. Just, you know." He shrugged, trying for casual and almost succeeding. "An offer."

There it was again. That gentle invitation, carefully phrased to give me room to decline. He'd been doing this for months, circling around the idea of asking me out without actually pushing. Always giving me space. Always letting me set the pace.

It would be so easy to say yes. To let someone in, even just a little. To have coffee with a kind man who saved kittens and didn't ask questions I couldn't answer.

But easy didn't mean safe.

"That's really thoughtful," I said, the words coming out softer than I intended. "I appreciate it. Things are just a bit overwhelming right now."

"Of course." He picked up his chai, and if there was disappointment in his expression, he hid it well. "The offer stands. Anytime."

"Thank you."

He headed for the door, then paused. "Oh, and Alexis? If you notice any changes with Sage, anything that concerns you, don't hesitate to bring her in. Even if it seems minor."

"I will."

"Good." He smiled, that warm, genuine smile that made something in my chest twist uncomfortably. "Take care of yourself, okay? Not just the cats."

Then he was gone, the bell chiming behind him, leaving me alone with the scent of chai and the ghost of almost-possibilities.

"Well," Poppy said from her perch near the window, her tone dryly amused. "That was subtle."

"What was?"

"The good veterinarian checking on Sage's progress." Her tail swished. "Funny how he needed to do that in person when you could have just called the clinic. Or how he lingered for ten minutes asking questions he already knows the answers to."

"He was being thorough."

"He was being interested." Poppy's amber eyes gleamed with knowing. "In you, not the kitten. Though Sage makes a convenient excuse."

I busied myself restocking napkins. "You're reading too much into it."

"Am I?" She settled into a more comfortable position, clearly enjoying this. "Because from where I'm sitting, that was the second man in as many days who's tried to spend time with you. And you've turned down both of them."

"I'm not interested in dating right now."

"You keep saying that. But I notice you didn't say you're not interested in them specifically." Poppy tilted her head. "Lionel brings you thoughtful gifts. Colton makes house calls for a kitten who doesn't need house calls. Both of them look at you like you hang the moon. And you keep building walls."

"I have reasons."

"You have fears," she corrected gently. "Which is different."

Before I could respond, the bell chimed again. More customers, blessedly ending this conversation. I threw myself into making drinks and taking orders, grateful for the distraction.

But Poppy's words lingered. Two men interested, both kind, both patient. Both offering exactly the kind of connection I'd told myself I couldn't have.

In the coven, relationships had been easy. Everyone knew what everyone else was. There were no secrets to hide, no carefully constructed lies to maintain. When Lily and I had stayed up late talking about the boys we liked, it had been simple. Uncomplicated. Safe.

Then I'd run, and simple had become impossible.

Now every interaction was a calculation. Every conversation a risk. Every moment of genuine connection just another opportunity to slip up, to reveal too much, to put myself in danger.

It was exhausting.

But it was necessary.

Wasn't it?

At nine-forty-five, the morning rush had ebbed to nothing. I flipped the sign to "Back at 11:00" and locked the door behind me, leaving Poppy to keep watch from her window perch. The walk to The Turning Page took only a few minutes down Main Street.

Maeve's bookshop was exactly what you'd expect from someone like her, and yet somehow more. Cozy, cluttered, and organized in a way that made sense only to its owner.

Books lined every wall from floor to ceiling, with more stacked on tables and chairs in precarious towers that should have toppled but never did. Little reading nooks tucked into corners and alcoves, each with a comfortable chair or window seat positioned to catch exactly the right amount of light, even on a gray morning like this.

The smell of old paper and tea filled the air, layered with something else I couldn't quite name. Herbs, maybe, or incense, or just the particular scent of a place where stories accumulated and settled into the walls.

Soft music played from somewhere in the back, though I couldn't see any speakers. The light felt different here too, warmer and softer than the gray morning outside, as if the shop existed slightly apart from the rest of Larkspur Valley. As if it occupied its own small pocket of reality where time moved differently and the ordinary rules didn't quite apply.

"Alexis!" Maeve appeared from behind a towering stack of mysteries, her curly hair even more wild than usual. "Perfect timing. I just put the kettle on. Come, sit."

She led me to a small reading nook in the back corner where two armchairs faced each other across a low table. A teapot and two cups sat waiting, steam rising gently.

"Chamomile," Maeve said, pouring. "I thought you might need something calming."

"Thank you." I accepted the cup, cradling it between my hands.

Maeve settled into the opposite chair and studied me with those perceptive eyes. "So. What did you want to ask me about?"

I'd rehearsed this on the walk over, trying to find a balance between curious and suspicious. "At dinner on Sunday, you mentioned that Orla Weston had been asking questions about Hazel. I was wondering what you knew about her. About all three of them, actually. Carla, Trish, and Orla."

"The three women who benefit most from Hazel's death," Maeve said, not bothering to pretend she didn't understand. "You're investigating."

My hands tightened on the cup. "I'm just trying to understand what happened."

"Mm-hmm." She took a sip of tea, considering. "Well, I'll tell you what I know, though it's not much for two of them. Trish I know well. Too well, some might say. The woman has been a thorn in everyone's side for years."

"How so?"

"Trish Lawrence is driven, selfish, and ambitious. Not necessarily bad qualities in business, but she has no sense of ethics or community. Everything is about winning for her, about being the best, the biggest, the most successful." Maeve set down her cup. "She opened Petals and Prose about five years ago, right after her divorce.

Poured all her settlement money into it. I think she saw Hazel's established business and decided she deserved that success without putting in the decades of work Hazel had."

"So she tried to compete."

"She tried to destroy." Maeve's tone hardened. "Undercut Hazel's prices even when it meant losing money. Spread rumors that Hazel's flowers came from inferior suppliers. Tried to poach Hazel's biggest clients with promises of discounts and free delivery. She even went to the town council trying to get Hazel's business license revoked over some made-up zoning violation."

"I remember one particularly nasty incident about three years ago," Maeve continued, her expression darkening. "Trish somehow got access to Hazel's supplier list and called every single one, claiming to be Hazel and canceling orders. Hazel showed up to work one Monday morning to find out she had no flowers coming for an entire week. No roses for Valentine's arrangements, no lilies for a funeral, nothing. She had to scramble, make personal calls, drive to Denver herself to pick up emergency supplies."

"That's sabotage."

"It was. And when Hazel figured out it was Trish, she still didn't retaliate. Just quietly restored her relationships with her suppliers and moved on. But Trish? She was furious that it didn't destroy Hazel's business. That's when the rumors started getting nastier. Claims that Hazel was senile, that she was mixing up orders, that her flowers were diseased." Maeve's hands tightened around her teacup. "None of it was true, but some of it stuck. Some customers started going to Trish instead, just to be safe."

"How did Hazel handle it?"

"With grace. As always. She'd just smile and say 'Quality speaks for itself' and keep doing beautiful work. Within six months, most of those customers came back, because Trish's flowers were cheaper and her service was terrible." Maeve paused. "But the thing is, Trish never stopped trying. Right up until Hazel died, she was looking for angles. Ways to undermine. Ways to win."

"Win what, though? It's a small town. There's room for two flower shops."

"For someone like Trish, there's never room for competition. Only for victory." Maeve took a long sip of tea. "She told someone at the Chamber of Commerce meeting last month that Hazel was 'past her prime' and should retire. That the town deserved 'fresh energy' in the floral business. People thought she was being inappropriate, but Trish doesn't care about inappropriate. She cares about getting what she wants."

"Did Hazel fight back?"

"Hazel ignored her. Just kept doing beautiful work and treating her customers well. Which, of course, made Trish even more furious." Maeve smiled sadly. "Hazel told me once that Trish reminded her of herself when she was younger. Too focused on external success, not enough on what really mattered."

That sounded like Hazel. Patient even with someone who was actively trying to hurt her business.

"And Carla?" I asked.

"Ah, the niece." Maeve refilled both our cups. "I don't know her as well. She's visited Larkspur Valley over the years, but never for long. Always seemed uncomfortable here, like she couldn't wait to leave. I got the impression there was tension between her and Hazel, though Hazel never spoke about it directly."

"Do you know why?"

"Only rumors. Some people said Carla resented Hazel for not leaving their family business to her mother, Hazel's sister. But the sister died years ago, and Carla expected to inherit eventually. Thought it was her birthright." Maeve's expression turned thoughtful. "There's something about inherited expectations that can poison a relationship. Carla saw that shop as already hers, which meant Hazel was just the obstacle standing between her and what she deserved."

"That's a dangerous way to think about someone."

"Isn't it?" Maeve agreed. "And now Hazel's gone, and Carla still doesn't have what she wants. That kind of frustration can make people do desperate things."

I thought about Carla's bitterness at the memorial service. Her anger about the will. Her demand to know what was in the box Hazel had left me.

"What about Orla Weston?" I asked. "You mentioned she'd been asking questions."

"Cordelia mentioned it to me last week. Said Orla had been curious about Hazel after the death. Asking about her routine, where she lived, whether she had family in town." Maeve paused. "Nothing unusual in itself, people are naturally curious after a death. But combined with other things about Orla, it made me wonder."

"What other things?"

"Here's the thing about Orla. She moved to Larkspur Valley about a year ago, just before you did, actually. Applied for the job at Cordelia's yarn shop out of the blue. No previous connection to the town that anyone knows of. Keeps to herself, doesn't socialize much. Pleasant enough when you talk to her, but there's something... opaque about her. Like you're talking to a mask, not a person."

A chill ran down my spine. A year ago. Right when I'd arrived in Larkspur Valley. Right when Hazel had welcomed me without questions.

Could that be a coincidence?

"Do you know where she came from? Before here?"

"Cordelia said somewhere in Wyoming. Casper, maybe? Or Cheyenne? She was vague about it." Maeve studied me over her teacup. "Why the sudden interest in Orla specifically?"

"She came into the café and knew I'd found Hazel's body. That information hadn't been widely shared yet."

"Interesting." Maeve's eyes sharpened. "Though in a town this size, information travels in unexpected ways. Still, you're right to wonder. Orla is the unknown variable here. Trish and Carla have obvious motives. But Orla? There's no clear reason for her to harm Hazel. Which either means she didn't do it, or there's something we don't know about."

We sat in silence for a moment, sipping tea and thinking.

"Can I ask you something?" I said finally. "At dinner, you said some answers are dangerous. What did you mean?"

Maeve smiled, but it didn't quite reach her eyes. "I meant that you're looking for truth in a situation where truth might expose you to danger. Whoever killed Hazel did it deliberately, with planning and poison. They're not going to take kindly to someone investigating."

"So you think I should stop."

"I think you should be careful. And I think you should consider that you might not be as alone in this as you believe." She held my gaze. "Larkspur Valley has a way of collecting people who don't quite fit elsewhere. People with secrets. People with gifts. You're not the only one, Alexis."

My heart hammered. "I don't know what you mean."

"Don't you?" She stood, signaling the end of our conversation. "Well, whether you do or don't, the offer stands. If you need help, ask. Some of us have been here longer and might have resources you don't."

She walked me to the door, and I stepped out onto Main Street with my head spinning. Maeve knew. Or suspected. Or was magical herself. I couldn't tell which, but the implication was clear: I wasn't as hidden as I thought.

The walk back to the café took only minutes, but my mind was racing the entire time. Trish had motive and history. Carla had expectations and bitterness. Orla had arrived a year ago under vague circumstances and was now asking pointed questions.

And I still didn't know which one of them had poisoned Hazel.

Back at the café, the cats demanded a full report while I made drinks for the lunch crowd. I filled them in quietly between customers, keeping my voice low.

"Orla arrived a year ago," Poppy repeated. "The same time you did."

"Could be coincidence," I said, but I didn't believe it.

"Or she was following you," Gus said grimly. "Tracking you. Waiting."

"But she didn't come for me. She killed Hazel." That was the part that didn't make sense. If Orla was from my past, if she'd been sent by the coven, why would she kill Hazel instead of exposing me or dragging me back?

Unless Hazel had gotten in the way somehow. Unless Hazel had protected me without my knowing.

The thought made my chest ache.

The afternoon dragged on. I served customers, cleaned, and tried not to spiral into paranoid theories about Orla being connected to my past. Around three-thirty, the bell chimed and Piper walked in with Eva and Ella.

"I hope this is okay," Piper said apologetically. "We didn't make it yesterday but I promised the girls we could visit the cats today."

"Of course it's okay." I smiled at Eva and Ella, who were already pressing their faces against the glass wall of the cat room. "They've been asking about you two."

"Really?" Ella's face lit up. "The cats were asking about us?"

"Absolutely." It wasn't even a lie. Rocky had mentioned them yesterday, wondering when they'd visit again.

"Can we go in?" Eva asked.

"Go ahead. Just be gentle."

The girls disappeared into the cat room, and I could hear their delighted giggles as the cats swarmed them. Rocky immediately started showing off, leaping from perch to perch. Even Millie crept out of her hiding spot to investigate, which was significant progress.

"Can we meet Sage?" Ella called out, her face pressed against the glass separating the viewing room from the main café. "The new kitten?"

"She's still too little," I said, smiling at Ella's eager expression. "She needs a few more weeks to get bigger and stronger. But next time you visit, I promise you can meet her. She's going to love you."

"Really?" Ella's eyes went wide. "You promise?"

"I promise."

That seemed to satisfy her, and she returned to playing with the other cats while Eva helped her find the toy basket.

Piper ordered a Chamomile Calm Latte and settled at a table where she could watch the girls through the glass.

"They needed this," she said. "Everything's been so heavy lately. Death is hard for kids to understand."

"It's hard for adults too," I said, bringing over her drink.

"Fair point." She took a sip. "How are you holding up? Really?"

"I'm okay. Better than I was." It was even partially true. Having a focus, having suspects, having something to do besides grieve, had helped.

"Mom said you seemed good at dinner. A little overwhelmed, maybe, but good. She was really happy you came." Piper smiled. "She's been trying to adopt you since you opened this place, you know. That's just how she is."

"She's very kind."

"She sees something in you that reminds her of herself. Someone who needs family but doesn't quite know how to accept it."

Piper glanced at me, then quickly away. "Sorry. That was too personal."

"It's okay." And surprisingly, it was. Maybe Flo did see something in me. Maybe that's why she kept trying, kept inviting, kept pushing gently at my walls.

Through the glass, I watched Eva and Ella playing with the cats. Ella was making a toy mouse dance for Poppy while Eva carefully brushed Gus, who was tolerating the attention with surprising patience.

"Alexis!" Ella called through the glass. "Gus says you make the best treats!"

I smiled, even as my heart skipped. Gus hadn't said anything to Ella. Gus couldn't have said anything to Ella.

Could he?

"He does love his salmon treats," I called back.

"Can I give him one?"

"Top shelf, blue container." I watched as Eva helped Ella reach the treats, and Gus's eyes lit up at the offering.

"Bribery," he announced. "I approve."

The girls played with the cats while Piper and I chatted about nothing important. School projects. The upcoming winter. Plans for Thanksgiving. Normal conversation that felt almost like friendship.

Finally, Piper glanced at her watch. "Girls, we need to let Alexis get back to work."

"Five more minutes?" Eva pleaded.

"Now, please. Grandma's expecting us for dinner."

The girls said elaborate goodbyes to each cat, making me promise they could visit again soon. As they headed for the door, Ella turned back.

"Alexis?"

"Yes?"

"Millie says thank you for the hiding spots. She feels safe here." Ella's face was completely serious, completely earnest. "I thought you should know."

My throat tightened. "Thank you for telling me."

After they left, I stood frozen behind the counter while the cats gathered around.

"She heard me," Millie whispered, sounding awed and frightened all at once. "That little girl heard me."

"She's sensitive," Poppy said carefully. "Some children are, before the world teaches them not to be."

I thought about Ella saying I "sparkled happiness." About her talking about the café's good energy. About her somehow knowing what Millie had said even though she couldn't possibly have heard it from across the room.

About how Piper had smiled indulgently when Ella said those things, thinking her daughter just had a vivid imagination.

She didn't know. Piper had no idea her daughter could actually hear what the cats were saying.

And I couldn't tell her.

Couldn't say "your daughter has the same gift I do." Couldn't offer to help Ella understand what she was hearing. Couldn't warn Piper that this was real, that Ella would need guidance, that ignoring it wouldn't make it go away.

Because telling them would mean revealing myself.

And I couldn't do that.

"That poor kid," Rocky said quietly, his usual chaos subdued.

He was right. Ella was six years old with a gift she didn't understand, and the one person in town who could help her had to stay silent. Had to pretend it was all imagination and whimsy while that little girl tried to make sense of voices no one else believed were real.

I'd never felt more alone. Or more useless.

"She'll be okay," Millie said softly, but she sounded like she was trying to convince herself as much as me. "Children are resilient."

"Or she'll learn to ignore it," Gus said. "Most people do, eventually. Convince themselves it was never real."

The thought of Ella losing her gift, suppressing it until she couldn't hear the cats anymore, made my chest ache. But maybe that would be safer for her. Maybe that would be better than living the way I did, always hiding, always afraid.

"Tomorrow," I said, my voice rough, "I watch Orla more carefully. Figure out if she connects to Hazel somehow. Figure out why she came here a year ago and what she was really doing."

"And Trish?" Poppy asked. "And Carla?"

"One of the three killed Hazel. For money, for business, for resentment." I wrapped my arms around myself, suddenly cold despite the warmth of the café. "Regular reasons. Regular human cruelty. That's what I have to believe."

"Why?" Gus asked.

"Because the alternative..." I couldn't finish. Couldn't say out loud what I'd been thinking since Maeve's cryptic comments and Orla's arrival timing and the growing feeling that something in Larkspur Valley wasn't quite normal.

Because the alternative was that this murder was connected to magic. To secrets. To the very thing I'd been running from.

And if that was true, then investigating it made me visible in ways I couldn't afford. Made me a target. Made me vulnerable to discovery by the people I'd spent years hiding from.

"Just focus on the facts," Poppy said gently. "Watch. Listen. Gather information. But don't jump to conclusions. Not yet."

She was right. I was letting fear and paranoia cloud my judgment. This was probably just a regular murder with regular motives. Trish wanted Hazel's customers. Carla wanted the shop. Orla... well, I didn't know what Orla wanted yet, but it was probably something mundane. Something explainable.

It had to be.

Because I couldn't handle it being anything else.

Outside, the threatened rain finally started to fall, soft and steady against the windows. The café felt warm and safe, but I couldn't shake the feeling that safety was an illusion. That something was coming that I wasn't prepared for.

Somewhere in Larkspur Valley, a killer was going about their evening. And tomorrow, I'd keep investigating.

One step at a time.

One suspect at a time.

Until I found the truth.

Even if I was terrified of what that truth might be.

Chapter Eleven

After Piper and the girls left, I closed the café early. Not by much, just thirty minutes, but I couldn't focus. Couldn't make small talk with customers. Couldn't pretend everything was normal when my entire understanding of Larkspur Valley had just shifted.

My hands shook as I locked the front door and flipped the sign to Closed. Through the glass, I could see Main Street going about its usual late afternoon routine. Tourists window shopping. Locals heading home from work. Everyone moving through their ordinary days while mine tilted on its axis.

Ella could hear cats talking. Six years old, and she had the same gift I did. Maybe stronger, if Millie was right about her hearing from across the room.

And Piper didn't know. Thought her daughter just had an active imagination. Smiled indulgently when Ella repeated what the cats said, like it was pretend.

I was the only one who knew the truth. The only one who could help Ella understand her gift. And I couldn't say a word without exposing myself.

I'd never felt more isolated.

The cats followed me upstairs without a word. They knew. Somehow, they always knew when I was reaching a breaking point.

Upstairs, I found Sage curled in her heated bed in my room, her tiny gray form rising and falling with steady breaths. She'd been napping since lunch, worn out from her morning explorations. Rocky paused in my bedroom doorway, glancing between me and the sleeping kitten, clearly torn between his protective duties and his concern for me.

I stood in front of the closet door for a long moment. My heart hammered against my ribs. The door was just a door, plain white wood with a simple brass knob. But behind it sat answers I'd been avoiding for weeks.

Then, before I could talk myself out of it, I opened it and pulled out the box.

It felt heavier than it had when Carla gave it to me. Or maybe that was just the weight of everything it represented: Hazel's secrets, her death, the truth I'd been too afraid to face. The cardboard was slightly worn at the corners, the packing tape yellowed with age. This wasn't something Hazel had sealed up after her death. This was something she'd prepared weeks, maybe months ago. Something she'd planned.

I carried it to my small kitchen table and set it down with more care than necessary. The packing tape was still intact, Hazel's handwriting still clear across the top: For Alexis Belrose. Her penmanship had been beautiful, all loops and careful curves. Old-fashioned, like everything about her. The sight of it made my throat tight.

"You're really going to do it," Poppy said softly. She'd positioned herself on the back of the couch, watching with those knowing amber eyes.

"I have to." I went to the drawer where I kept odds and ends and pulled out a box cutter. My hands shook slightly as I walked back to the table. The blade caught the afternoon light filtering through the windows, and for a moment I just stared at it.

One cut. That's all it would take. One slice through the tape and I'd know.

I stood there, box cutter in hand, staring at the sealed cardboard.

Just cut the tape. Just open it. Just see what she left you.

But I couldn't move.

My fingers had gone numb around the box cutter's handle. My breath came shallow and quick, the way it did when I was about to have a panic attack. The box sat there, innocuous and terrifying, waiting.

What if it was proof that Hazel had known I was a witch? What if she'd left evidence that could expose me? Letters about my abilities. Documentation of times she'd seen me do something impossible. Notes about the cats and how they seemed to understand me too well. What if opening this box destroyed the last year of relative peace I'd managed to build?

What if it told me something about her death that I wasn't ready to know?

What if she'd known who was going to kill her? What if she'd written it down and I was about to become the only person with evidence that could point to a murderer? What if that made me the next target?

"It's okay to be scared," Millie said from her spot on the armchair, her gray fur fluffed up with concern.

"I'm not scared." But my voice shook, giving me away. The box cutter felt slippery in my damp palm.

"Yes, you are," Gus said, not unkindly. "And that's okay. Whatever's in there, it's going to change things. You're allowed to be scared of that."

From my bedroom, I heard a small mew. Sage had woken up, probably sensing the tension in the apartment. A moment later, Rocky appeared in the doorway, the tiny kitten following close behind him like a gray shadow.

"What's happening?" Sage's voice was still soft, still gaining strength. "Why is everyone worried?"

"It's okay, little one," Rocky said, his tone surprisingly gentle. "Alexis is just dealing with something difficult."

Sage blinked up at me with enormous eyes, then padded across the floor to sit at my feet. Her presence, small and trusting, made something in my chest crack.

I set the box cutter down on the table, my hand trembling so badly the metal clattered against the wood. "I just need a minute. I need to clear my head."

"Take your time," Poppy said. "The box isn't going anywhere."

I grabbed my jacket from the hook by the door and headed back downstairs. The cats didn't follow, understanding that I needed to be alone. Even Sage stayed upstairs, though I could feel her worried gaze following me as I left.

Outside, the afternoon had turned gray and cold. The clouds that had threatened rain all morning were finally making good on their promise, a light drizzle beginning to fall. I pulled my jacket tighter and started walking, the dampness seeping through the fabric almost immediately.

I had no destination in mind. I just walked, letting my feet carry me down Main Street while my mind spun in circles. The box sat on my table, waiting. Hazel's secrets, waiting. The truth, waiting.

And I was running again. Not physically this time, but emotionally. Running from answers I'd claimed I wanted.

The rain picked up, cold drops sliding down the back of my neck. I passed The Turning Page, where warm light spilled from the windows and I could see Maeve arranging books in the display. She glanced up and waved, but I pretended not to see. I couldn't face her knowing smile right now, couldn't handle her gentle questions about the magic in my blood.

Past The Gilded Dragon, where comic books and graphic novels filled the windows. Lionel was probably inside, surrounded by his beloved stories. He'd given me that graphic novel about dreams and reality. Had he somehow known I needed stories about people who lived between worlds?

Past Mountain Brew Coffee, where tourists huddled under the awning, trying to stay dry. Past the yarn shop, its windows dark. Orla wasn't there. Orla, who walked past my café at 9:45 every morning now instead of 10:15. Orla, who I still knew nothing about.

I walked until my feet ached and my jeans were soaked through and I was shivering from more than just the cold.

I was so lost in thought that I didn't realize where I was until I looked up and found myself standing in front of Hazel's flower shop.

The windows were dark, the interior shadowy. A small wreath hung on the door with a sign: Closed until further notice. Through the glass, I could see the shapes of flowers in various states of wilting, arrangements that would never be picked up, a business frozen in time.

A massive arrangement of lilies drooped near the counter, their white petals browning at the edges. Roses in a crystal vase had dropped their petals in a sad circle on the floor. Baby's breath, once cloud-like and delicate, had dried to brittle brown lace. It was like watching beauty decay in slow motion, life draining away while the world moved on.

Hazel would have hated this. She'd always been so particular about her flowers, so insistent that they be fresh and perfect. Seeing her life's work dying felt like a violation.

"Pathetic, isn't it?"

I jumped and turned to find Carla standing a few feet away, an umbrella open over her head. She must have come from the side entrance that led to Hazel's apartment. Her coat was expensive-looking, perfectly tailored, but her eyes were red-rimmed like she'd been crying.

"I didn't mean to intrude," I said.

"You're not intruding. It's a public sidewalk." Carla's gaze returned to the shop window. "I've been trying to decide what to do. The lawyer says I can't change anything for six months, but someone needs to deal with the flowers. They're all dying."

Rain dripped from my hair into my eyes. I wiped it away, suddenly aware of how bedraggled I must look compared to Carla's polished appearance. "I'm sorry."

"Are you?" She looked at me directly, and I saw something raw in her expression. "Or are you just saying what you think you should say?"

I didn't have an answer for that. Was I sorry? For Hazel's death, yes. For Carla's pain, maybe. But for the complicated mess between them, the years of hurt and misunderstanding, I wasn't sure there was room for my pity.

Carla sighed and stepped closer to the window, studying the wilting arrangements. Her breath fogged the glass. "I used to visit her when I was young. My mother would bring me here, and Aunt Hazel would let me play with the flower clippings while they talked. I thought it was magical, the way she could take all these separate pieces and make them into something beautiful."

It was the most human I'd ever heard her sound. Not bitter or sharp, just sad. Remembering something that had been good before it all went wrong.

"She was good at making things beautiful," I said quietly.

"She was good at a lot of things." Carla's voice had gone soft, almost wistful. "Making flower arrangements. Running a successful business. Being respected in the community. Everything except maintaining relationships with her own family."

I wanted to defend Hazel, to say that relationships were complicated and maybe Carla shared some of the blame. But standing here in the rain, looking at the evidence of Hazel's life's work dying in the darkness, I couldn't find the words.

"Did you open the box yet?" Carla asked abruptly.

"No."

"Why not?"

"I don't know." The honesty surprised me. "I'm scared of what might be in it."

"Scared?" Carla turned to face me fully, her umbrella tilting. Rain began hitting her shoulder, but she didn't seem to notice. "Of what? Old letters? Family photos? What could possibly be scary about a box of mementos?"

"What if it tells me things about her I don't want to know? What if it changes how I remember her?" The words came out quieter than I intended. "Sometimes not knowing is easier."

Carla stared at me for a long moment. The rain drummed on her umbrella, a steady rhythm that filled the silence between us. Then her expression softened slightly, something like understanding crossing her face.

"At least you can admit you're scared. That's more honest than most people are."

We stood in silence, two women who'd both lost Hazel in different ways, looking at the dark shop with its dying flowers. The rain fell harder, turning the street into a river of gray water. Somewhere a car splashed past, its tires hissing on the wet pavement.

"The lawyer told me more about the will," Carla said finally. "Apparently, if after six months he determines the shop can't be successfully maintained or if there's no suitable buyer, it's to be donated to the town. The building would be torn down, turned into some kind of community garden or green space. Hazel's way of making sure her flowers would always be part of Larkspur Valley."

"That would be a huge undertaking. The building, the apartment above..."

"Exactly. It would require permits, demolition crews, making sure the neighboring buildings aren't damaged in the process. Thousands of dollars in costs." Carla's laugh was bitter. "Leave it to Aunt Hazel to make her last wishes so complicated and expensive that even in death, she's making everyone else deal with the consequences of her idealism."

"That sounds like her."

"It's infuriating." But Carla's voice had lost some of its edge. "And perfect. And exactly the kind of thing she'd do. One last way to control everything from beyond the grave while pretending it's about the greater good. Even dead, she's determined that her vision for this town matters more than what anyone else wants."

"Or maybe she really did want what was best for the community."

"Maybe." Carla closed her umbrella with a snap, and rain immediately began soaking into her expensive coat. She didn't seem to notice. "I'm going back to my hotel. I can't stand looking at this place anymore, knowing it's slipping through my fingers."

She started to walk away, then paused and turned back. Her hair was getting wet, dark strands sticking to her face. "Alexis?"

"Yes?"

"When you do open that box, if there's anything in there about why she made the choices she did, about why she cut me out, I'd appreciate knowing. Not for legal reasons. Just..." She swallowed hard. "I'd like to understand."

"If there's anything like that, I'll tell you. I promise."

She nodded once, sharp and final, then walked away. Her footsteps echoed on the wet sidewalk, growing fainter until they disappeared into the sound of the rain.

I stayed there for a few more minutes, looking at the flower shop. Thinking about Hazel and Carla and complicated family relationships. About expectations and disappointments and the ways we hurt the people we love without meaning to. About the box sitting on my kitchen table and all the answers it might contain.

Carla was bitter, angry, hurt. She had motive and opportunity. She inherited something, even if it wasn't what she'd wanted.

But was she a murderer?

I didn't know anymore.

The drizzle turned to proper rain, cold and insistent. I finally turned away from the shop and headed back toward my café, my shoes squelching with every step. Water ran down my face, into my eyes, soaking through every layer of clothing. By the time I climbed the stairs to my apartment, I was damp and cold and no clearer on anything than I'd been before.

The cats were waiting, arranged around the living room like a furry intervention committee. Five pairs of eyes tracked my progress as I dripped onto the floor. Sage had positioned herself between

Rocky and Poppy, her small presence somehow making the intervention feel even more serious.

"Feel better?" Poppy asked.

"Not really." I shrugged off my wet jacket and hung it up, watching water drip from the hem. "But I ran into Carla. Had an interesting conversation."

I filled them in while I changed into dry clothes, my fingers clumsy with cold as I peeled off wet jeans and pulled on soft sweatpants. My favorite sweater, the one Hazel had complimented once. The memory stung.

When I came back out, the box was still sitting on my kitchen table, untouched. Waiting. Always waiting.

Sage had moved closer to it, sniffing curiously at the cardboard. "What's in the box?" she asked, her voice carrying that kitten curiosity that hadn't yet learned some questions were complicated.

"I don't know," I admitted.

"Are you going to open it now?" Rocky asked, his orange tail twitching with nervous energy.

I looked at it for a long moment. Thought about Carla's request to understand. Thought about my conversation with Maeve and her careful non-answers. Thought about Ella hearing Millie across a crowded room and what that meant for both of us. Thought about Orla and her precise timing and Trish and her bitter rivalry and poison and secrets and truth piling up like snow in a storm.

"No," I said finally. "Not yet. I need to be ready, and I'm not ready yet."

"When will you be ready?" Gus asked, his grumpy face somehow conveying more concern than criticism.

"I don't know." I picked up the box, feeling its weight in my hands. Hazel's handwriting stared up at me, patient and permanent. "But not today."

Sage watched me with those enormous eyes, her head tilted. "It's okay to be scared," she said softly, echoing Millie's words from earlier. "Rocky says being scared just means something matters."

Out of the mouths of kittens. I felt my throat tighten.

"You're a smart little one," I told her, then carried the box back to the closet.

I set it carefully in the corner where it had been, in the darkness where I didn't have to look at it. Where I could pretend it didn't exist for a little longer.

I closed the closet door and leaned against it, feeling like a coward and not caring.

Whatever was in that box, it had waited this long. It could wait a little longer.

Because right now, I needed to focus on the living. On finding Hazel's killer. On protecting myself and this town and whatever magical secret we were all apparently sharing. On understanding the community I'd been so busy hiding from that I'd missed seeing it clearly.

The box could wait.

Justice couldn't.

"Okay," I said, turning to face the cats. My voice came out stronger than I felt. "Tomorrow, I watch Orla more carefully. I find out where she goes, who she talks to, what she does when she's not at the yarn shop. There has to be something that connects her to Hazel. Some reason she would have killed her."

"And if there's no connection?" Poppy asked.

"Then I move on to Trish or Carla. One of them did this. I just have to figure out which one."

"And when you do?" Millie's voice was barely a whisper. "What then?"

That was the question I didn't have an answer for. How did I prove what I knew without revealing how I knew it? How did I give Iris the evidence she needed without exposing myself? How did I stop a killer without becoming vulnerable to the very thing I'd been running from for years?

"I'll figure it out," I said with more confidence than I felt. "One step at a time."

Sage padded over and sat on my foot, a tiny warm weight. "We'll help," she announced with absolute kitten confidence. "Rocky says that's what families do."

The word hit me harder than I expected. Family. These cats, this apartment, this café. Somewhere along the way, without meaning to, I'd built something that felt like family. Not perfect, not traditional, but mine.

And Hazel had been part of that, however briefly. She'd welcomed me, guided me, given me space to breathe and be.

I owed her the truth.

Outside, the rain fell harder, drumming against the windows. Somewhere in Larkspur Valley, a killer was going about their evening, thinking themselves safe from discovery.

They were wrong.

The box could wait.

But justice couldn't.

Chapter Twelve

Wednesday morning arrived with clearer skies and a plan I wasn't entirely confident in. But sitting around waiting for answers wasn't working. I needed to get closer to Orla Weston, and the yarn shop seemed like the most logical place to start.

"This is a terrible idea," Gus said from his bed by the fireplace. He'd been saying variations of this since I'd mentioned the plan last night.

"Noted." I refilled the pastry case with Flo's morning delivery, arranging the cranberry scones and blueberry muffins with hands that weren't quite steady. "But I don't have a better one."

"You could just follow her home. See where she lives, what she does after work." Rocky was pacing on one of the cat trees in the viewing room, making the other cats give him annoyed looks. The fluffy orange long-hair, Butterscotch, had already retreated to a higher perch to escape his restless energy.

"That's called stalking, and it's illegal." I wiped down the counter for the third time, the motion automatic and soothing. "Going to a yarn shop and showing interest in a hobby is perfectly normal."

"You don't know anything about knitting," Poppy pointed out from her window perch. "Or crochet. Or any kind of needlework."

"Which is why I'm going to learn. Or at least pretend to learn long enough to observe Orla in her natural environment." I checked the clock. Nine-thirty. The yarn shop would be open now, and the morning café rush was over. "As soon as the last customer leaves, I'll head over."

From upstairs, I heard a small mew. Sage had been quiet all morning, probably sensing the tension in the apartment. She'd been sleeping in later these days, conserving her energy for afternoon playtime with Rocky.

"What about Sage?" Rocky asked, his pacing stopping suddenly. "I should stay with her. What if she needs something while you're gone?"

"She'll be fine for an hour," Poppy said. "She's getting stronger every day. Besides, all of us will be here."

But Rocky looked torn, glancing between me and the stairs that led to where Sage was sleeping, his protector instincts clearly warring with his concern for me.

"Stay with her," I said gently. "Make sure she's okay. The others will keep watch down here."

His relief was immediate. "Really? You're sure?"

"I'm sure. She needs you more than I do right now."

Two people remained in the café: a regular who always lingered over his laptop for hours, and a tourist studying a map of hiking trails. I busied myself wiping down already-clean tables, refilling napkin dispensers, anything to look occupied while I waited.

Finally, after what felt like an eternity but was probably only ten minutes, the tourist left. Then the laptop regular glanced at his watch, packed up, and headed out with a wave.

The café was empty.

"What if she recognizes what you're doing?" Millie's voice was barely above a whisper. "What if she knows you're investigating?"

That was the fear that had kept me awake half the night. "Then I'll play dumb. Say I'm just trying to find closure, trying to understand what happened to Hazel. People expect grief to make you act strangely."

"Be careful," Millie said, and the worry in her voice made my chest tight. "That woman is dangerous."

"I'll be in a public shop surrounded by yarn and probably half a dozen elderly ladies. What's she going to do?"

The cats exchanged looks that clearly said I was being naive. Maybe I was. But what was the alternative? Sit here and wait for Iris to solve a murder with no leads? Wait for a killer to get comfortable, to disappear, to never face justice?

No. I had to do something.

"One hour," I promised. "If anything feels wrong, I'll leave immediately."

"You'd better," Gus growled.

I grabbed my jacket and headed out, locking the café door behind me and flipping the small sign I'd made: Back in 1 hour. My hands shook slightly as I pocketed my keys.

The walk to the yarn shop took less than five minutes, but I used every second to prepare. What would I say? How would I act? I needed to seem genuinely interested in learning a new hobby, not like someone interrogating a murder suspect. Natural. Casual. Just a woman looking for a distraction from grief.

Main Street was busy with the mid-morning crowd. Tourists browsing shop windows, locals running errands, the normal rhythm of a small mountain town going about its day. Everyone so ordinary, so unsuspecting. None of them knew that somewhere among them walked a killer.

The morning sun felt warm on my face, but I couldn't shake the chill that had settled into my bones. I passed The Turning Page and saw Maeve through the window, shelving books. She glanced up and our eyes met for just a second. Something in her expression made me think she knew exactly where I was going and why. But she just gave me a small nod and returned to her work.

Cordelia's Yarn Haven was three blocks down Main Street, tucked between Mountain Brew Coffee and a vintage clothing boutique called Retro Revival. The storefront window displayed an elaborate arrangement of yarn in autumn colors, cascading from ceiling to floor like a fiber waterfall. Several knitted samples hung on display: delicate lace scarves, chunky hats with pompoms, even a complicated-looking sweater with an intricate cable pattern that must have taken months to complete.

I stood outside for a moment, looking through the glass. I could see movement inside, shadows of people browsing. Normal. Safe. Just a yarn shop.

I took a breath and pushed through the door.

A bell chimed overhead, cheerful and bright, and I was immediately hit with the smell of wool and something floral. Lavender, I realized. Sachets hung from various displays, filling the air with the scent. The shop was larger than it looked from outside, with floor-to-ceiling shelves lined with yarn in every color imaginable. Reds that ranged from pale pink to deep burgundy. Blues from sky to navy. Greens in every shade of forest and sea. Purples, oranges, yellows, neutrals. An entire rainbow organized by color and weight, labeled with neat handwritten tags.

A few small tables in the center of the shop held pattern books and knitting needles of various sizes. One wall was dedicated to crochet hooks, displayed like tiny instruments in graduated sizes.

Another section had finished samples: baby blankets, shawls, Afghans, things I didn't even have names for.

"Welcome, welcome!" Cordelia Kelder swept toward me like a colorful tornado, and I had to resist the urge to take a step back. She wore a hand-knitted cardigan in shades of purple and pink that should have clashed but somehow worked, the stitches so even and perfect they looked machine-made. Her silver hair was piled on top of her head in an elaborate bun secured with what looked like knitting needles, and multiple necklaces jangled as she moved. "Alexis! From the cat café! What a lovely surprise!"

"Hi, Cordelia." I managed a smile, hoping it looked natural. "I was thinking about taking up a new hobby. Knitting or crochet, maybe?"

"Oh, how wonderful!" Her face lit up like I'd just announced I'd won the lottery. "I always say there's nothing quite as therapeutic as working with yarn. Keeps the hands busy and the mind calm. Perfect for someone who's been through what you've been through lately." She reached out and patted my arm, the gesture motherly and slightly overwhelming.

She said it kindly, but I still felt the weight of it. Everyone in this town knew everyone else's business. Knew I'd found Hazel's body. Knew we'd been friends. Knew I was grieving.

"I thought it might help," I agreed, which wasn't entirely a lie. Having something to do with my hands while I thought about murder might actually be useful.

"Absolutely, absolutely. Now, have you ever knitted before? Or crocheted? They're different, you know. Some people think they're the same, but they're not at all. Knitting uses two needles and creates a fabric with interlocking loops. Crochet uses one hook and creates a different structure entirely. Both beautiful, but very different techniques—"

"I haven't tried either." I glanced around the shop, trying to seem casual while really looking for Orla. "I'm completely new to this."

"Even better! I love teaching beginners. There's something so special about watching someone create their first project, seeing that moment when the stitches start to make sense." Cordelia beamed at me. "Orla!" She called toward the back of the shop. "Come help our newest student!"

My heart rate kicked up a notch. This was it. The moment I'd been planning for.

Orla emerged from a storage room carrying a box of yarn, and I had to consciously keep my expression neutral. She wore her usual unremarkable clothes: gray slacks, a cream-colored blouse, sensible shoes. Her graying hair was pulled back in a low ponytail, not a strand out of place. She had that same pleasant but blank expression I'd come to associate with her, like a mask that never quite slipped.

The same woman who'd come into my café days ago, warned me that investigating Hazel's death was dangerous, then disappeared before I could ask any real questions. Now here she was, looking at me with polite unfamiliarity, as if we'd never spoken at all.

"Alexis wants to learn to knit," Cordelia announced cheerfully. "Can you show her the beginner supplies while I help Mrs. Chen find that mohair blend she wanted?"

"Of course." Orla set down her box and turned to me with that practiced smile. No flicker of recognition. No acknowledgment of our previous conversation. Just the courteous attention of a shopkeeper to a new customer. "Knitting or crochet? Cordelia mentioned both."

"I'm not sure. What would you recommend for a complete beginner?"

"Crochet is a bit more forgiving," she said, leading me toward the wall of hooks. "With knitting, if you drop a stitch, it can unravel several rows. With crochet, you only lose the stitch you were working on. Easier to fix mistakes."

"Then crochet it is." I watched her select a hook from the display, her movements efficient and practiced. "I need all the help I can get."

"Everyone starts somewhere." She handed me a medium-sized hook. "This is a good all-purpose size. And for yarn, I'd suggest something smooth and light-colored for your first project. Makes it easier to see your stitches."

We spent the next fifteen minutes selecting supplies: a beautiful blue yarn that reminded me of summer skies, a basic hook, a simple pattern book for beginners. Orla explained the basics patiently, demonstrating how to hold the hook, how to make a slip knot, how to begin a foundation chain. Her teaching style was methodical and clear, and I found myself actually paying attention despite my ulterior motives.

"You mentioned you're grieving," she said suddenly, and I had to force myself not to react too strongly. "I'm sorry for your loss. Hazel Blaine, wasn't it?"

There it was. The opening I'd been waiting for, though she'd brought it up more naturally than I'd expected.

"Yes. We were friends. I still can't quite believe she's gone." All true, which made the lie easier.

"It's always hardest when it's unexpected." Orla's expression remained pleasantly sympathetic, but something in her eyes sharpened slightly. "I heard it wasn't an accident. That Sheriff Scott is investigating it as a homicide."

"That's what I've heard too." I kept my voice neutral, curious but not pressing. "Did you know Hazel?"

"A little. She used to come in for yarn. Made the most beautiful lace shawls. Had a real talent for it." Orla wrapped my purchases in tissue paper with precise, careful movements. "Always pleasant to talk to. Such a shame what happened."

"The sheriff thinks it was poison," I said, watching her reaction carefully. "Some kind of plant-based toxin."

For just a moment, something flickered across Orla's face. Surprise? Recognition? It was gone before I could identify it, replaced by that pleasant mask again.

"How terrible," she said, and her voice was appropriately horrified. "Who would do such a thing?"

"That's what everyone's trying to figure out." I accepted the bag she handed me, making sure to look sad rather than suspicious. "I keep wondering if I missed something. If there were signs."

"You can't think that way," Orla said, but there was something in her tone that felt rehearsed. "Sometimes terrible things happen and there's nothing anyone could have done to prevent them."

"I suppose you're right." I paid for my supplies and tucked the bag under my arm. "Thank you for your help. I'm sure I'll be back soon when I inevitably mess this up and need more yarn."

"That's what we're here for." She smiled, but it didn't reach her eyes. "Actually, if you're interested, we have a crochet circle Thursday evenings. Beginners welcome. It's a nice group, and having people to help you when you get stuck is invaluable."

"That sounds great. What time?"

"Seven o'clock. We meet in the back room. Bring your project and we'll help you get started."

"I'll be there. Thank you, Orla."

"My pleasure."

I left the shop with my supplies and more questions than answers, the bell chiming behind me like a goodbye. The conversation with Orla had felt off somehow. Too careful. Too measured. Like she'd been expecting me to ask about Hazel. Like she'd had her answers prepared.

Or maybe I was just paranoid. Maybe grief and suspicion were making me see conspiracy where there was only coincidence.

The walk back to the café felt longer than it should have. My hands were shaking slightly, and I realized I was clutching the yarn bag too tightly, crinkling the paper. I forced myself to breathe, to look normal, to be just another person walking down Main Street on a Wednesday morning.

Back at the café, the cats were waiting. Poppy, Gus, and Millie were arranged in the viewing room like a furry tribunal, eyes fixed on the door the moment I walked in. From upstairs, I could hear Rocky's voice, talking softly to Sage.

"Well?" Poppy demanded immediately, before I'd even set down my bag.

"She's good." I set the yarn bag on the counter and leaned against it, suddenly exhausted. "Very good. She didn't give anything away. Seemed surprised when I mentioned the poisoning, but it could have been genuine surprise or practiced surprise. I couldn't tell."

"Did she say anything useful?" Gus asked, jumping down from his perch to pace in front of me.

"She said she knew Hazel a little. That Hazel used to come in for yarn." I thought about it, trying to remember every detail of the conversation. "Hazel knitted lace shawls, apparently. Orla called them beautiful. Said Hazel had a real talent for it."

"So they knew each other," came Rocky's voice from the stairs. He appeared with Sage following close behind him, the tiny kitten moving with much more confidence than she had just days ago.

"Casually, at least." I pulled out my new crochet hook and yarn, staring at them without really seeing them. The blue was pretty, the hook solid and simple. Tools for creating something. Not tools for solving a murder. "But that doesn't tell us if Orla had a reason to kill her. Doesn't tell us anything, really, except that Hazel had been in that shop. Had probably talked to Orla. Maybe more than once."

Sage padded over and sniffed the yarn bag curiously. "What's this?"

"Yarn. For making things." I reached down to stroke her soft head. "I'm learning to crochet."

"Why?" Her innocent question made me smile despite everything.

"To get close to someone I need to watch."

"Oh." She seemed to accept this as perfectly logical. "Rocky says you're very good at watching people."

"Rocky talks about me, does he?"

"All the time," Rocky said, sounding slightly embarrassed. "She asks questions."

"Unless Hazel figured out something about Orla," Poppy said slowly, her amber eyes thoughtful. "Figured out who she really was or why she was really here. And Orla killed her to keep that secret."

It was possible. If Orla was connected to something dangerous, and if Hazel had somehow discovered that connection, she might have confronted Orla. Might have tried to protect someone without anyone knowing. Might have put herself between danger and an innocent person.

And died for it.

The thought made me feel sick, my stomach churning with guilt and grief.

"Or maybe Orla is just a yarn shop employee," I said, but my voice lacked conviction. "Maybe she's nobody. Maybe this whole thing is a waste of time and the real killer is Carla or Trish."

"Do you believe that?" Millie asked softly.

"No," I admitted. "Something about her felt... wrong. Too controlled. Too perfect. Like she was playing a role."

"Then we keep watching," Poppy said firmly. "Keep investigating. Keep gathering information."

"She mentioned a crochet circle on Thursday evenings," I said. "She leads it. Maybe I should go. Observe her in a different setting, see if she lets her guard down around other people."

"That's tomorrow," Millie pointed out, her voice worried.

"I know." Tomorrow felt too soon and not soon enough all at once. Every day that passed was another day Hazel's killer walked free. Another day I failed to get justice. But rushing in without a plan, without more information, could be dangerous. "I need to actually learn some basic stitches first, or it'll be obvious I'm not really there to learn."

The rest of Wednesday passed in a blur of customers and coffee and attempting to learn basic crochet stitches from YouTube videos on my phone during slow periods. I'd prop the phone against the espresso machine, watch a few seconds of demonstration, then try to replicate it with my yarn and hook.

The yarn was forgiving, like Orla had said, soft and smooth and easy to work with. But my fingers felt clumsy and my mind kept wandering to poison and secrets and that flicker of something in Orla's eyes when I mentioned the poisoning. My stitches came out uneven, too loose in some places and too tight in others, the tension all wrong.

"You're thinking too much," Poppy observed from her window perch.

"I have a lot to think about."

"Focus on one stitch at a time. Like you're pouring one drink at a time. Not the whole day. Just this moment."

She was right, but it was hard to focus when my brain kept replaying the conversation with Orla, analyzing every word, every pause, every micro-expression.

By closing time, I had managed to create a lumpy, uneven chain stitch about six inches long. It was terrible, but it was something. Proof that I'd been practicing. Proof that I was genuinely trying to learn.

"Very artistic," Gus said, examining my work with a critical eye. "If by artistic you mean looks like a cat threw up yarn."

"It's my first day."

"And hopefully your last. Stick to making coffee."

"Can't. I need to be able to go to that crochet circle tomorrow without looking completely incompetent."

"I hate to break it to you," Rocky said, "but you already look completely incompetent."

"Thanks for the vote of confidence."

But I kept at it that evening after closing, sitting on my couch with the cats arranged around me. Sage had claimed a spot on my lap, her small weight warm and comforting. She watched my hands move with the fascination only a kitten could have, occasionally batting at the yarn when it dangled within reach.

"No attacking the yarn," I told her gently. "I need this to look halfway decent by tomorrow."

"But it moves," she protested.

"Everything moves to you." Rocky settled beside us, close enough that Sage could lean against him. "You'd chase a dust mote if it floated by."

"Dust motes are interesting," Sage said seriously, and I had to smile.

I practiced the same basic stitch over and over, watching more videos, reading instructions in the pattern book Orla had sold me. Chain stitch. Single crochet. Double crochet. The terms started to make sense, the movements becoming slightly less awkward.

It gave my hands something to do besides clench with frustration. Gave my mind something to focus on besides that box in the closet, still waiting, still holding Hazel's secrets.

Tomorrow, I'd go to the crochet circle. I'd sit in a room with Orla and strangers, all of us working with yarn and hooks. I'd watch her teach and interact with other people. Maybe she'd reveal something. Maybe I'd see a crack in her careful facade. Maybe someone else would mention Hazel, and I'd see how Orla really reacted when she wasn't expecting the question.

Or maybe I was chasing shadows. Maybe the real killer was Carla with her bitterness and inheritance, or Trish with her rivalry and rage. Maybe I was wasting time learning a hobby I'd never actually wanted, sitting in yarn shops and pretending to care about stitches while a murderer laughed at how easily they'd gotten away with it.

But I had to try.

For Hazel.

Even if it meant sitting in a room full of strangers, pretending to care about yarn, while really watching for signs of murder.

Outside my apartment window, the stars came out over the mountains, bright and cold and distant. The same stars that had been shining the night Hazel died. The same stars that would keep shining whether I found her killer or not.

Sage had fallen asleep in my lap, her breathing soft and steady. Rocky dozed beside us, one paw stretched out to touch the kitten. Poppy watched from the armchair, Millie from behind the fern, Gus from his bed by the fireplace that wasn't lit yet.

My found family, keeping vigil while I tried to learn to crochet and catch a killer at the same time.

Tomorrow, I'd get closer to the truth.

Or at least, I'd learn to crochet.

One way or another, it was progress.

Chapter Thirteen

Thursday evening came too quickly. I stood in front of my closet at six-thirty, staring at my limited wardrobe options like they held the answers to the universe.

The crochet circle started at seven. The yarn shop was a five-minute walk. Which meant I had twenty-five minutes to decide what to wear and stop my stomach from churning.

"Just pick something," Poppy said from her perch on my bed. The other cats were arranged around the room like an audience at a particularly boring theater production, watching my minor breakdown with varying levels of concern and amusement.

From the doorway came a small mew. Sage sat there, having navigated the stairs on her own. I'd been letting her explore downstairs in the café for the past few days, always supervised, helping her build confidence in moving through the space. She was getting bolder, more sure of herself. Rocky had been with her earlier but was now sprawled on my armchair, giving her space to explore independently.

"You made it all the way upstairs by yourself," I said, momentarily distracted from my wardrobe crisis.

"Rocky showed me the safe way," Sage announced proudly. "No falling."

"Good job." I turned back to the closet, pulling out a dark green sweater, holding it up against myself in the mirror, putting it back. Too severe. "I can't just pick something. I need to look casual but put-together. Interested in crochet but not trying too hard. Normal."

"You're overthinking this," Gus observed from his spot on the armchair. "It's a yarn circle, not a job interview."

"I know that." I grabbed a gray cardigan, considered it, shoved it back into the closet. Too drab. Too forgettable. Or maybe that was good? No, too drab. "I just need to look right."

"Why are you so nervous?" Rocky asked, tilting his head in that way that made him look far too perceptive for an orange cat.

"I'm not nervous."

"You've changed clothes three times already," Poppy pointed out. "And you're sweating even though it's sixty degrees in here."

I sat down on the edge of my bed, admitting defeat. My hands were trembling, and there was a tight knot in my stomach that had been there since I woke up this morning. "Fine. I'm nervous. Are you happy?"

"Why?" Millie asked softly from her hiding spot under the bed. I could just see her gray face peering out.

That was the question, wasn't it? I took a breath, trying to articulate what was churning in my chest. Trying to name the anxiety that had been building all day.

"Because this is a group of people. A social gathering. And I'm going to have to sit there for at least an hour, maybe two, making small talk and pretending to care about stitches and patterns while really watching Orla for signs that she's a murderer." The words came faster now, tumbling out. "And the whole time, I'll have to be careful not to say anything that reveals what I am. Not to slip up. Not to let my guard down even for a second because one wrong word, one strange comment, and everything I've built here could collapse."

The cats were silent, letting me continue.

"And it's not just that." My voice caught, rough with emotion I hadn't realized was so close to the surface. "It's that this is about Hazel. About finding out who killed my friend. And it's so personal and so real and I'm terrified I'm going to mess it up. That I'll miss something important or say something wrong or that Orla will realize I'm investigating her and then..." I trailed off, unable to finish the thought.

"Then you'll be in danger too," Poppy finished quietly.

"Yeah." The word came out as barely more than a whisper.

"So don't go," Gus said, and there was surprising gentleness in his gruff voice. "Stay here. Stay safe. Let Iris handle it."

I looked at him, this grumpy old cat who pretended not to care about anything except treats and naps. "You know I can't do that."

"I know." He sighed, a very human sound. "Doesn't mean I have to like it."

"Wear the blue sweater," Millie said suddenly, her voice stronger than usual. "The soft one. It makes you look friendly but not like you're trying too hard. And it matches your eyes."

I looked at her, surprised. Millie rarely offered opinions on anything that didn't involve hiding spots or treats or whether a particular shadow was threatening.

"The blue one," she repeated with more confidence. "Trust me."

I pulled out the sweater she meant: a soft cornflower blue that I'd bought months ago and barely worn because it felt too bright, too noticeable. But when I held it up, I saw what Millie meant. It was cheerful without being loud, casual without being sloppy. I paired it with dark jeans and the boots I wore most days. Looked at myself in the mirror.

Millie was right. I looked casual, approachable, normal. Like someone who might genuinely want to learn to crochet, not someone investigating a murder. Like someone who belonged in a small-town craft circle.

"Thank you," I said, meaning it.

"You're welcome. Now go catch a killer." Coming from timid, fearful Millie, the words carried extra weight. If she could be brave enough to say that, I could be brave enough to walk into a yarn shop.

I grabbed my bag with my yarn and hook, gave each cat a quick scratch behind the ears. Sage bumped her head against my hand when I reached her. "Be safe," she said softly.

"I will."

I headed downstairs before I could talk myself out of it.

The walk to Cordelia's Yarn Haven felt longer than five minutes. Each step felt deliberate, heavy, like I was walking toward something inevitable and possibly dangerous. My stomach twisted with each block I passed, and I had to force myself not to turn around and run back to the safety of my apartment.

The evening air was cool but not cold, carrying the scent of pine from the mountains and something savory cooking from one of the restaurants. Main Street was quieter in the evening, most shops closed, just a few restaurants and bars lit up with activity. A couple walked past me, laughing about something, completely unaware of the tension coiling in my chest.

I passed The Turning Page, dark now. Passed Mountain Brew Coffee with its warm lights but empty tables. Passed shops I'd walked by a hundred times but really looked at now, trying to memorize details, trying to distract myself from where I was going.

"Alexis!"

I jumped, nearly dropping my bag. Dr. Colton Dover was crossing the street toward me, wearing khakis and a button-down shirt instead of his usual veterinary scrubs. He had a jacket slung over one arm and that easy smile that made everyone in town trust him with their pets.

"Dr. Dover. Hi." My voice came out steadier than I felt.

"Colton, please. We've been through enough kitten emergencies for the formality." His smile widened. "You look nice. Going somewhere?"

"Crochet circle at Cordelia's." I gestured vaguely in the direction of the yarn shop. "Thought I'd try something new."

"That's great!" He sounded genuinely pleased, like I'd told him I'd accomplished something significant. "It's good to see you out and about. You work so hard at the café, I worry you don't take enough time for yourself."

Something warm unfurled in my chest at his concern, even as I felt guilty for not deserving it. "Thanks. Are you headed somewhere?"

"Ventura's Steakhouse." He gestured down the street. "Meeting my parents and brother to celebrate my parents' fifty-first anniversary. Mom wanted the filet, Dad wanted an excuse to tell embarrassing stories from their wedding, and my brother wanted free food. So here we are."

"Fifty-one years. That's impressive."

"It is." His expression softened. "They're good people. Still hold hands when they think no one's watching." He paused, studying me with those perceptive eyes that probably served him well with frightened animals. "How's Sage doing? Settling in okay?"

"She's doing really well. Getting braver every day. She came upstairs by herself today."

"That's wonderful. Kittens are resilient little things. Give them safety and love and they bounce back faster than you'd think." He shifted his jacket to his other arm. "Well, I should let you get to your circle. But I'm really glad you're doing this. Taking time for yourself, I mean. You deserve it."

"Thanks." I managed a smile that almost felt real. "Have a good dinner."

"You too. I mean, have a good circle." He laughed at himself. "Enjoy the yarn."

I watched him walk away toward the steakhouse, something settling in my chest. It was nice, being noticed. Being worried about. Having someone see that I worked hard and thinking I deserved a break. Even if he had no idea what I was really doing tonight.

The moment of warmth faded as I turned back toward the yarn shop. The building came into view, lit up warm and welcoming. Through the large front windows I could see a group of women already gathered around one of the tables that had been pushed together. They were laughing about something, heads bent together over their work. Normal. Pleasant. Safe.

Except one of them might be a murderer.

My steps slowed. I could still leave. Turn around right now. Make an excuse tomorrow about feeling sick or getting called away for an emergency or the café being too busy. No one would think twice about it.

But then I'd be no closer to answers. No closer to justice for Hazel. No closer to understanding what had really happened in that alley.

I stopped about ten feet from the door, my heart hammering. This was it. Last chance to back out.

I thought about Hazel. About her kindness and her patience and how she'd welcomed me without questions. About how she'd deserved so much better than dying alone in an alley. About how someone had poisoned her, planned it, executed it, and was walking around free while she was gone forever.

I pushed through the door.

The bell chimed, cheerful and bright, and several faces turned toward me. My cheeks immediately felt hot. I wasn't used to being looked at, being noticed, being the center of attention even for a few seconds.

"Alexis! Wonderful! Come in, come in! You're just in time." Cordelia waved enthusiastically from behind the counter where she was arranging teacups and a plate of cookies. She wore another elaborate hand-knitted cardigan, this one in shades of orange and gold that caught the warm light.

I recognized a few faces from the café: Pearl Van from the book club, her gray hair pulled back in a neat bun. Mabel Smalls with her ever-present sharp eyes and suspicious expression, like she was perpetually waiting to catch someone in a lie. And two other women I'd seen around town but whose names I couldn't remember.

And at the head of the table, arranging pattern books and example stitches with precise movements, was Orla Weston.

She looked up as I entered, and our eyes met for just a second. Was that recognition? Wariness? Or just neutral acknowledgment? I couldn't tell.

"Everyone, this is Alexis Belrose," Cordelia announced, as if they didn't all know exactly who I was. Small towns didn't allow for anonymity. "She runs The Cozy Purrch and she's brand new to crochet. Let's make her feel welcome!"

There was a chorus of friendly greetings, voices overlapping: "Welcome!" "So glad you came!" "We love beginners!"

Pearl patted the empty chair next to her with a warm smile. "Sit here, dear. I promise we don't bite. Well, Mabel might, but only if you make a political comment she disagrees with."

"I do not bite," Mabel said primly, but there was amusement in her eyes.

I sat, hyperconscious of every movement. Was I sitting too stiffly? Too casually? I pulled out my yarn and hook with hands that I hoped weren't visibly shaking, setting them on the table in front of me like props in a play I didn't know how to perform.

The table itself was covered with projects in various stages of completion. Pearl had what looked like a baby blanket in soft yellow. Mabel was working on something with a complicated stitch pattern in deep purple. The atmosphere should have been cozy and welcoming, but all I could feel was the weight of maintaining my facade.

"I love that color," one of the women I didn't know said, gesturing to my blue yarn. She was probably in her fifties, with kind eyes behind wire-rimmed glasses and a project that looked like a blanket in her lap, already at least three feet long. "Very soothing. Reminds me of summer skies."

"Orla helped me pick it out," I said, glancing at Orla, who gave a small nod of acknowledgement but didn't smile.

"She has excellent taste in yarn," the woman continued enthusiastically. "I'm Beatrice, by the way. Beatrice Frost. I work at the library with Pearl. Reference desk."

"Nice to meet you."

"And I'm Dorothy Webb," the other unfamiliar woman said. She was older, probably in her seventies, with perfectly coiffed white hair that looked like it had been set at a salon that morning, and a string of pearls around her neck. Everything about her suggested old money and careful grooming. "I've been coming to these circles for fifteen years. Best evening of my week. Better than most of the social functions my late husband used to drag me to, I'll tell you that."

"Dorothy's husband was on the town council," Pearl explained quietly. "She's been much happier since he passed. Terrible thing to say, but it's true."

"Not terrible at all," Dorothy said with a slight smile. "Milton was a bore and everyone knew it."

Cordelia bustled over with a tray of tea and cookies, the cups rattling slightly. "Help yourselves! I made chamomile and peppermint. And the cookies are snickerdoodles, fresh this morning. Now, Orla, why don't you get our newest student started while the rest of us work on our projects?"

Orla set down her delicate work and moved to sit across from me, pulling her chair around so we were at a slight angle. Close enough for instruction but not uncomfortably close. Everything about her movement was controlled, measured, precise.

"Did you practice the chain stitch I showed you?" Her voice was pleasant, professional, the same tone she'd used in the shop.

"I tried." I pulled out my lumpy six-inch chain, feeling absurdly embarrassed about showing her my terrible work. "I'm not sure I'm doing it right."

"Let me see." She examined my work with a critical but not unkind eye, her fingers moving along the stitches, testing the tension. "Your tension is too tight here, and too loose here. But the basic motion is correct. That's the important part. The tension will even out with practice. Let me show you again."

She demonstrated the stitch, her fingers moving with practiced ease. Hook in, yarn over, pull through. Again. Again. The motion looked simple, almost meditative, when she did it. I watched, trying to focus on the mechanical process rather than on her face, her expressions, any sign that she was anything other than a patient yarn shop employee teaching a beginner.

But I couldn't help noticing details. The way her shoulders relaxed slightly when she worked. The small furrow between her eyebrows when she concentrated. The callus on her right index finger from years of holding a hook.

"Now you try," she said, handing back my hook.

I attempted to replicate her movements, hyper-aware that everyone at the table was working on their own projects but probably also watching the new person struggle. My fingers felt clumsy, the yarn kept twisting wrong, and my stitches came out uneven.

"Good," Orla said, though my work looked nothing like hers. "Better tension that time. Keep practicing that until it feels natural, then we'll move on to the single crochet stitch. It takes time. Some people pick it up quickly, others need weeks. There's no rush."

She returned to her seat at the head of the table and picked up her own project: something intricate and lacy in cream-colored thread that looked like it required both skill and infinite patience.

I practiced my chain stitch, trying to make my tension even, while my ears strained to catch every word of every conversation. Looking for clues. Looking for anything. The soft click of hooks against yarn. The quiet murmur of advice and laughter. The domestic simplicity of it all felt surreal when I was here to investigate murder.

Around the table, the women chatted easily, their voices creating a comfortable hum. Pearl was telling Dorothy about a new mystery novel that had come into the library. Beatrice was helping Mabel with a complicated pattern. Cordelia moved between the counter and the table, making sure everyone had tea, offering advice, adjusting someone's project with gentle hands.

Watching them, something twisted in my chest. A memory, sharp and unexpected.

This was what we'd done in the coven. Not crochet specifically, but gathering together in the evenings, working on projects with our hands while we talked and laughed and just existed together. Lily and I would sit side by side, making sachets or grinding herbs or stitching protective sigils into fabric. Elder Miriam would lead discussions about the craft, about magic, about life. The other women would offer advice, share stories, create that sense of community that made you feel like you belonged to something larger than yourself.

I'd given that up. Walked away from those warm evenings, that easy fellowship, that feeling of being known and accepted. And here I sat in a yarn shop, surrounded by women doing almost the same thing, except I couldn't truly be part of it. Couldn't let my guard down. Couldn't be honest about who I was or what I was doing here.

The ache of it surprised me. I'd thought I was past missing what I'd left behind. But sitting here, watching these women create together, I felt the loss of it all over again.

"Such a shame about Hazel," Dorothy said suddenly, and the table went quiet. Even the clicking of hooks stopped for a moment. "I still can't believe it. She was always so careful. So healthy. I remember her telling me just last month that she'd had her annual physical and was fit as a fiddle."

"The sheriff told me it's being investigated as a murder now," Mabel said, her sharp eyes scanning the table like she was taking inventory of everyone's reactions. "Poisoning, apparently. Some kind of plant-based toxin, from what I heard."

My hook slipped, and I had to restart my chain, trying to keep my hands steady. This was it. This was where I might learn something useful.

"Poisoning?" Beatrice looked shocked, her kind face crumpling with distress. "Who would poison Hazel? She was the sweetest woman. She never had an unkind word for anyone."

"That's what we'd all like to know," Pearl said grimly, setting down her work. "That nice woman, murdered in her own alley. In her own space. It's terrible. Makes you feel like nowhere is safe anymore."

"I heard the niece is contesting the will," Cordelia contributed from the counter, where she was refilling the tea kettle. "Trying to get the flower shop. Can you imagine? The woman's barely cold and Carla's already got lawyers involved. It's unseemly."

"Grief makes people do strange things," Orla said quietly. All eyes turned to her, and I watched carefully, looking for any crack in her composure. "Sometimes when we lose someone, we grasp at anything we can control. Inheritance, property, possessions. It feels like holding onto the person when really it's just holding onto things. Objects that can't love us back."

It was surprisingly insightful. Unexpectedly philosophical. And it made me wonder what Orla had lost besides her sister. What she'd grasped at. What objects she'd tried to hold onto in place of people.

"Still," Dorothy said with a sniff, adjusting her pearls, "there's grieving and then there's being greedy. From what I hear, Carla barely visited Hazel in the last decade. Couldn't be bothered to drive up from Denver more than once a year, if that. And now suddenly she cares about the flower shop?"

"And then there's Trish Lawrence," Mabel added with obvious distaste, her nose wrinkling like she'd smelled something unpleasant. "Trying to swoop in and buy the shop. That woman has no shame. Never has."

"She's always been like that," Pearl agreed, picking up her yellow blanket and working a few stitches before setting it down again, too agitated to focus. "Competitive to the point of cruelty. I remember when she tried to undercut Hazel on the library's flower budget. Offered to do the arrangements for half price just to steal the contract. Half price! Can you imagine?"

"Did it work?" I asked, trying to sound curious rather than investigative.

"Of course not. Hazel's arrangements were worth every penny, and we all knew it. She had an eye for color and form that Trish has never had. Trish's flowers never lasted more than a few days. Brown edges on the petals by day three, every single time." Pearl shook her head, genuine anger in her voice. "She never understood that it wasn't just about price. It was about quality and care and relationships. About knowing what the library needed for each display, each season."

The conversation drifted after that to other topics: the upcoming Harvest Festival, someone's grandchild who was applying to colleges, a recipe for pumpkin bread that Cordelia swore was the best she'd ever tasted. But I kept working on my chain stitch, kept watching Orla from the corner of my eye.

She was good at this. Good at seeming engaged without really participating. She'd nod at the right moments, smile slightly when something funny was said, offer a small comment here or there. But she never truly joined in, never revealed anything real about herself beyond the most basic surface details.

It was exactly what I did. The same techniques I used to stay hidden, to keep people at arm's length, to seem normal while protecting my secrets. The same careful balance of friendliness and distance.

Which meant either she was also hiding something significant, or I was projecting my own paranoia and survival instincts onto an innocent woman who just happened to be reserved by nature.

"Alexis, dear, how's your chain coming along?" Cordelia called from across the room, making me jump slightly.

I held up my work, which had progressed from six inches to about ten, though the tension was still wildly inconsistent. Some stitches were so tight I could barely get the hook through. Others were so loose they looked like they might unravel if I breathed on them wrong.

"Wonderful! You're a natural. Ready to try the next stitch?"

"I think so." I wasn't sure at all, but I nodded anyway.

Orla set down her delicate shawl, the cream thread gleaming in the light, and came back around to sit across from me. "Single crochet is the foundation of most patterns. Once you master this, you can make almost anything. Dishcloths, scarves, blankets, even stuffed animals if you're patient enough."

She demonstrated, her fingers moving in a rhythm that seemed simple when she did it but became impossibly complicated when I tried to replicate it. Hook in through the chain, yarn over, pull through one loop. Yarn over again, pull through both loops on the hook.

"Hook through, yarn over, pull through, yarn over again, pull through both loops," she recited patiently as I fumbled through my first attempt, the yarn twisting awkwardly. "It takes time. The motion needs to become automatic. Don't get frustrated."

"I'm not frustrated." But I was, and not about the crochet. I was frustrated that I'd learned nothing useful tonight. That Orla remained an enigma wrapped in neutral politeness. That I was no closer to answers than I'd been before walking through the door. That

I was sitting here pretending to care about stitches when what I really wanted was to know if the woman teaching me had killed my friend.

"You knew Hazel, didn't you?" I asked, trying to sound casual. Just making conversation. Just connecting over shared acquaintances. "From when she'd come in for yarn?"

"A little." Orla's expression didn't change, but something in her posture shifted. More alert, maybe. Or maybe I was imagining it. "She was always very pleasant. Loved yarns in earth tones and jewel tones. Browns and greens and deep blues. Said they reminded her of her garden, of growing things."

"Did she come in often?"

"Every few weeks. She'd browse for a while, touch all the yarns, talk about what she was working on." Orla's voice remained steady, conversational. "She'd been making a lap blanket in forest green. Never got to finish it, I suppose."

The thought of Hazel's unfinished project sitting somewhere made my throat tight.

"Did she ever mention family? Or problems with anyone?"

Now Orla's eyes met mine directly, and I saw a flicker of something. Suspicion? Understanding? Warning? "Why do you ask?"

"Just trying to understand what happened. She was my friend." I tried to keep my voice steady, curious but not interrogative. "I'm trying to make sense of it."

"The sheriff is investigating. Perhaps it's best to let her do her job." Orla's tone was gentle but firm, like she was giving advice to a child who didn't understand the danger they were courting. "Murder investigations are dangerous things for civilians to involve themselves in. Questions can draw attention. Attention can be dangerous."

Was that a warning? A threat? Or genuine concern? I couldn't read her expression at all.

Before I could respond, Mabel spoke up from across the table, her voice carrying that sharp edge of authority. "Orla's right. Leave it to Iris. She's good at what she does. We elected her for a reason. Let her handle the investigating while you handle your café."

The conversation moved on, someone asking about the Harvest Festival decorating committee, but I felt Orla's eyes on me for several more seconds before she returned to her seat. Watching. Evaluating. Wondering what I really wanted to know and why.

I'd pushed too hard. Been too obvious. Asked too many questions in too short a time. She knew I was digging into Hazel's death, and now she'd be on guard. Now she'd be watching me as carefully as I was watching her.

The rest of the evening dragged on like hours stretched into years. I practiced my stitches, my fingers moving mechanically. Joined in the occasional conversation, laughing when others laughed, nodding at the right moments. Tried to look like someone who was genuinely interested in learning a new hobby rather than someone investigating a murder.

But the whole time, I felt Orla's awareness of me. Not watching directly, but conscious of my presence. Like two predators circling, both pretending to be prey.

At eight-thirty, people started packing up their projects. I'd managed to create a small, lumpy square of single crochet stitches that looked more like a dishrag someone had used to clean up a crime scene than anything useful. The edges pulled in weird directions, the stitches varied wildly in size, and there were several holes where I'd missed stitches entirely.

"You did wonderfully for your first session," Cordelia said warmly, squeezing my shoulder in a motherly way that made me flinch slightly. "Same time next week?"

"Maybe. I'll have to see how busy the café is." I packed up my supplies quickly, eager to escape the warm lights and friendly faces and the weight of maintaining my facade for two hours straight.

"You're always welcome here, dear," Dorothy said, already wearing her coat, her pearls gleaming under the shop lights. "We're a friendly group. Well, most of us are friendly. Mabel is suspicious, but she means well."

"I'm discerning," Mabel corrected. "There's a difference."

Outside, the evening air was cool and crisp, shocking after the warm stuffiness of the shop. I started walking back toward my café, my mind spinning, trying to process everything that had happened or hadn't happened.

The streets were quieter now, most people home for the evening. A few bars were lit up, laughter spilling out into the street. But mostly it was dark storefronts and the distant sound of cars on the highway that ran behind town.

The evening had been both helpful and frustrating. I'd learned that Hazel had regularly visited the yarn shop, which meant more opportunities for Orla to have interacted with her. More chances for conversations, for arguments, for Hazel to notice something about Orla that shouldn't be noticed. I'd learned that Orla had lost a sister, which might explain some of her reserve, her careful distance from others, but didn't tell me anything about whether she was a murderer.

And I'd learned that I was terrible at subtle investigation. That my questions were too direct, too pointed, too obviously leading somewhere. That I needed to be more careful or I'd end up revealing more about myself than I learned about Orla.

Back at the apartment, I found Sage curled on the couch where she'd clearly been waiting. She lifted her head when I entered.

"You're back," she said, blinking sleepy eyes.

"I'm back." I sat beside her, and she immediately climbed into my lap.

"How did it go?" Poppy asked from her perch. The other cats emerged from various spots around the apartment.

I dropped my bag on the couch beside me, exhausted in a way that had nothing to do with physical tiredness. "I don't know. I asked too many questions. Orla warned me off investigating. But I didn't learn anything useful. Nothing that tells me if she killed Hazel or if I'm just paranoid."

"So it was a waste?" Rocky asked, his tail twitching with agitation.

"Maybe. Or maybe I learned that Orla is watching me as carefully as I'm watching her." I pulled out my terrible square of stitches, holding it up to the light. It looked even worse in my apartment than it had in the shop. "And that I'm never going to be good at crochet. This is pathetic."

Sage sniffed at the yarn. "It's lumpy."

"Very lumpy," I agreed.

"But you're going back next week?" Millie asked, her voice worried.

I thought about it. About sitting in that room full of people, maintaining my careful facade for hours. About watching Orla watch me. About the exhaustion of being around others while carrying so many secrets, so much fear, so much purpose hidden under a layer of false normalcy.

"I don't know," I admitted, setting down the lumpy square. Sage batted at it experimentally. "Maybe I'm approaching this wrong. Maybe I need to focus on Trish or Carla instead. They have clearer motives. Maybe I should talk to them directly instead of sitting in craft circles hoping to overhear something useful. Or maybe I just need to accept that without being able to tell Iris what the cats saw, I'm never going to prove anything."

The thought was depressing. Crushing, even.

"Don't give up," Poppy said firmly, her amber eyes intense. "You learned that Hazel went to the yarn shop regularly. That's something. It means she and Orla had opportunities to interact beyond just passing on the street. To talk. To share information. Maybe to argue."

She was right. It wasn't much, but it was more than I'd known before. It was a connection, however small. It was progress, even if it felt like failure.

I just needed to figure out what to do with it.

Tomorrow, I'd regroup. Rethink my approach. Maybe talk to Iris again, see if the investigation had uncovered anything new. Maybe follow up on Trish or Carla, see if one of them had a more obvious connection to the murder.

Tonight, I just needed to process the fact that I'd survived a social gathering without exposing myself, even if I hadn't learned much. That I'd maintained my cover for two hours. That despite feeling like I'd failed, I'd actually done what I set out to do: observe Orla in a different setting, confirm that Hazel had been in that shop regularly, establish myself as someone who might keep coming back.

That had to count for something.

Sage had fallen asleep in my lap, her small weight comforting. Outside my window, Larkspur Valley settled into evening routines. Lights came on in windows. People went about their lives, cooking dinner and watching TV and putting children to bed. Completely unaware that a killer walked among them.

But I knew.

And somehow, someway, I was going to prove it.

Even if it meant attending more crochet circles and fumbling through more terrible stitches. Even if it meant enduring more hours of careful social performance.

Justice for Hazel was worth any amount of discomfort.

I just had to keep reminding myself of that.

Chapter Fourteen

That night brought restless sleep and strange dreams.

I was drifting somewhere between waking and sleeping, that hazy space where reality blurs at the edges, when Rocky's voice cut through the fog.

"Alexis. Wake up."

His tone was wrong. Too sharp, too urgent. I surfaced from sleep like coming up from deep water, disoriented and cotton-headed. The bedside clock glowed 2:47 in harsh red numbers.

"What's wrong?" My voice came out rough.

"Listen." Rocky was at the window, his orange fur silvered by moonlight. "Something's happening across the alley."

I sat up, the last remnants of sleep falling away. Poppy was already at the window beside Rocky, her calico body tense. Gus had abandoned his usual spot by the fireplace and was pacing near the bedroom door. Even Millie had emerged from her hiding spot behind the fern, her gray face anxious.

"What kind of something?" I kept my voice low, though I wasn't sure why. Instinct, maybe. The same instinct that made the hair on the back of my neck stand up.

"Sounds. Movement." Poppy's tail lashed once. "At the flower shop. Or above it."

Hazel's apartment. The one Carla had been slowly cleaning out over the past weeks, sorting through her aunt's life. The apartment that should have been empty at three in the morning, locked, undisturbed.

I slipped out of bed, my bare feet silent on the hardwood floor. The apartment was dark except for ambient streetlight filtering through the windows. I moved to join the cats, staying back from the glass, and peered across the narrow alley toward the building that housed Hazel's Blooms.

At first, I saw nothing. Just the familiar outline of the building, dark windows reflecting moonlight, the quiet stillness of a small town at three in the morning.

Then I heard it. A sound so faint I might have imagined it. A scraping, sliding sound. Metal on wood, maybe. Or glass.

"There." Rocky's whisper was barely audible. "Second floor window. The one facing us."

I strained my eyes, watching the window he indicated. Hazel's bedroom window. And then I saw it too. A flicker of light. Brief, quickly extinguished, but unmistakably there. Someone was inside with a flashlight.

My heart kicked into high gear, adrenaline flooding my system. Someone was breaking into Hazel's apartment. Someone was searching for something.

But what? The police had already processed the scene, taken what they needed for the investigation. What could still be there that was worth breaking in for?

"I need to call 9-1-1." I spoke quietly, backing away from the window. "Someone's broken in."

"But you can't tell them we heard it," Gus said urgently, following me. "You can't explain how you knew."

He was right. I couldn't say that my cats had alerted me to the break-in. That would raise questions I absolutely could not answer. Questions that would expose exactly what I was, what I could do.

I needed a cover story. Something believable. Something normal.

"I'll say I couldn't sleep." My mind raced, constructing the lie even as I reached for my phone on the nightstand. "That I was awake, heard a faint sound. Stepped out onto my balcony to check, and that's when I heard glass breaking and saw the flashlight."

"Will she believe that?" Millie asked nervously.

"She'll have to." I grabbed my robe from the hook by the door, pulling it on over my pajamas. "It's plausible. More plausible than telling her my cats woke me up to report suspicious activity."

I dialed 9-1-1, my fingers steadier than I expected. The phone rang twice before a crisp voice answered.

"9-1-1, what's your emergency?"

"This is Alexis Belrose at The Cozy Purrch Café on Main Street. Someone's broken into the building across the alley from me. Hazel's Blooms. I can see a flashlight moving in the second-floor apartment."

"Are you in immediate danger?"

"No. I'm in my own apartment. But someone's definitely inside that building. I heard glass breaking."

"Stay where you are. Keep your doors locked. Officers are on their way."

The line clicked off. I lowered the phone, suddenly aware of how fast my heart was beating. How badly my hands wanted to shake.

"What now?" Rocky asked.

"Now we wait." I moved back to the window, careful to stay in shadow. "And we watch."

Sage appeared from the bedroom doorway, blinking sleepily. She'd been woken by the commotion but seemed more curious than scared. Rocky immediately moved to her side, touching noses with her reassuringly.

The flashlight in Hazel's apartment kept moving, room to room. I heard another sound, louder this time. Something heavy falling or being knocked over. The intruder was getting frustrated, maybe. Getting reckless.

Minutes crawled by. Five. Seven. The flashlight kept moving, room to room. I heard another crash and another loud bang.

Then, the sound of sirens in the distance. Faint at first, then growing steadily louder.

The flashlight in Hazel's apartment stopped moving. Froze in place. Then disappeared completely, snuffed out like a candle.

"They heard the sirens," Poppy said. "They're running."

I pressed closer to the window, my breath fogging the glass. The alley below was empty, dark, quiet. If the intruder had fled, I couldn't see them. They must have gone out the back, through the rear entrance that led to the service alley behind Main Street.

The sirens grew louder, closer. Red and blue lights painted the buildings, flashing rhythmically. A patrol car pulled up in front of Hazel's shop, then another. Doors opened. Figures in uniform emerged, moving quickly but cautiously.

One of them was Iris. Even from this distance, I recognized her silhouette, the authoritative way she moved. She gestured to the other officers, directing them. Two went around back. One stayed at the front. Iris approached the door to the shop, her hand on her weapon.

I needed to go down there. Needed to be the concerned neighbor who'd called in the break-in. Needed to play my part convincingly.

"Stay here," I told the cats. "Stay away from the windows. If anyone asks, you were all asleep."

"You're the only weirdo who can hear us," Gus said dryly. "Who exactly is going to ask us?"

Despite everything, despite the adrenaline and fear, I stopped and laughed. A short, slightly hysterical sound. "You're right. I'm being ridiculous."

"Be careful," Millie said softly, and the moment of levity passed.

I grabbed my keys and phone, pulled on the sneakers I'd left by the door, and headed downstairs.

Good. I unlocked the café door, locked it behind me, and stepped out into the narrow alley. The cold night air bit through my robe, making me shiver. Or maybe that was just adrenaline.

Iris spotted me immediately as I came around to the front of Hazel's building. Her expression was unreadable in the flashing lights, but her body language was tense.

"Alexis. You called this in?"

"Yes. I couldn't sleep, was awake. I heard a faint sound and saw a flashlight moving through Hazel's window."

Iris studied me for a long moment. "You could hear that from across the alley?"

"Not at first. The initial sound was really faint. That's why I stepped out onto my balcony to see if I could pinpoint where it was coming from. That's when I heard glass break more clearly and saw the light moving inside."

It was thin, but it was plausible. The buildings were close together, the alley narrow. Sound could carry, especially in the dead of night when everything else was quiet.

"Did you see anyone leave the building?" Iris asked.

"No. I called 9-1-1 immediately. By the time I looked back, the flashlight was gone. They must have heard the sirens."

"Probably." Iris turned toward the building. "Wait here."

She moved to join the other officers. They'd gotten the door to the shop open and were cautiously making their way inside. I hugged my robe tighter around myself, the November chill seeping through the fabric.

More lights came on in neighboring buildings. Other people woken by the sirens, curious about the commotion. I saw faces in windows, silhouettes watching. Mabel Smalls appeared on her porch three doors down, wrapped in a thick bathrobe, her silver hair in curlers.

"Alexis?" she called. "What's happening?"

"Someone broke into Hazel's place," I called back. "I heard it and called the police."

"Oh my stars." Her hand went to her chest. "In our town. Breaking into a dead woman's home. What is this world coming to?"

I had no answer for that.

The officers were inside for what felt like forever but was probably only ten or fifteen minutes. When Iris finally emerged, her expression was grim.

"Whoever was in there is gone. They went out the back, broke a window to get in. Made a mess searching the place."

"Searching for what?" I asked, genuinely confused.

"That's a good question." Iris looked tired, older than her years in the harsh glow of the patrol car lights. "The apartment had already been processed as part of the investigation. We'd removed what we needed. There shouldn't have been anything valuable left."

"This is connected to Hazel's death, isn't it?" I asked. "Someone's looking for evidence."

"Maybe." Iris didn't confirm or deny. "Or it's someone looking to steal whatever they could. Sometimes people target the homes of the recently deceased, figuring there might be valuables and no one around to notice."

But she didn't sound convinced. Neither was I.

Iris pulled out a small notebook. "I need to get your statement while it's fresh. What time did you first hear something?"

"Around two forty-five. I couldn't sleep, was just lying in bed. Then I heard this faint sound."

"What kind of sound?"

"Scraping, maybe? Or something sliding. It was really faint. That's why I got up and went to the balcony to see if I could figure out where it was coming from."

Iris scribbled notes. "And that's when you heard the glass break?"

"Yes. And I saw the flashlight moving in the window. That's when I called 9-1-1."

"Did you see the intruder? Any glimpse of them at all?"

"No. By the time I got to the window, they were already inside. I just saw the flashlight beam moving around."

"And you didn't hear or see them leave?"

"The sirens started, and the flashlight went out. They must have gone out the back."

Iris closed her notebook. "You did the right thing, calling it in immediately. But Alexis, you need to be more careful. Lock your doors. Lock your windows. Don't open the door to anyone you don't know. Whoever killed Hazel is still out there, and tonight proves they're getting desperate."

"I understand."

Iris nodded, satisfied. "Go home. Lock your doors. Try to get some sleep."

I crossed back to the café, acutely aware of eyes watching from windows, neighbors observing. The gossip would be all over town by morning. Alexis Belrose called in a break-in at Hazel's place. Alexis heard something in the middle of the night. Alexis was the hero who scared off an intruder.

Or, depending on who was doing the talking, Alexis was poking her nose where it didn't belong and got lucky she didn't get hurt.

Inside the café, the cats were waiting exactly where I'd left them. Rocky with Sage, Poppy and Gus near the door, Millie peeking from behind a counter.

"What happened?" Rocky asked immediately.

I locked the door behind me, checked it twice. "Whoever broke in got away before the police arrived. They went out the back when they heard the sirens. Made a mess searching Hazel's apartment."

"Looking for something," Poppy said.

"But what?" I sagged against the counter, suddenly exhausted. The adrenaline was wearing off, leaving me shaky and hollow. "The police already processed the scene. What could still be there worth breaking in for?"

A thought flickered. The box. The sealed box Carla had given me, still sitting unopened in my closet. Could they have been looking for that? Or whatever was in it?

But that didn't make sense. No one knew Carla had given it to me. And I didn't even know what was inside.

"I'm just being paranoid, right?" I said to no one in particular.

"Maybe," Gus said. "Or maybe whoever killed Hazel is getting desperate. Taking risks. Making mistakes."

"That's what scares me." I pushed off the counter, heading for the stairs. "Desperate people are dangerous people."

"Or they get more dangerous," Rocky said quietly.

He was right. A cornered animal was unpredictable, vicious. A killer who felt threatened might decide that eliminating the threat was easier than hiding from it.

I might have just painted a target on my back by calling in that break-in. By proving I was paying attention, watching, aware.

Upstairs, I checked every window lock. Checked the door lock three times. Drew the curtains closed. The apartment suddenly felt less like a sanctuary and more like a trap, exposed on all sides, vulnerable.

"We'll keep watch," Poppy said, settling near the window despite the drawn curtains. "We'll listen for anything unusual."

"All of us," Gus agreed. "We'll rotate. Someone awake at all times."

"You don't have to do that."

"Yes, we do." Rocky's voice was firm. "You protected Sage. You protect all of us. Now we protect you."

My throat tightened. "Thank you."

Sage padded over and bumped her head against my leg. "You're family," she said simply. "That's what family does."

Out of the mouths of kittens.

I settled on the couch, knowing sleep was impossible now. The cats arranged themselves around the apartment, some visible, some in shadow. My guardians, my witnesses, my found family.

Across the alley, lights still flashed red and blue. Iris and her officers processing the scene, documenting the break-in, looking for clues that wouldn't lead them anywhere useful because the killer had been smart enough to leave nothing behind.

But they'd made a mistake coming here tonight. They'd revealed how desperate they were.

And desperate people made mistakes.

I just had to be patient enough to catch them making one.

Chapter Fifteen

Friday morning, I came downstairs at six-thirty to find a piece of paper on the floor just inside the café door.

I'd barely slept after the break-in at Hazel's apartment. Maybe two hours of restless dozing before giving up entirely. My body was running on adrenaline and coffee I hadn't made yet.

For a moment, I just stared at the paper. White against the dark wood floor, folded once. Innocuous. Ordinary. But wrong. Nothing should be inside my locked café that I hadn't put there myself.

My heart rate kicked up before I even touched it.

Someone had slipped it under while the café was closed. While I'd been upstairs, watching the police process Hazel's apartment across the alley. After whoever broke in had been searching for something they didn't find.

And now this.

A soft chirp made me turn. Sage sat at the bottom of the stairs, having followed me down. She was getting confident navigating them now, though Rocky usually stayed close. This morning, he appeared a moment later, trotting down with easy confidence.

"You okay?" Rocky asked, his orange tail twitching. "You smell scared."

"There's something on the floor. A note." My voice came out steadier than I felt. "After everything that happened tonight, now there's a note."

My vision blurred as I picked up the paper, my fingers clumsy with adrenaline. The smell hit me immediately. Perfume. Heavy, floral, overwhelming. Too strong. Too deliberate.

Trish Lawrence came to mind immediately. That was her signature scent. But something about that felt wrong. Too obvious.

I unfolded the paper carefully.

One word, printed in large, bold letters: STOP.

"That's bad," Rocky said from the counter. "That's a threat."

"I know." I set the paper down, not wanting to touch it anymore but needing to keep it visible. Evidence.

"What does it mean?" Sage asked, her small voice worried. "Stop what?"

"Stop asking questions about Hazel's death," Rocky said grimly.

He was right. First the break-in across the alley, now this. Someone was getting desperate.

"I need to talk to everyone. Can you get the others?"

The cats assembled quickly. Poppy and Gus came down together, Millie crept along the wall. Rocky went straight to Sage, touching noses with her.

"So someone left a threatening note," Gus said, limping over to examine it. "First they break into Hazel's apartment. Now they're threatening you directly. This is escalating."

"Did anyone see who left it?" Poppy asked. "Or hear anything besides what Smoke already told us?"

"I heard something around three-thirty," Smoke confirmed. "Footsteps outside, very soft. I went to the window but couldn't see much. Just a figure in dark clothing. Bulky coat. They knelt down at the door, pushed something under, and left toward the back street."

The alley. Where Hazel had died.

"Right after the break-in," I said quietly. "This must be from the same person."

"Gus, can you smell anything else on it? Anything besides the perfume that might point to who left it?"

He approached carefully, his whiskers twitching as he took in the scents. His nose wrinkled. "The perfume is overwhelming. Paper underneath, standard. Toner from a laser printer. But that perfume is covering everything else. Too strong. Deliberately strong, maybe."

"Trish's signature scent," I said.

"If it is Trish, she's not being subtle about it," Gus said. "Which seems stupid for someone who just committed murder."

"Unless she's just arrogant," Rocky suggested.

"Or someone else wants us to think it's her." I stared at the paper. "Anyone could spray perfume on paper. Buy a bottle that smells like what she wears."

Which meant either Trish had left the note and was foolish enough to leave her signature scent, or someone wanted me to think she had. Someone clever enough to recognize that a too-obvious clue might work. Someone who'd just broken into Hazel's apartment looking for evidence and decided I was getting too close.

"What are you going to do?" Poppy asked.

"Tell Iris. She needs to know."

I went through my morning routine on autopilot. Feeding the cats their breakfast, Sage eating alongside the others now with her mix of wet and dry food. Prepping the café, grinding beans, checking supplies. Everything normal except for the threatening note sitting on my counter and the memory of police lights flashing across the alley just hours ago.

At eight, I unlocked the door and flipped the sign to "Open."

The morning crowd trickled in. Felix Wren first, ordering his Ginger Spark. Cordelia minutes later, bubbling with yarn shipment news. Followed by Mabel commenting on how tired I looked.

"Didn't sleep well," I said, which was the understatement of the year.

At eight-fifteen, Sheriff Iris Scott walked through the door.

She looked exactly as exhausted as I felt, dark circles under her eyes. She walked straight to the counter.

"Black coffee. Large. And whatever pastry has the most sugar."

I poured her coffee and selected a cinnamon roll dripping with icing.

"Were you able to get any sleep after processing the scene?"

"Maybe an hour." She wrapped both hands around the coffee cup like she was trying to absorb its warmth. "What about you?"

"Not much." I pulled out the note. "And not to make your day more difficult, but I found this under my door this morning. Someone slipped it through during the night."

Iris set down her coffee, instantly alert. She pulled gloves from her pocket and put them on before touching the note. She unfolded it, read the single word, then lifted it to her nose.

"Stop." Her eyes cut to me. "Stop what, Alexis?"

"I don't know."

"I think you do." Iris set the note down carefully. "I told you to stop investigating. And now someone is leaving threatening notes. This is connected to you asking questions, not to last night's break-in."

I hesitated. Part of me wanted to lie, to say I'd been home all evening. But Iris would find out. She always did. And she'd know exactly why I'd gone to that crochet circle, no matter what excuse I gave.

"At the crochet circle yesterday evening, people were talking. About Hazel, about the investigation. I wasn't asking questions. I was just listening."

"Why were you at a crochet circle?" Iris held the note closer. "Taking up new hobbies right after your friend's murder?"

The words stung. "With Hazel gone, I was just trying something new. Trying to fill the time. Trying not to sit alone thinking about the fact that she's dead."

Some of the sharpness left Iris's expression. She sniffed the paper again. "Did you put perfume on this?"

"No. That's how I found it."

"Heavy floral perfume. Trish Lawrence wears perfume like that. Her signature scent." Iris was already connecting dots. "Was Trish at the crochet circle?"

"No. Just Cordelia, Orla, Mabel, Pearl, Beatrice, and Dorothy."

"But Trish's shop is only three doors down from Cordelia's. She could have seen you going in. Could have decided you were getting too close." She paused, thinking. "Or whoever broke into Hazel's place could have seen the police presence, realized someone had called it in, and decided to send you a warning."

She pulled out her phone and took photos. "I'm going to have a conversation with Ms. Lawrence this morning. This constitutes harassment at minimum."

"What if it wasn't her?" The words came out before I could stop them. "What if someone just made it smell like her perfume to throw us off?"

Iris looked at me sharply. "That's a very specific suspicion. Why would you think that?"

"Anyone could spray perfume on paper. It's almost too obvious, isn't it?"

"True. But most people wouldn't think of that level of deception. The simple explanation is usually correct."

She folded the note carefully and tucked it into an evidence bag. "And Alexis, I'm going to say this one more time: stop investigating. This note is a warning. Someone is watching you. Someone knows you've been asking questions. And whoever broke into Hazel's apartment last night is getting desperate. Next time, it might be more than just paper under your door."

"I understand."

"Do you? You went to a crochet circle where one of your suspects works. That's not someone who understands the danger they're in." Her voice was firm but not entirely unkind. "I know you want justice for Hazel. But you're putting yourself in danger, and I can't protect you if you keep doing reckless things."

"You're right."

"I mean it. Whoever killed Hazel has already killed once. They broke into her apartment last night looking for something. And now they're leaving you threatening notes. They're not going to hesitate to do worse if they feel threatened. And this note? This means they already feel threatened by you."

She left with her coffee and cinnamon roll, the note secured in her evidence bag. I watched her go, feeling relief and dread. Relief that I'd told her. Dread because I knew I wasn't going to stop.

The morning dragged on. Every customer made me wonder: was it you? Did you break into Hazel's apartment? Did you leave that note? Are you watching me right now to see if I'm scared enough to stop?

Around one o'clock, Flo came in with her afternoon pastry delivery.

She took one look at me and frowned. "You look terrible. What's wrong?"

"Just tired."

"Alexis." She put her hands on her hips. "I've known you for a year now, and you've never been a good liar. What's really wrong?"

"Someone broke into Hazel's apartment last night. I heard it, called the police. Then this morning, someone left a threatening note under my door. Just one word: stop."

Flo's face went pale. "Oh, honey. This is getting serious."

"The sheriff thinks it's because I've been asking questions about Hazel's death."

"Have you been?"

"Not really. I went to a crochet circle and people were talking about it. Just listening to gossip."

"Oh, honey." Flo pulled me into a hug. "You need to be careful. Whoever killed Hazel, they're dangerous. They've already killed once. And now they're breaking into places, leaving threats."

"I know. The sheriff is handling it."

"Good. Let her handle it." Flo squeezed my shoulder. "Your job is to stay safe and make coffee and take care of those cats. Promise me you'll be careful?"

"I promise."

She left looking worried, and I felt guilty for making her worry.

By closing time, I was ready to collapse. I locked the door and stood in the empty café feeling the day's tension catch up with me.

"Breathe," Poppy said. "You're safe now. The café is locked."

I followed her instructions until my heart rate slowed.

Upstairs, the cats gathered around as I made dinner. Pasta with sauce from a jar. I fed them their evening meal, Sage eating enthusiastically alongside the others.

"So, what now?" Rocky asked. "Do we stop? Do we listen to the note and back off?"

"No." The word came out sharp and definitive. "Someone trying to scare me off means I'm getting close to something. Means they're worried. The break-in, the note, it all means they're desperate."

"It also means you're in danger," Poppy pointed out. "Real danger."

"I've been in danger before. Running from my coven, hiding what I was. This is just a different kind. More immediate, maybe. But I've survived worse."

"At least before you were running away from danger," Gus said. "Now you're deliberately walking toward it. That's not survival. That's something else."

He was right. But I couldn't stop now. Not when someone had confirmed that I was on the right track. Not when Hazel deserved justice.

"I'll be more careful. More subtle. I won't ask obvious questions. But I'm not stopping. I can't stop. Not now."

Outside my window, night fell over Larkspur Valley. Somewhere out there, someone who'd killed once, who'd broken into a dead woman's home, who was threatening me, was getting more desperate by the hour.

But they didn't know what I was. Didn't know that I'd spent years learning to hide, to watch, to survive in a world that wanted to control me. Didn't know that I'd run from people far more dangerous than a small-town murderer.

They thought a simple note would scare me away.

They were wrong.

I just had to figure out who they were before they decided words weren't enough.

Before they moved from threats to action.

Before I became the next body in an alley.

Sage curled up beside me, purring softly. She trusted me to keep her safe. They all did.

I couldn't let them down.

And I couldn't let Hazel down either.

I sat there in the growing darkness, unable to shake the restless energy thrumming through me. The walls felt too close. The apartment too small. My thoughts kept circling back to the break-in, the note, the threats, the danger. I needed to move, to do something, but I had nowhere to go.

"You're going to wear a hole in the floor with all that anxious energy," Poppy observed from her perch. "You need a distraction."

"I'm fine."

"You're not fine. You're wound so tight you're vibrating." She tilted her head, studying me. "Didn't that comic shop owner invite you to something tonight? Game night?"

I blinked. "Lionel's game night. That's tonight. Friday night."

"He's invited you multiple times," Poppy continued. "Multiple times you've said no. Maybe tonight you should say yes."

"I can't just show up. I never go. He probably doesn't expect me anymore."

"So surprise him." Her amber eyes were knowing. "You need to get out of this apartment. You need to be around people, do something normal. Stop thinking about murder and threats for a few hours. Otherwise you're going to drive yourself crazy sitting here all night."

"And stop talking to your cats," Gus added from his spot on the armchair. "People will think you're one of those crazy cat ladies."

"I am a crazy cat lady," I pointed out.

"True. But you don't need to advertise it by spending Friday night having conversations with us instead of actual humans."

"Point taken."

They were both right. The thought of sitting here alone, replaying every moment of the day, analyzing the note and the perfume and who might have left it, that would drive me insane. I needed a distraction. Something to occupy my mind.

"You know what? I think you're right." I stood up, careful not to disturb Sage. "That's probably what I need. Just a few hours of normalcy."

"Good," Poppy said. "Go. We'll be fine here. Rocky will keep watch."

"You sure?"

"Go," she repeated firmly. "Before you change your mind."

I grabbed my jacket and headed for the door before I could talk myself out of it.

Justice for Hazel was worth any risk.

I just had to make sure I survived long enough to deliver it.

Chapter Sixteen

I stood on the sidewalk outside The Rebel Rogue, staring at the warm light spilling from the windows. Laughter and voices drifted out, muffled but unmistakably cheerful. Through the glass, I could see people gathered around tables, bent over what looked like board games and character sheets.

I'd felt braver standing in my apartment at home. Now the thought of being around people was terrifying.

My hand went to my jacket pocket, checking for my phone like I might need an emergency escape route. The threatening note flashed through my mind. The break-in at Hazel's apartment. Someone had stood at my door in the dark while I'd been upstairs. Someone wanted me to stop. Someone might be watching me right now.

Or maybe I was being paranoid. Maybe I just needed to go inside, play some games, and remember what it felt like to be a normal person doing normal things on a Friday night.

Before I could talk myself out of it, I pushed through the door.

The bell chimed, and several faces turned toward me. The shop smelled like paper and cardboard and something sweet, probably whatever snacks were laid out on the counter. Shelves lined every wall, organized with obvious care. Comic books in protective sleeves, graphic novels arranged by genre, board games stacked neatly on dedicated shelves. It was exactly the kind of space someone who genuinely loved what they did would create.

"Alexis?" Lionel looked up from where he was setting up what appeared to be a complicated board game, his face breaking into a surprised smile. "You came. You actually came."

"I hope it's okay that I just showed up. I know I never responded to your invitations, I just thought maybe tonight I could use the distraction." The words tumbled out too fast, betraying my nervousness.

"Are you kidding? This is great." He was already moving toward me, that golden retriever energy in full effect. His strawberry blonde hair was even more disheveled than usual, and he wore a t-shirt with some superhero I didn't recognize. "Come in, come in. Let me introduce you to everyone."

He guided me toward the group with a hand that almost touched my back but didn't quite, like he wasn't sure if the gesture would be welcome. I appreciated the restraint.

"Everyone, this is Alexis. She runs The Cozy Purrch, which has the best coffee in three counties and cats you can hang out with while you drink it. Alexis, this is everyone."

"Helpful," said a man with kind eyes behind wire-rimmed glasses. He stood and offered his hand. "I'm Gabe. I work at Mountain Market. You probably don't recognize me because I'm usually in the back doing inventory, but I've been in your café a few times."

"Nice to officially meet you." His handshake was firm but not aggressive.

"Esther James," said a woman in her forties with graying hair pulled back in a ponytail. She had the look of someone who'd spent years perfecting the art of patient explanation. "I teach English at the high school. I've heard wonderful things about your café from some of my students. Apparently it's the cool place to study."

"I didn't know that." The thought made me oddly pleased.

"Rory Scout." A man with sun-weathered skin and calloused hands nodded at me from his seat. Construction worker, I'd guess from his build and the way he moved like someone used to physical labor. "And that's my coworker Dawson over there." He gestured to a younger man who gave me a friendly wave.

"Cooper Sparks," said a lean man with a postal service logo on his jacket. "I deliver your mail sometimes. Well, not personally. I mean, I work for the post office. You know what I mean."

"I do," I said, trying to put him at ease with a smile.

And then my eyes landed on Dr. Colton Dover, sitting at one of the tables with what looked like character sheets spread in front of him. He looked different in jeans and a casual button-down instead of his vet scrubs, more relaxed somehow. He smiled when he saw me, surprise and pleasure crossing his face.

"Alexis. I didn't know you were into gaming."

"I'm not, really. Lionel's been inviting me for a while, and I finally decided to take him up on it." I was hyperaware of how that sounded, like I'd come specifically for Lionel, which wasn't true but also wasn't entirely false. I'd come because I needed a distraction, because Poppy had suggested it, because sitting alone in my apartment was driving me slowly insane.

"Well, I'm glad you're here." Colton's smile was warm, genuine. "It's good to see you out."

Something shifted in the air, subtle but noticeable. Lionel's posture changed slightly, straightening. Colton's gaze flicked from me to Lionel and back. Some kind of masculine assessment happening that I didn't have the energy to decode.

"So what are we playing?" I asked, trying to redirect attention away from whatever dynamic was unfolding.

"We've got a few options," Lionel said, his voice maybe slightly more enthusiastic than before. "There's a group playing a role-playing game over there, that's more Colton's speed. And we've got board games here. Ever played Catan? Ticket to Ride? Codenames?"

"I haven't played any games since I was a kid."

"Perfect. You're getting the full introduction tonight." He was already pulling out a box. "We'll start with something simple. Cooperative game, so we're all working together. Less pressure."

The next hour passed in a surprisingly pleasant blur. The game Lionel chose involved us working together to stop various diseases from spreading across a world map, which felt a little too on-the-nose given current events but was actually engaging once I understood the mechanics. Esther was clearly the strategist, planning several moves ahead. Gabe was cautious, always considering worst-case scenarios. Rory played with the kind of methodical patience you'd expect from someone who measured twice and cut once.

And Lionel was encouraging, explaining rules when I got confused, celebrating small victories, never making me feel stupid for being new.

"You're good at this," he said when I successfully stopped an outbreak in Asia. "Natural strategic thinking."

"It's just a game."

"Games reveal character." He grinned. "You're willing to take calculated risks but not reckless ones. You think about consequences. You work well with others even when you're uncomfortable."

I wasn't sure how to respond to that, so I focused on drawing my next card.

During a break between rounds, Cooper got up to grab drinks from the cooler Lionel had set up. "Anyone else want something? I'm buying." He paused. "Wait, is it buying if it's free? I'm acquiring beverages for people."

"I'll take a water," Esther said. "Thanks, Cooper."

"Can you believe that break-in at Hazel's place?" Cooper said as he distributed drinks. "I heard about it this morning. Someone broke in Thursday night, went through her whole apartment."

My attention sharpened, but I kept my expression neutral, studying my game cards like they required intense concentration.

"I heard the same thing," Gabe said, shaking his head. "What kind of person breaks into a dead woman's apartment? What were they even looking for?"

"That's what I want to know," Esther said. "Sheriff Scott was tight-lipped about it when I bumped into her this morning, but you could tell she was concerned. First a murder, now a break-in. What's happening to our town?"

"It feels wrong," Rory agreed. "Larkspur Valley's always been safe. People don't lock their doors half the time. And now we've got murder and breaking and entering within two weeks of each other."

"They're probably connected," Dawson said. "Has to be, right? Someone killed Hazel, and now someone's looking for something in her apartment. Evidence, maybe."

"Or something valuable," Cooper suggested. "Though I can't imagine what. Hazel wasn't exactly wealthy."

"Did they find anything?" I asked, then immediately regretted the question when everyone looked at me. Too interested. Too specific. Again.

"Not that I heard," Gabe said. "Whoever it was got scared off when someone called the police. Ran out the back before they could be caught."

"Actually, that was Alexis," Colton said from the table behind us. "I heard she's the one who called it in. Heard the break-in happening from her café."

Everyone turned to look at me with new interest.

"You were there?" Esther asked. "That must have been terrifying."

"I couldn't sleep, heard some noise across the alley. Saw a flashlight moving in the window and called 9-1-1." I tried to sound casual, like it had been no big deal. "By the time the police got there, whoever it was had already run."

"Still," Lionel said, his voice concerned. "That's scary. Knowing someone was that close."

"It's all scary," I admitted quietly. "Hazel's death, the break-in. It doesn't feel safe anymore."

A somber silence settled over the table. Esther reached over and squeezed my hand briefly.

"Sheriff Scott will figure it out," she said with conviction. "She's good at her job. And in the meantime, we all need to be more careful. Lock our doors, pay attention to our surroundings."

The conversation shifted, but the mood had changed. What started as a fun Friday night now carried an undercurrent of unease. Everyone was thinking about it, about murder and break-ins and the violation of safety they'd all taken for granted.

"So have you been super busy at the post office?" Gabe asked Cooper, clearly trying to lighten things up. "With the holidays coming up?"

"Starting to pick up. You know how it is. Everyone ordering online." Cooper seemed grateful for the change of subject. "Though I will say, we've had some interesting activity lately. That Carla woman, Hazel's niece, has been in almost every day. Sending certified letters, receiving packages. Very official-looking stuff."

"Legal documents, probably," Esther said. "Didn't she hire a lawyer to contest the will?"

"That's what I heard." Gabe set down his bottle. "She came into the market three days ago, and she was on her phone the entire time she was shopping. Loud conversation about property rights and business valuations. Made sure everyone could hear her."

"Tacky," Esther murmured. "I actually ran into her at Mountain Brew last week. Got stuck behind her in line." She glanced at me apologetically. "Sorry. They just open earlier. I have to be at school before eight when your shop opens."

"There's enough business for both shops," I said with a smile. "But mine's better."

Esther laughed. "I'll stop by my first day off. I promise!"

"I'll hold you to that."

"Anyway," Esther continued, "Carla was complaining to whoever would listen about how her aunt had never appreciated her, had pushed her away, and now she was just trying to get what was rightfully hers."

"Did she seem angry?" I asked.

"More entitled than angry," Esther said thoughtfully. "Like the world owed her something. Why do you ask?"

"Just curious. It's a sad situation all around." I kept my voice carefully neutral. "Hazel was such a kind person."

"How are you really holding up?" Colton asked from the table behind us, his voice gentle. "I know you two were close."

I felt several pairs of eyes on me. Right. I'd forgotten that Colton knew. That he'd checked in on me before. That I couldn't just pretend Hazel had been a casual acquaintance.

"I'm managing," I said quietly. "Some days are harder than others."

"It is sad," Lionel agreed, his voice gentle. "And it's okay to be affected by it, Alexis. You don't have to pretend it doesn't hurt just because we're playing games."

The conversation moved on, shifting to holiday plans and whether the town's Christmas decorations were going to be as elaborate as last year's. I half-listened, my mind still turning over what I'd learned. Carla at the post office constantly, sending certified letters. Legal documents. Making scenes about her inheritance. And she'd been pushing the narrative that Hazel had pushed her away, setting up justification for whatever legal action she was taking.

It painted a picture of someone desperate, grasping, maybe desperate enough to kill.

"Your turn, Alexis," Gabe said gently, pulling me back to the present.

"Sorry. Distracted." I played my card, automatically following the strategy Esther had laid out earlier.

"Everything okay?" Lionel's voice was low, concerned. He'd moved his chair slightly closer, and I could smell his cologne. Something clean and understated, like soap and fresh paper.

"Fine. Just tired. Long day."

His eyes searched my face like he was trying to read what I wasn't saying, but he didn't push. Just nodded and returned to the game.

We finished our round, successfully saving the world from pandemic doom, and I felt an absurd little thrill of accomplishment. Esther high-fived me, Gabe gave me a respectful nod, and Lionel beamed like I'd won an Olympic medal.

"See? Natural," he said.

Rory and Dawson joined our table for the next game, and the conversation shifted again. This time, Rory was the one who brought up something interesting.

"I got a call yesterday about a construction project," he said, shuffling cards for whatever game we were setting up next. "Expansion work on that flower shop, Petals and Prose. You know, Trish Lawrence's place."

"She's expanding?" Gabe raised his eyebrows. "Business must be good."

"That's what I thought. So I went by this morning to take measurements and give her a quote." Rory shook his head. "She was very clear about what she wanted. Bigger workspace, more storage, dedicated area for wedding consultations. Said she needed to scale up her operation now that she's, and I quote, 'the only game in town.'"

The words hung in the air, sharp and uncomfortable.

"That's cold," Dawson said. "Hazel's barely gone and she's already capitalizing on it."

"That's business, I guess," Rory said, though his tone suggested he didn't approve. "But yeah, the timing feels wrong. And the way she said it, there was this satisfaction in her voice. Like she'd been waiting for this opportunity."

"Did she say anything else?" I asked.

"Just that she'd been planning this expansion for a while but was waiting for the right moment." Rory dealt cards with practiced efficiency. "She kept talking about how she was going to transform the floral business in Larkspur Valley, bring in more sophisticated arrangements, corner the wedding market. Very ambitious. Very confident."

"Confident enough to have made sure there wouldn't be competition?" The words were out before I could stop them.

The table went quiet. Everyone looked at me.

"That's a serious accusation," Esther said carefully.

"Not an accusation. Just an observation." I tried to backtrack, make it sound less pointed. "I mean, Sheriff Scott is investigating, right? So someone must have had a motive."

"True," Gabe said slowly. "And Trish did have motive. They'd been rivals for years. Hazel had most of the long-term contracts, the loyal customers. Trish was always trying to undercut her, steal business. Never worked though. Hazel was too good at what she did."

"Was," Esther repeated quietly. "Past tense. That's so strange. She was just here, you know? Just alive. And now she's not."

The mood at the table had shifted from playful to somber. I felt guilty for causing it, for bringing murder and suspicion into what was supposed to be a fun evening.

"Sorry," I said. "I didn't mean to bring down the mood. Let's play."

"No, it's okay," Lionel said, and his hand briefly touched my shoulder, a gesture of comfort. "It's on everyone's mind anyway. Might as well acknowledge it instead of pretending everything's normal when it's not."

The game continued, but the easy laughter had dimmed slightly. I noticed Colton watching me from his table, his expression thoughtful, like he was trying to figure something out. When our eyes met, he smiled, but there was a question in it.

Partway through the game, I excused myself to use the bathroom, needing a moment to process everything I'd learned. The small bathroom at the back of the shop was decorated with framed comic book covers and a poster that said "In this bathroom, we believe in second chances" with a resurrection joke I didn't quite understand.

I splashed water on my face, staring at my reflection. I looked tired. Stressed. The kind of tired that sleep wouldn't fix.

But I'd learned things tonight. Carla was aggressively pursuing the inheritance, making sure everyone knew she felt entitled to it. Trish was expanding her business with disturbing timing and troubling satisfaction. Both of them had motive. Both of them had opportunity.

And Orla? Orla remained a mystery I hadn't solved.

When I returned to the group, I found Lionel and Colton standing near the counter, ostensibly examining a new graphic novel shipment but clearly having been discussing something. They both looked up when I approached, and there was that assessment again. That male sizing-up that happened when two people realized they were interested in the same thing.

Or in this case, the same person.

I wasn't ready for this. Wasn't ready for any kind of romantic complication. My life was complicated enough without adding relationship dynamics to the mix. But I couldn't deny that both of them were attractive, both were kind, both had been nothing but patient and welcoming.

"Everything okay?" Colton asked.

"Fine. Just needed a minute." I gestured back to the table. "I should get back to the game."

"Actually," Lionel said, checking his watch, "we're wrapping up for the night. It's almost ten. But I'm really glad you came, Alexis. It was great having you here."

"I had fun." And I had, despite the somber turns in conversation. "Thanks for letting me come."

"You didn't crash. You were invited. Multiple times." His smile was warm, reaching his green eyes. "I hope you'll come back next week?"

"Maybe." I wasn't ready to commit, wasn't sure if I could manage another evening of pretending to be normal while carrying so many secrets. "We'll see how the week goes."

"That's fair." He walked me to the door, and I was aware of Colton watching us, pretending to help Esther pack up game pieces. "Hey, Alexis?"

"Yeah?"

"If you ever need to talk about anything, anything at all, I'm a good listener. No judgment. No pressure. Just, if you need someone." He looked almost embarrassed making the offer. "I know you keep to yourself, and that's fine. But the offer's there."

Something in my chest tightened. He was being genuinely kind, offering friendship without expectation of anything in return. It was disarming.

"Thanks, Lionel. That means a lot."

I said goodbye to the rest of the group, accepted Gabe's invitation to stop by the market sometime, promised Esther I'd think about hosting a student study group at the café, and carefully avoided making eye contact with Colton because I wasn't ready to navigate whatever was happening there.

The cold night air hit me when I stepped outside, clearing my head. The street was quiet, most shops closed, just a few bars lit up down the block. I started walking back toward the café, my mind churning through everything I'd learned.

Carla was desperate, aggressive, entitled. Trish was opportunistic, calculating, satisfied. Either of them could have done it. Either of them had reason.

But which one had actually stood in that alley and poisoned Hazel? Which one had watched her die? Which one had broken into her apartment looking for evidence? Which one had left that threatening note under my door?

I was so lost in thought that I almost didn't hear the footsteps behind me. Almost didn't register that someone was following me down the dark street, their pace matching mine.

My heart rate spiked. The threatening note flashed through my mind. The break-in. Someone desperate enough to search a dead woman's home. Someone who knew I was asking questions. Someone who might have followed me from game night.

Stop.

I walked faster, my hand going to my phone in my pocket. The footsteps behind me sped up too.

"Alexis, wait."

I spun around, ready to run or scream or both.

Colton held up his hands, apologetic. "Sorry, I didn't mean to scare you. I was heading the same direction and thought I'd walk with you. Make sure you got home safe. But I should have called out sooner. I'm sorry."

My heart was still hammering, adrenaline making my hands shake. "It's fine. You just startled me."

"You looked pretty deep in thought. Thinking about the game?"

"Something like that." I started walking again, and he fell into step beside me. My pulse was still racing, the fear taking longer to subside than it should.

"You seemed really interested in the conversation about Hazel's death. More than just grief." His voice was gentle, not accusatory. "You're investigating, aren't you?"

I debated lying, but something about the quiet street and the genuine concern in his voice made me give him part of the truth.

"I'm just trying to understand what happened. She was important to me. She helped me feel welcome when I first moved here. I need to know who did this to her."

"I get that. But be careful." He was quiet for a moment. "Whoever killed Hazel broke into her apartment just last night. They're desperate. Desperate people are dangerous. And for what it's worth, I think Sheriff Scott is good at her job. She'll figure it out."

"I hope so."

We walked in silence for another block before he spoke again. "Lionel really likes you."

The observation caught me off guard. "We're just friends."

"Maybe to you. But he looks at you like you're the most interesting person he's ever met." Colton's tone was carefully neutral. "Just thought you should know. In case you weren't aware."

"And why are you telling me this?"

He smiled, rueful. "Because I'm a terrible strategist and I just told my competition that he has a shot."

Oh.

"I'm not really looking for anything right now," I said carefully. "My life is complicated. I'm not in a place where I can offer anyone anything real."

"That's fair. And I respect that." We'd reached my café, the dark windows reflecting the streetlights. "But when you are ready, if you are ready, I'd like to throw my hat in the ring. No pressure. Just, putting it out there."

He was being so direct, so honest. It was refreshing and terrifying in equal measure.

"I'll keep that in mind." It was the best I could offer.

"That's all I ask." He gave me that warm smile again. "Get some rest, Alexis. And lock your doors. Lock your windows. After the break-in, after that note you got, someone's escalating. Be careful."

"Not paranoid. Practical." I thought of the note under my door, the perfume, the threat. The intruder searching Hazel's apartment. "Thanks for walking with me."

"Anytime."

I watched him walk away, then let myself into the café. Locked the door behind me, checked it twice. Checked the windows. The building felt different now, vulnerable. Someone had been at my door. Someone had been across the alley. Someone was watching, waiting.

Upstairs, the cats were waiting. Sage was curled on the couch, Poppy on her perch, the others scattered around like they'd been casually lounging but I knew they'd been watching the door.

"How was it?" Poppy asked.

"Informative." I dropped my jacket on the chair and started filling them in. Carla's aggressive legal maneuvering. Trish's suspiciously timed expansion. The conversations, the clues, the pieces slowly coming together. And everyone talking about the break-in, about how their safe small town didn't feel safe anymore.

"And the people?" Rocky asked. "Were they nice?"

"They were." I thought about Lionel's enthusiasm, Colton's directness, the way everyone had welcomed me without question. "It was good. Being around people. Feeling normal for a few hours."

"See?" Poppy looked smug. "I told you that you needed it."

"You were right." I sat on the couch, and Sage immediately climbed into my lap. "You were absolutely right."

Outside my window, Larkspur Valley was quiet, peaceful, settled into Friday night routines. Somewhere out there, a killer walked free. Someone who'd murdered Hazel, broken into her apartment, threatened me with a note. Someone getting more desperate by the day.

But tonight, I'd gathered more pieces of the puzzle. Tonight, I'd remembered what it felt like to be part of a community, even if I could only show them a carefully curated version of myself.

Tomorrow, I'd figure out what to do with everything I'd learned.

Tonight, I'd just be grateful that I'd gone, that I'd pushed through my fear, that I'd let myself have a few hours of something close to happiness.

It wasn't much. But it was something.

And right now, something was enough.

Chapter Seventeen

Saturday morning came with frost on the windows and gossip on everyone's lips.

I'd barely unlocked the café door when Felix Wren shuffled in, more alert than usual. Last night's game night felt like it had happened weeks ago instead of hours. I'd stayed up too late replaying the conversations, analyzing what Rory had said about Trish's expansion plans, what Cooper had mentioned about Carla's constant trips to the post office. My eyes felt gritty from lack of sleep, but at least I'd learned something useful.

"Did you hear?" he asked, forgoing his usual distracted greeting. "Sheriff Scott went to see Trish Lawrence yesterday afternoon. Questioned her for over an hour at her shop."

"I hadn't heard." The lie came easily, even though I'd been the reason for that visit.

"Everyone's talking about it." He ordered his Ginger Spark and leaned against the counter. "Apparently someone left you a threatening note, and it smelled like Trish's perfume."

My stomach dropped. "How do you know about the note?"

"Cordelia." Of course. "She was at the general store yesterday evening, and Jasper mentioned it. You know how news travels."

I did. In a town of five thousand, everyone knew everyone else's business by sundown.

The morning continued in the same pattern. Every customer who came in had heard about the note, about Trish being questioned, about the investigation taking a new turn. Mabel Smalls had the most detailed information, naturally.

"Iris kept her at the flower shop for ninety minutes," Mabel reported over her Lavender Dreams tea. "Asked her where she was Thursday night when the note was left. Trish said she was home alone, watching television. No witnesses. No proof."

"That's not much of an alibi," I said carefully.

"Exactly what Iris thought, apparently. But it's not no alibi either. She could have been home. Or she could have been here, leaving threatening notes under your door." Mabel's sharp eyes studied me. "You should be careful, dear. Whoever killed Hazel might decide you're too much trouble."

"The sheriff said the same thing."

"And she's right. Let her handle this. That's what we pay her for."

But I couldn't let it go, and we both knew it.

At 8:15, Iris walked in looking like she'd slept as poorly as I had.

"Black coffee," she said, and I noticed the dark circles under her eyes.

"Long night?" I poured her usual.

"Long week." She accepted the cup and took a long drink. "Half the town thinks I should arrest Trish Lawrence immediately. The other half thinks I'm harassing a local business owner. Can't win."

"Did she have an alibi?" I kept my voice neutral, curious but not pushy.

Iris gave me a look that said she knew exactly what I was doing. "I probably shouldn't tell you this," Iris said, then sighed. "But you're going to ask questions anyway, and I'd rather you have accurate information than half-truths from town gossip."

She looked at me before speaking again. "Weak one. Says she was home alone Thursday night. Can't prove it, but I can't disprove it either." She paused. "The perfume on the note is definitely her brand. Same one she was wearing when I questioned her. But like you said yesterday, anyone could have put perfume on paper."

"So, you're not sure it was her."

"I'm not sure of anything yet." Iris's frustration was evident. "The autopsy confirmed poison, but we still don't know how it was administered or when. We have three women with motives but no solid evidence against any of them. And now we have a threatening note that may or may not have been left by the person who wears that particular perfume."

Three women. So, Iris was still looking at Carla and Orla too, not just Trish.

"What kind of poison was it?" I asked. "If you can say."

"I probably shouldn't." But she was tired, and maybe she thought sharing a little information might keep me from doing something stupid. "Plant-based alkaloid. Something you'd find in certain herbs or flowers. Causes disorientation, loss of balance, eventual loss of consciousness if the dose is high enough."

My mind raced. Plant-based. Herbs or flowers. Which meant someone with knowledge of plants. Like someone who ran a flower shop. Or someone who ran a competing flower shop. Or someone who worked in a yarn shop but might have other knowledge.

Or a witch who specialized in herbal magic and healing teas.

My blood ran cold at the thought.

"You okay?" Iris asked, noticing my expression.

"Fine. Just thinking about Hazel ingesting poison without realizing it. It's horrible."

"It is." Iris finished her coffee and set down the cup. "I'm following every lead I have. But Alexis, you need to stay out of it. No more crochet circles. No more casual conversations where you just happen to ask about suspects. No more investigating."

"I understand."

"I hope so. Because that note wasn't idle. Someone is watching you. Someone knows you're asking questions. And I don't want to be investigating your death next."

She left, and I stood behind the counter trying to process everything. Plant-based poison. Herbs or flowers. Someone with botanical knowledge.

"That doesn't narrow it down much," Poppy observed from her window perch. Sage was curled beside her, soaking up the weak morning sun. "Hazel knew plants. Trish works with flowers. You work with herbs in your teas."

"Don't remind me." The fact that the murder weapon was something I understood, something I used in my own magic, made me feel sick.

The morning rush picked up, keeping me busy. But around ten-thirty, the bell chimed and Esther James walked in, looking pleased with herself.

"I told you I'd stop by my first day off," she said with a smile, approaching the counter. "Kept my promise."

"You did." I returned her smile, genuinely happy to see a friendly face. "What can I get you?"

"That's the question, isn't it?" She studied the menu board with interest. "I usually just have coffee at home or at Mountain Brew. Basic stuff. But since I'm here, what do you recommend?"

I looked at her, really looked at her, the way I'd learned to do when making healing teas. Saw the slight tension in her shoulders, the tiredness around her eyes despite the smile, the way she was already thinking ahead to whatever she needed to do next.

"How's your day looking?" I asked.

"Grading essays this afternoon. Thirty-two of them on symbolism in 'The Great Gatsby.' I love my job, but sometimes..." She trailed off with a rueful laugh.

"You need focus and energy," I said, already reaching for the right teas and herbs. "Something to help you concentrate but not make you jittery. And something to keep your energy steady through the afternoon."

"That sounds perfect."

I brewed her a blend of green tea with a touch of ginseng for clarity, peppermint for focus, and a hint of honey for sustained energy. As I worked, I let just a whisper of intention flow into it. Nothing that would change her, just a gentle nudge toward alertness and concentration. The kind of thing that would feel like a really good cup of tea rather than anything magical.

When I handed it to her, she took a careful sip and her eyebrows rose. "Wow. This is really good. How did you know?"

"Just a hunch," I said with a small smile. "You mentioned grading essays. Figured you'd need something to help you power through."

"You figured right." She took another sip, already looking more relaxed. "I definitely need to focus. Thirty-two essays, and I swear half of them think the green light is just a green light."

I laughed. "Sounds rough."

"It's the job." She glanced around the café, taking in the cozy atmosphere, the cats visible through the archway. "This place really is lovely. I can see why my students like studying here. It's peaceful."

"That's the goal."

"Well, you've succeeded." She paid for her drink, leaving a generous tip. "I'm glad I stopped by. And I'm glad you came to game night last night. It was nice having someone new there."

"Thanks for making me feel welcome."

"Anytime. That's what we do in this town." She headed toward the door, then paused. "And Alexis? Be careful, okay? With everything that's going on. I know you cared about Hazel. But the sheriff's right. Let her handle it."

"I will."

She gave me a knowing look that said she didn't quite believe me, but she smiled anyway and left.

I watched her go, feeling a small warmth in my chest. A potential friend. Someone who saw me as a person, not just the café owner or a suspect or a witch in hiding. Just Alexis, who made really good tea and had shown up to game night.

It was a small thing, but it mattered.

But around eleven, the bell chimed and this time the person walking in didn't look friendly. No, this person looked determined.

Carla Lynch looked different than the last time I'd seen her. Less rigid, almost animated. There was color in her cheeks and energy in her step.

"Alexis," she said, approaching the counter. "I heard about the note. Are you all right?"

"I'm fine. Just a little shaken."

"I can imagine." She glanced around the café, making sure no one was close enough to overhear. "I also heard that Trish woman is a suspect now. Good. I've had my eye on her since this whole thing started."

"Your eye on her?"

"She's been circling the flower shop like a vulture. Showed up at my hotel twice trying to 'discuss options' for the property. Made my skin crawl." Carla leaned against the counter. "I told the sheriff that Trish had plenty of motive. She's been trying to destroy Aunt Hazel's business for years. Maybe she finally decided to destroy Hazel herself."

There was something almost gleeful in her tone. Relief, maybe, that suspicion was pointing elsewhere. That she might not be under scrutiny anymore.

"The sheriff is investigating everyone," I said carefully.

"Of course. But Trish is the obvious choice, don't you think? She had motive, she had opportunity, and now her perfume is all over a threatening note." Carla's eyes glittered. "I hope Iris arrests her soon. It would be fitting. Trish spending years trying to ruin Hazel, and ending up in prison for murder instead."

"What about Orla Weston?" I asked, watching her face carefully. "She works at the yarn shop. She would have known if Hazel came in regularly."

"Who's Orla Weston?"

"She works for Cordelia. Has been here about a year."

Carla shrugged. "Never heard of her. Has she done something suspicious?"

"I don't know. Maybe." Or maybe I was fixated on her because my instincts said she was wrong, dangerous, connected to something I didn't understand yet.

"Well, the sheriff will figure it out. But my money's on Trish." Carla straightened. "I just wanted to check on you. Make sure you were safe after that note."

"That's kind of you."

"We're both victims here, in a way. Both lost Hazel. Both caught up in this mess." She started toward the door, then paused. "Have you opened that box yet? The one Aunt Hazel left you?"

My hands stilled on the cloth I'd been using to wipe the counter. "Not yet."

"Why not? It's been over a week."

"Because I'm not ready."

"Not ready." She shook her head, something bitter creeping back into her expression. "Must be nice, having the luxury of not being ready. Some of us had to deal with lawyers and funeral arrangements and contested wills whether we were ready or not."

"Carla—"

"It's fine. I'm sure whatever's in that box is very important. Very personal. I hope it's worth the wait." She left before I could respond, the bell chiming sharply in her wake.

"She's still angry," Poppy observed from her window perch.

"Wouldn't you be?" I asked. "She expected to inherit, got nothing, watched Hazel give things to other people instead of her. That kind of disappointment breeds resentment."

"Resentment enough to kill?" Gus asked from his bed. Rocky was sprawled nearby, keeping one eye on Sage as she batted at a toy mouse.

That was the question. Carla was bitter, hurt, angry. She'd felt passed over and rejected. She'd come to Larkspur Valley expecting to finally get what she thought she deserved, only to be shut out again.

But did that make her a murderer?

"I don't know," I admitted. "She has motive. She had opportunity, probably. She knew where Hazel lived, knew her routines. But something about her doesn't feel like a killer. She's too open about her anger. Too obvious."

"Maybe that's the point," Rocky suggested. "Maybe she's so obvious that no one thinks she'd actually do it."

"Or maybe," Millie said softly from her hiding spot behind the counter, "she's just a bitter woman who lost her aunt and is taking it out on everyone else because she doesn't know how else to grieve."

I thought about that. About grief expressing itself as anger, as resentment, as lashing out. I'd seen it before. Done it myself, in different ways.

"The sheriff is still watching all three of them," I said. "Trish, Carla, and Orla. She hasn't ruled anyone out."

"But she told you to stay out of it," Poppy reminded me.

"I know."

"Are you going to listen?"

I looked around my café, at the customers enjoying their drinks, at the cats lounging in various spots, at the life I'd built here over the past year. A life that felt threatened now, disrupted by murder and notes and the constant fear that I was being watched.

"I'm going to be more careful," I said finally. "But no, I'm not stopping. Whoever left that note wanted to scare me. Wanted me to back off because I'm getting close to something."

"Or because you're in danger and they're giving you a chance to save yourself," Gus pointed out.

"Either way, I can't stop now. Not when Hazel deserves justice. Not when someone thinks they can threaten me into silence."

The cats didn't argue, though their expressions ranged from worried to resigned.

The rest of Saturday passed slowly. More customers, more gossip about Trish and the investigation, more speculation about who could have killed beloved Hazel Blaine.

Around three in the afternoon, a woman came in who I vaguely recognized. She was probably in her late fifties, with kind eyes and gray-streaked brown hair pulled back in a simple ponytail. She ordered a chamomile tea and then lingered near the cat room, watching through the glass.

After a few minutes, she approached the counter. "I was here a few days ago," she said, her voice soft. "I've been thinking about it ever since."

"I remember," I said, and I did. She'd spent nearly an hour in the cat room, sitting quietly while the cats investigated her.

"I just fell in love with Cinnamon. The tortoiseshell with the sweet face." Her smile was tentative, hopeful. "I was hoping, if it's okay, I'd like to apply to adopt her."

Something warm bloomed in my chest, pushing back against the darkness of the past week. "Of course. I'd love that."

"I'm a widow," she said as I pulled out the adoption paperwork. "My name is Elsie. Elsie Porter. My husband Gerald passed five months ago. Cancer." She said the word like it tasted bitter. "Cancer is a thief. It took him slowly, piece by piece, until there wasn't anything left but pain and then nothing at all."

"I'm sorry." The words felt inadequate, but she nodded like they helped anyway.

"I just don't like being all alone in that house. It's too quiet. Too empty. I thought maybe a cat would help. Some company. Something to take care of that isn't just me rattling around by myself."

We went through the paperwork together, and I found myself telling her about Cinnamon's personality, how she loved sunny spots and would chirp when she wanted attention, how she was gentle and patient and would be perfect for someone who needed quiet companionship.

"She sounds wonderful," Elsie said, signing the last form with a trembling hand.

I brought Cinnamon out in a carrier I kept for adoptions, along with some starter supplies. Elsie's eyes filled with tears when she peered through the carrier door at the pretty tortoiseshell face looking back at her.

"Thank you," she whispered. "You have no idea what this means."

"Promise me you'll come back and visit? Let me know how she's settling in?"

"I promise. We'll come by next week." She smiled through her tears. "Both of us."

I watched her leave, Cinnamon's carrier held carefully in both hands, and felt a surge of satisfaction. Two lonely souls finding each other. Something good in a week that had been mostly darkness and death and fear.

But the feeling faded quickly as my mind returned to its usual spiral. Hazel, lying in that alley. Three women with motives. A threatening note. Plant-based poison that I could have made myself if I'd wanted to.

The satisfaction of the adoption couldn't quite overshadow the weight of everything else.

By closing time, I was exhausted from maintaining my facade, from pretending I knew less than I did, from keeping all my secrets carefully locked away.

Upstairs, I made dinner and tried not to think about plant-based poisons and how easy it would be to brew such a thing if you knew what you were doing. Tried not to think about the fact that I had that knowledge, had used similar herbs for healing, could theoretically have done exactly what the killer had done.

The thought made me sick.

I fed the cats their evening meal, watching as they gathered around their bowls. Even Sage ate with enthusiasm now, her small body growing stronger every day. She'd come so far from the fragile, frightened kitten I'd rescued. Rocky still kept close, but she didn't need him quite as much anymore.

I settled on the couch with my terrible crochet project, forcing my fingers through the motions of chain stitches while my mind wandered.

Trish had a weak alibi and an obvious motive. But would she really kill someone over a business rivalry?

Carla had bitterness and disappointment. But would she kill her own aunt over an inheritance?

Orla had arrived at the same time I did, knew about Hazel's routines, and had given me a warning about investigating. But what was her motive?

I didn't have enough pieces yet. Didn't have enough proof.

But I was getting closer. I could feel it.

The threatening note proved it.

Someone was scared.

And scared people made mistakes.

I just had to be patient enough to catch them making one.

Outside, night fell over Larkspur Valley. The temperature dropped, frost forming on the windows again. Winter was coming, and with it, the sense that time was running out.

Justice delayed was justice denied.

And Hazel had been waiting for justice long enough.

Tomorrow, I'd figure out my next move. Tonight, I just needed to survive another day of carrying secrets and watching suspects and pretending I was nothing more than a woman who made coffee and loved cats.

When really, I was so much more.

And so much more dangerous than any of them realized.

If they pushed me too far, they'd find out exactly what a witch could do when someone she loved was taken from her.

I just hoped it wouldn't come to that.

Chapter Eighteen

Sunday morning, I woke to the realization that if I spent another day trapped in my apartment or café, I was going to lose my mind.

"I need to get out," I announced to the cats over breakfast. "Go somewhere. Clear my head."

"Where?" Poppy asked.

"I don't know. Maybe a hike. Up toward Rowan's Ridge. Fresh air, exercise, no people asking me about murder investigations or threatening notes."

"Can I come?" Rocky asked immediately, his tail shooting straight up with excitement.

I looked at him, this bundle of chaotic energy who'd been cooped up inside for days while I spiraled. "Actually, yes. You could use the exercise. We both could."

"Really?" He started zooming in circles. "Really really? We're going on an adventure?"

"We're going on a hike. A calm, peaceful hike."

"That sounds like an adventure!"

Sage watched from her spot on the couch, her gray head tilted. "Can I come too?"

"Not this time, little one. The trail is too steep and long for you. But Rocky will tell you all about it when we get back."

"I'll tell you everything!" Rocky promised, still zooming.

Twenty minutes later, I had Rocky in his harness and leash, something I'd bought months ago on a whim and rarely used. He tolerated the harness with surprising patience, too excited about going outside to complain.

"We'll be back in a few hours," I told the other cats. "Hold down the fort."

"Be careful," Poppy said. "Someone left you a threatening note two days ago. Maybe going into the woods alone isn't the smartest plan."

"I'm not alone. I have Rocky."

"I have sharp claws!" Rocky announced proudly. "And excellent hearing! And I can climb trees really fast if we need to escape!"

"See? We'll be fine."

The trail to Rowan's Ridge started at the edge of town, winding up through pine forests and aspens that had already lost most of their leaves. The morning air was crisp and cold, turning my breath to fog, but the sun was bright and the sky was that brilliant blue you only get in autumn.

Rocky walked beside me with surprising focus, his orange fur bright against the brown trail. Every few minutes he'd stop to investigate a particularly interesting smell or watch a bird, but mostly he trotted along, clearly thrilled to be outside.

"This is amazing," he said after we'd been walking for twenty minutes. "Why don't we do this every day?"

"Because you'd probably chase a squirrel and I'd spend three hours trying to find you."

"I wouldn't chase a squirrel." He paused. "Unless it was a really interesting squirrel. Then maybe."

Despite everything, I smiled. This was exactly what I'd needed. Space. Quiet. Just me and a cat and the mountains that surrounded Larkspur Valley.

We climbed higher, the trail growing steeper. My legs burned pleasantly, and my mind started to clear. Up here, away from the café and the customers and the constant weight of investigation, I could think more clearly.

Plant-based poison. Someone with botanical knowledge. Three suspects with three different motives.

But which one had actually done it?

Trish, with her years of competition and her obvious desire for that prime location?

Carla, with her bitterness and her disappointed expectations?

Or Orla, with her careful facade and her perfect timing of arriving just when I did?

"You're thinking too much," Rocky observed. "I can tell. Your face gets all scrunchy."

"My face does not get scrunchy."

"Does too. You should see it. Like this." He made an exaggerated expression that probably looked nothing like me.

"Very helpful, thank you."

We reached a clearing about halfway up the trail, and I stopped to catch my breath. The view was spectacular: Larkspur Valley spread out below, the lake glittering in the sunlight, Main Street a ribbon of buildings and trees. From up here, everything looked peaceful, orderly, safe.

From up here, you couldn't see the darkness hiding underneath.

"It's pretty," Rocky said, sitting beside me. "I can see the café from here. See? That building with the cat room window."

He was right. I could just make out The Cozy Purrch, a small shape among other small shapes.

My home. My business. My carefully constructed life.

A life that was now threatened by whoever had killed Hazel.

We stayed there for a few more minutes, then headed back down. The descent was easier, faster, and Rocky seemed disappointed when the trail ended and we were back on the streets of Larkspur Valley.

"Can we do that again?" he asked. "Tomorrow?"

"Maybe. We'll see."

I was half a block from the café when I saw her.

Trish Lawrence stood in front of my door, arms crossed, face tight with anger. She wore another too-bright dress under a jacket, and yes, I could smell her perfume from here.

My steps slowed.

"Keep walking," Rocky said quietly. "Don't let her think she can intimidate you."

Good advice from an impulsive cat.

I walked up to my door, Rocky at my side, and met Trish's eyes directly. "Can I help you?"

"You can stop telling the sheriff I threatened you." Her voice was sharp, accusatory. "I didn't leave that note."

"I didn't tell her you left it. I gave her the note I found under my door. She observed that it smelled like your perfume. Draw your own conclusions about what that means."

"I'm drawing the conclusion that someone is trying to frame me." Trish's hands clenched. "That note reeked of my perfume. Too much. Like someone doused it deliberately to make sure everyone would know."

That was actually perceptive. And aligned with what I'd been thinking.

"Have you told the sheriff that?" I asked.

"Yes. She said she'd consider all possibilities." Trish's expression shifted slightly, some of the anger giving way to something that looked almost like fear. "I didn't kill Hazel. I wanted her business, yes. I wanted that location. I wanted to finally win. But I would never kill someone over it."

"Then who did?"

"How should I know? Maybe her bitter niece who got cut out of the will. Maybe some random person with a grudge. Maybe—" She stopped, seemed to reconsider her words. "I don't know. But it wasn't me."

We stood there in silence, two women staring at each other in front of a cat café on a Sunday morning.

"For what it's worth," I said finally, "I don't think you did it either."

Trish blinked, surprised. "You don't?"

"The note was too obvious. Too much perfume, too deliberate. It felt like someone wanted to point the sheriff in your direction." I unlocked my door, Rocky slipping inside ahead of me. "But that doesn't mean I know who actually did it."

"If you figure it out," Trish said quietly, "tell the sheriff, not me. I don't want to be anywhere near this mess anymore."

She walked away, her heels clicking on the sidewalk, and I stood in my doorway watching her go.

"Do you believe her?" Rocky asked.

"I think I do. Which means I've been wasting time looking at the wrong suspect."

Inside, I let Rocky out of his harness and climbed the stairs to my apartment. The other cats were waiting, demanding a full report on the hike, wanting to know if Rocky had behaved himself. Sage bounced over, her energy matching Rocky's enthusiasm.

"Did you see birds? Did you climb trees? Was it scary?" she asked, her questions tumbling over each other.

"I saw lots of birds," Rocky said proudly. "And I didn't chase any of them. Well, I wanted to, but I didn't."

I told them about the trail, the view, the confrontation with Trish. But my mind was elsewhere, circling back to the same conclusion I'd been avoiding.

If not Trish, then Carla or Orla.

Carla, who'd been obvious about her bitterness but maybe too obvious.

Or Orla, who'd been careful, calculated, present at exactly the wrong times.

I needed more information. Needed something that would definitively point to one of them.

And there was only one place I was going to find it.

I walked to my bedroom closet and opened the door. The box sat where I'd left it, sealed and waiting, Hazel's handwriting stark across the top.

For Alexis Belrose.

"You're going to open it," Poppy said softly from the doorway.

"I'm going to open it."

I carried the box to my kitchen table. Set it down carefully. Pulled out the box cutter I'd abandoned weeks ago.

My hands were shaking.

Whatever was in this box, Hazel had wanted me to have it. Had sealed it, had left instructions, had known she might die and had prepared for that possibility.

Which meant she'd known something. Had suspected something. Had maybe even known who would kill her.

And she'd left the evidence for me.

I took a breath and pressed the blade against the tape.

"You don't have to do this alone," Millie said, and suddenly all five cats were there, arranged around the table like a support group. Even Sage had jumped up onto a chair to watch, her small gray face serious.

"Thank you," I whispered.

Then I pulled the blade through the tape, the sound of it splitting sharp in the quiet apartment.

The seal was broken.

Whatever secrets Hazel had left me, I was about to discover them.

I just had to be brave enough to look inside.

My hands hovered over the cardboard flaps.
One more breath.
Then I opened the box.

Chapter Nineteen

The flaps lifted easily, and I found myself staring into the box.

For a moment, I couldn't move. Couldn't breathe. Whatever was in here would change everything, and once I looked, once I knew, I couldn't unknow it.

"It's okay," Poppy said softly. "We're here."

I reached in and pulled out the first item.

A book. Leather-bound, old, the kind of journal that had been handled countless times. The cover was worn smooth, and when I opened it, I recognized Hazel's handwriting immediately.

But it wasn't a regular journal.

It was a grimoire.

My hands went numb.

Page after page of spells, herb combinations, moon phases, incantations. Notes in the margins about successes and failures. Sketches of protective sigils. Instructions for brewing potions I recognized, healing teas I'd made myself, truth serums that worked exactly like mine.

Hazel had been a witch.

"Oh," Millie breathed. "She was like you."

I couldn't speak. Could only stare at the pages, at the proof that Hazel had been hiding the same secret I'd been hiding. That we'd been the same, and I'd never known.

That we could have been honest with each other, and I'd wasted that chance.

I set the grimoire aside with trembling hands and reached back into the box.

A second journal, this one newer. I opened it and found a different kind of writing. A history. A story.

The coven war began in 1987...

I read slowly, my heart hammering. Hazel had been part of a coven in Oregon. A peaceful coven that practiced light magic, healing, protection. But another coven, one that practiced darker magic, had wanted their territory, their power, their influence.

The war had lasted three years. Magical battles that looked like accidents to outsiders. Houses burning down. People disappearing. Death masquerading as misfortune.

And it had ended when Hazel killed the leader of the dark coven.

A woman named Moira Weston.

Weston.

My blood turned to ice.

I flipped through the journal faster now, finding the entry I was looking for.

I had no choice. Moira would have destroyed us all. Her death ended the war, scattered her coven, brought peace. But her sister swore vengeance. Swore she'd hunt me to the ends of the earth. So I ran.

I changed my name. Moved across the country. Tried to build a new life. And for forty years, I thought I'd succeeded.

Until Orla Weston walked into Cordelia's yarn shop.

The words blurred. I had to read them again to make sure I'd understood.

Orla Weston. Sister of the woman Hazel had killed. Here in Larkspur Valley, working three doors down from Hazel's flower shop, waiting for the perfect moment to take her revenge.

I reached back into the box with trembling hands.

Photographs. Old ones, faded with time. A group of women standing together, arms around each other, smiling. Hazel among them, younger, her dark hair not yet gray. And in another photo, a different group. Harder faces. Dark energy even in a still image.

One woman stood in the center, tall and commanding.

On the back, in Hazel's handwriting: *Moira Weston, 1990*.

I held the photo up to the light, studying Moira's face. Then I understood.

Orla looked like her. Older, grayer, more weathered. But the bone structure was the same. The eyes were the same.

She'd been here for a year. Working at the yarn shop. Watching Hazel. Planning.

And I'd led a completely separate life, never knowing that another witch was three blocks away, never knowing we were both hiding from our pasts in this small mountain town.

I pulled out more items. Protective charms, small sachets that smelled of herbs I recognized. Each one labeled with a date and a purpose.

For Alexis - Protection from Detection - October
For Alexis - Safe Sleep - November
For Alexis - Clear Mind - January

She'd been making charms for me. Protecting me. For months.

The tears came then, hot and bitter. Hazel had known what I was. Had been watching over me. Had been keeping me safe without me ever knowing.

And I'd kept her at arm's length. Had never trusted her with the truth.

"There's something else," Gus said quietly. "At the bottom."

I wiped my eyes and reached in one more time.

An envelope. Thick paper, sealed with wax. My name across the front in Hazel's careful script.

I broke the seal and pulled out several pages of a handwritten letter.

My dear Alexis,

If you're reading this, then Orla has finally done what she came here to do. I'm sorry you had to find me in that alley. Sorry you had to carry that weight. Sorry for so many things.

I knew what you were from the moment you walked into my flower shop, lost and scared and trying so hard to seem normal. It takes one witch to recognize another, even when we're both hiding. I saw the magic in you, the power you were trying to suppress, the fear that someone would find you.

I understood that fear because I'd been living with it for forty years.

I won't burden you with the full story of my past - you'll find that in the journals I've left you. What matters is this: I killed a woman named Moira Weston to stop a coven war. It was necessary. It was right. But her sister Orla never forgave me.

Orla Weston arrived in Larkspur Valley in October of last year. I recognized her immediately - she looks so much like her sister. I knew why she'd come. Knew what she planned. But I couldn't run again. I was too old, too tired, too done with running.

So, I prepared. Made these protections for you. Wrote this letter. Left instructions for my will that would buy you time. Six months before any decisions are made about the shop - six months for you to figure this out, to understand, to protect yourself.

Because here's what you need to know, what I should have told you when you first arrived: Larkspur Valley sits on a convergence of ley lines. It's a place of power, a place that draws magical beings unconsciously. That's why you felt pulled here. That's why I stayed here. That's why Orla found us both.

You're not the only magical person in this town, Alexis. There are others:

Maeve Atwater *- Seer. She knows more than she tells, sees more than should be possible. She's been here longer than anyone, watching over the town's magical community.*

Atticus Law *- Can speak to animals. He thinks it's just an affinity, doesn't realize it's actual magic. Keep an eye on him - when he figures it out, he'll need guidance.*

Ella Hendry *- Only six years old, but already showing signs of sensitivity. She can sense magic, feel emotions, maybe even hear animals speak. She's young enough that she doesn't question it yet. Protect her if you can.*

My hands were shaking so hard I almost dropped the letter.

Ella could hear the cats. I'd thought I was imagining it, but Hazel had known. Had been watching her too.

I forced myself to keep reading.

There are others, though I haven't identified them all. Some know what they are. Most don't. We hide from each other as much as from the outside world, afraid of exposure, afraid of betrayal.

But you should know: This place that drew you here for safety might also draw what you're running from. Whatever coven, whatever past, whatever darkness you fled - it could follow you here, just as Orla followed me.

Be cautious. Be prepared. And know that you don't have to face it alone.

I wish I'd been brave enough to tell you all this while I was alive. Wish we'd had the chance to be honest with each other. But I was afraid - afraid that revealing myself would put you in danger, would make Orla realize you were special, would paint a target on your back.

So, I stayed silent. Kept my distance. Protected you from the shadows.

And now I'm gone, and you're reading this, and I hope you can forgive me for all the things I never said.

Trust Maeve. She'll help you if you let her. Watch Orla - she's patient and dangerous and won't stop until she feels her sister's death is avenged. And please, Alexis, don't blame yourself for my death. This was always going to end this way. At least I got one more year. One more year watching you build a life here. One more year of Tuesday morning teas and Sunday evening dinners and believing that maybe, just maybe, we'd both finally found a home.

Be careful. Be strong. Be the witch I know you are.

With love and hope, Hazel

P.S. - The grimoire is yours now. Use it wisely. And the charms I made for you will last another three months before they need to be renewed. By then, I hope you'll have learned to make your own.

The letter slipped from my fingers onto the table.

Hazel had known everything. Had known I was a witch from the first day. Had known Orla was hunting her. Had known she was going to die.

And she'd spent her last year protecting me instead of saving herself.

The grief hit like a physical blow. I bent over the table, pressing my forehead against the cool wood, and sobbed.

She'd been my friend. My only real friend. And we could have been so much more if I'd just been brave enough to trust her. If I'd just told her the truth.

But I'd been too afraid. Too cautious. Too used to hiding.

And now she was gone, and all I had left were her journals and her charms and a letter that explained everything too late.

A soft weight landed on the table beside me. Sage, having climbed up to be closer. She pressed her small gray body against my arm, purring.

"She loved you," Poppy said softly. "She knew what you were and she loved you anyway."

"She died protecting me." My voice was broken, raw. "Orla came for her, but Hazel made sure I stayed hidden. Made sure I stayed safe. She died so I could live."

"Then don't waste it," Gus said, his voice rough. "Don't let her sacrifice be for nothing. Catch her killer. Make sure Orla pays for what she did."

I sat up, wiping my face. Sage stayed close, her steady purr a small comfort. The table was covered with evidence: grimoires, journals, photographs, charms, the letter.

Everything I needed to understand what had happened.

Everything except proof that would hold up in a non-magical court of law.

Iris couldn't know about ley lines and coven wars and forty-year-old revenge. She needed evidence she could use. Physical proof. Witnesses.

And I was the only witness who knew the whole truth.

"We have to be smart about this," I said, my voice steadier now. "Orla has been planning this for a year. She's patient. Careful. She won't make obvious mistakes."

"So, we make her make mistakes," Rocky said. "We push her. Make her react."

"That's dangerous," Millie worried.

"Everything about this is dangerous." I gathered up the items from the box, handling them carefully. Sage watched with those serious gray eyes, understanding more than a kitten should. "But we have something Orla doesn't know we have. We have Hazel's story. We have her warning. We know who Orla really is and why she's here."

"And we have magic," Poppy added. "If it comes down to it, you can defend yourself."

I thought about that. About using magic openly. About exposing myself. About all the things I'd been afraid of for so long.

But Hazel had died protecting me. The least I could do was be brave enough to use what I was to catch her killer.

"Tomorrow," I said, standing up. Sage jumped down from the table, landing lightly on the floor. "Tomorrow I'll figure out how to trap her. How to make her reveal herself. How to give Iris the evidence she needs."

"And tonight?" Gus asked.

"Tonight, I read these journals. Learn everything Hazel knew about Orla. Find her weaknesses." I picked up the grimoire, feeling its weight, its power. "And I remember what it means to be a witch."

I'd been running for so long. Hiding. Suppressing my power. Afraid of being found.

But I was done running.

Orla Weston had come to Larkspur Valley to kill the witch who'd killed her sister.

And she'd succeeded.

But now I knew. Now I understood. Now I had Hazel's knowledge and her magic and her blessing.

And I was going to make sure Orla never hurt anyone again.

For Hazel.

For justice.

For every witch who'd ever had to hide what they were because the world was too dangerous to show their truth.

Outside, the sun set over the mountains, painting the sky in shades of orange and pink. Beautiful and terrible and full of promise.

Tomorrow, everything would change.

Tonight, I just needed to prepare.

The box sat empty on my table, its contents spread around me like pieces of a puzzle I was finally beginning to understand.

Hazel had given me everything I needed.

Now I just had to be brave enough to use it.

Chapter Twenty

Monday morning, I opened the café running on three hours of sleep and too much caffeine.

I'd spent most of the night reading Hazel's journals, learning about the coven war, about Moira Weston's cruelty, about the magical battle that had ended with Hazel having no choice but to kill or be killed. About Orla's vow of vengeance, spoken over her sister's body.

About forty years of running and hiding that had finally ended in a Larkspur Valley alley.

The morning rush was brutal. Everyone wanted coffee, everyone wanted to chat, and I wanted to scream that I'd discovered my friend was murdered by someone seeking revenge for a forty-year-old death and could they please just take their lattes and leave me alone.

But I smiled and made drinks and deflected questions about the investigation and waited.

At 8:15, Iris came in for her black coffee. She looked tired but determined.

"Morning," I said, handing her the cup.

She took it, studying me for a moment like she was waiting for me to ask questions, to push for information. When I didn't, something shifted in her expression.

"Have you had any more incidents? More notes?"

"No. Everything's been quiet." I kept my voice casual, normal. "I listened. No more investigating."

It was a lie, and a blatant one, but Iris seemed to accept it at face value. Her shoulders relaxed slightly.

"Good. I'm glad you're staying safe." She took a sip of coffee. "I'll keep you updated when I can."

She left, and I stood behind the counter feeling only slightly guilty about the deception.

The morning dragged on. I kept glancing at the clock, waiting for a reasonable time to close for a lunch break. Finally, at eleven-thirty, I made my decision.

"I'm going out for an hour," I told the cats. "Poppy, you're in charge of watching the café."

"Where are you going?" she asked, though her tone suggested she already knew.

"To see Maeve."

"Be careful."

"I will."

Sage looked up from where she'd been napping in a sunny spot. "You're going to catch the bad person?"

"I'm going to try, little one." I scratched behind her ears. "Rocky, keep an eye on her while I'm gone?"

"Always do," he said, moving closer to Sage.

I flipped the sign to "Back at 12:30" and locked the door behind me.

The walk to The Turning Page took five minutes that felt like an eternity. My heart hammered the entire way, and my hands were clammy despite the cold air. This was it. The moment I stopped hiding. The moment I admitted to another magical person what I was.

The moment I asked for help.

The bookshop was empty when I walked in, the bell chiming softly overhead. Maeve appeared from between the stacks almost immediately, as if she'd been waiting.

"Maeve..." I started, and suddenly couldn't find the words. How did you tell someone you'd read a dead witch's letter that said they were a Seer? How did you admit what you were after a year of carefully hiding it?

But Maeve just smiled, warm and knowing and completely unsurprised.

"So you know now," she said simply. "Good. Let's get down to business."

She led me to the back room, past the reading nook where we'd had tea, to a small office I'd never seen before. Books lined every wall here too, but these were different. Older. Leather-bound. The kind of books that hummed with power even from across the room.

Maeve closed the door and gestured for me to sit in one of two chairs facing each other across a cluttered desk.

"I've been waiting for you to open that box," she said, settling into the opposite chair. "Hazel sealed it two months ago, right after she realized Orla knew who she was. She knew what was coming."

"Why didn't she run?" The question burst out. "Why didn't she leave, go somewhere else, stay alive?"

"Because she was tired of running. And because you were here." Maeve's eyes were kind but direct. "She knew what you were the moment you arrived. Another witch in hiding, scared and alone. She wanted to stay, to watch over you, to make sure you didn't face the same fate she was facing."

My throat tightened. "She died protecting me."

"She died doing what she thought was right. And now we honor that by making sure Orla pays for what she did." Maeve leaned forward. "You've been investigating. Trying to figure out how to prove Orla killed Hazel. But you can't tell the sheriff about coven wars or magical revenge, can you?"

"No. I need real evidence. Something Iris can use."

"Then we give her a confession." Maeve pulled out a piece of paper and a pen. "Orla is patient and careful. She's been planning this for a year. She won't crack under normal questioning. But she doesn't know that we know who she really is. She doesn't know Hazel left you everything."

"So we use that." I was starting to see it. "We make her think she got away with it. Make her comfortable. Then we spring the trap."

"Exactly." Maeve started writing, her handwriting neat and precise. "Here's what I'm thinking. Orla knows you've been investigating. She's been watching you, probably left that note herself to throw suspicion on Trish. She thinks you're getting close but she doesn't know how close."

"So I back off. Make her think the note worked. Make her think I'm scared and stopping."

"Yes. Give it a few days. Let her relax. Then we set up a confrontation." Maeve looked up from her notes. "But not a direct one. We need her to confess somewhere Iris can hear it. Somewhere public enough that Orla won't suspect a trap."

"How do we make her confess?" That was the sticking point. "She's too careful. Too controlled."

"You said Hazel left photos. Of Moira Weston, Orla's sister." Maeve's eyes gleamed with sudden understanding.

"Yes. An old photograph from before the coven war ended."

"What if you told Orla you found something in the box? Something that belonged to her sister. And when she touches it..." Maeve was already pulling books from her shelves, her movements quick and purposeful.

"We spell the photograph." I saw it immediately, my heart racing. "A compulsion to confess. To boast about what she's done. She touches it and suddenly she wants to tell me everything."

"Exactly. But there's a complication." Maeve set a thick tome on the desk between us. "She'll talk about magic. About covens and revenge and witch killings. Iris can't hear that."

My excitement faltered. "Then how—"

"So we add a translation layer. A spell that changes the words as they leave her mouth." Maeve opened the book, revealing pages of ancient text with notes in the margins. "When Orla says 'coven,' Iris hears 'family.' When she says 'magic,' Iris hears 'weapon' or 'poison' or whatever makes sense in context. When she talks about killing a witch, Iris hears about killing a woman."

I leaned forward, studying the pages. The text was in a language I half-recognized, something old and powerful. "I've read about layered spells like this. Never attempted one, but I understand the theory."

"Theory and practice are very different things." Maeve's eyes were appraising. "You're strong, Alexis. Stronger than most witches I've met. That's why your old coven wanted you, isn't it? They wanted to harness that power for darker purposes."

I nodded, uncomfortable with the reminder. "But strength without experience is just raw potential. I've spent years suppressing my magic, not developing it. I can brew a perfect truth serum, but something this complex..."

"That's why we'll do it together." Maeve traced a finger down the page. "The compulsion spell is straightforward. You could probably manage that on your own. Make her want to talk, to boast, to reveal everything she's accomplished. But the translation spell is far trickier. We'll need to be very specific about which words get changed and what they become."

"How specific?"

"Every magical term needs a mundane equivalent that makes sense in context. 'Coven' becomes 'family.' 'Spell' or 'curse' becomes 'plan' or 'method.' 'Magical poison' becomes just 'poison.' We're not changing the story, just the vocabulary." Maeve pulled out more books, stacking them on the desk. "It's delicate work. We'll need to cast it together, weaving our power through the photograph so it activates the moment Orla touches it."

"When?" My hands were shaking with a mix of fear and determination.

"Tomorrow evening. After you close the café. Bring the photograph of Moira Weston, and we'll do the spell work here." Maeve met my eyes seriously. "This is powerful magic, Alexis. The kind that leaves traces. The kind that could expose us if anyone looks too closely. Are you sure you want to do this?"

I thought about Hazel, lying in that alley. About a year of friendship I'd wasted by being too afraid to trust her. About Orla Weston walking free while Hazel was dead.

"I'm sure."

"Good." Maeve studied me for a moment. "You've been wondering about Ella, haven't you? About why she has the gift when her mother and sister don't."

The question caught me off guard, though I'd been thinking about it since reading Hazel's letter. "I know magic doesn't pass down simply, like eye color or height. It's more complicated than that. But the specifics..." I shook my head. "My own mother never had any powers. I spent my childhood trying to understand why I was different, why I had to hide what I could do. No one ever explained it to me."

"Because most magical families don't understand it themselves," Maeve said, settling back in her chair. "They just know it happens. But I've spent decades studying patterns, watching families. Think of it like musical ability. Some families produce generations of musicians, others produce one prodigy in a hundred years. Sometimes it skips generations entirely. Sometimes siblings have vastly different levels of ability."

"So Ella has it and Piper doesn't because..."

"Because everyone has a spark of magic in them, but in most people it never ignites." Maeve gestured as she explained. "They live their whole lives never knowing they could have accessed something more. In others, the spark catches. Sometimes through trauma, sometimes through exposure to other magical beings, sometimes for no reason anyone can understand."

"And some people ignore it," I said, understanding dawning. "Even when they feel something different about themselves."

"Exactly." Maeve nodded approvingly. "I'd bet anything that Piper has felt things. Sensed things. Had moments where she knew something she shouldn't know. But she's explained it away. Rationalized it. Convinced herself it's normal because accepting that it's magic would mean accepting a world she's not ready to believe in."

"But Ella is young enough that she doesn't question it yet."

"Children accept magic more easily. They haven't been taught yet that it's impossible." Maeve's expression grew thoughtful. "In five or ten years, if no one teaches Ella what she is, she'll probably start suppressing it too. Convincing herself she's just imaginative. Just sensitive. Just different in ways that can be explained without resorting to magic."

I thought about my own childhood, feeling different, sensing things others couldn't, having abilities I couldn't explain. My mother had been loving but completely mundane, and there had been no one to tell me what I was until the coven found me. "That's what happened to me. My mother couldn't help me understand because she didn't have magic herself. She never knew what I was going through."

"Hazel knew what she was from a young age because she grew up in a family that practiced openly," Maeve said gently. "But when the coven war happened, when people died, she realized that being known as a witch could get you killed. So she ran. Changed her name. Buried her magic deep. Became someone new."

"And Carla?"

"Carla probably has a spark too. But she's spent forty-five years being completely mundane, completely normal. If she has any sensitivity at all, she's buried it so deep she'll never find it again." Maeve paused. "Sometimes I wonder if that's why there was such tension between her and Hazel. On some level, maybe Carla sensed that her aunt was different, special in a way she couldn't name. And that created resentment."

It made sense. All of it. "What about Atticus? Hazel's letter said he could speak to animals but doesn't realize it's magic."

"Atticus is an interesting case." Maeve leaned forward. "He has significant ability, but he's rationalized it his entire life. He thinks he's just good with animals, that he has an affinity, a talent for reading their body language and behavior. He doesn't question why he can understand what they need without them making a sound, why he always seems to know when an animal is in distress before anyone else does."

"So, his spark ignited, but he doesn't recognize it as magic."

"Exactly. And he might live his whole life that way, using his gift but never acknowledging what it truly is." Maeve smiled slightly. "One day he might figure it out. When he does, he'll need someone to explain it to him. To help him understand what he is."

"And Hazel wanted that person to be me."

"She wanted you to watch over the magical community here. The ones who know what they are and the ones who don't." Maeve's eyes were serious. "Larkspur Valley draws us here, Alexis. The ley lines, the convergence of power. But once we're here, we need someone to help us navigate it. Hazel was that person for decades. Now she wants you to take her place."

The weight of that responsibility settled on my shoulders. "I don't know if I can."

"You can. You already have been, in small ways. Helping people through your teas, using your intuition to know what they need." Maeve leaned forward. "That's what Hazel did. Small magic, quiet magic, the kind that helps without being obvious. That's what this town needs."

"After we catch Orla."

"After we catch Orla," Maeve agreed. "Then Wednesday morning, we spring the trap." Maeve closed the book with a decisive thump. "You invite Orla for coffee at 8:00, right at opening time. A few witnesses won't hurt anything, and it makes the confession public. Tell her you found something in Hazel's box that she needs to see. Make it sound urgent, mysterious. She won't be able to resist."

"She'll want to know what I found. What I know." I was building the scenario in my mind. "She'll be curious, maybe worried. And when I show her the photograph of her sister..."

"She touches it, and the compulsion takes hold. She'll want to tell you everything. How clever she was, how patient, how she finally got her revenge after forty years." Maeve's smile was grim. "And Iris will hear every word, translated into terms she can understand and use."

"How do we make sure Iris is there? She usually comes at 8:15, but if Orla arrives at 8:00..."

"I'll make sure Iris knows to stop by early that day." Maeve's smile turned mysterious. "I have my ways of influencing things without being obvious about it. A casual mention that I had a feeling something important would happen Wednesday morning at your café. She's learned to trust my intuitions over the years."

I believed her. If she was a Seer, she probably saw dozens of possible futures, knew which threads to pull to make the right one happen.

"There's one thing I don't understand," I said slowly. "If you're a Seer, if you can see possibilities, why didn't you see what Orla was planning? Why didn't you warn Hazel?"

Maeve's expression grew sad. "Because Hazel asked me not to. She came to me two months ago, told me she'd recognized Orla, knew what was coming. She asked me to promise not to interfere, not to warn her, not to try to save her."

"Why would she do that?"

"Because she'd been running for forty years and she was tired. Because she believed Orla deserved her revenge, in a way. Because she wanted it to end." Maeve's voice was gentle. "But she also asked me to watch over you. To make sure that when the time came, you'd have help. That you wouldn't face this alone."

My eyes burned. "She thought of everything."

"She loved you like a daughter. Or maybe like the person she'd been forty years ago, before everything went wrong." Maeve stood, indicating our meeting was over. "Go back to your café. Act normal. If you see Orla, be pleasant but distant. Don't give her any reason to suspect you're planning something."

"I won't."

"And Alexis?" Maeve's expression grew serious. "Tomorrow evening, when we cast the spell, bring your grimoire. Hazel's grimoire. We'll need its power as well as ours."

I nodded, understanding. This wasn't just about catching a killer. It was about using Hazel's own magic to ensure her murderer faced justice. It was poetry, in a dark sort of way.

"Tomorrow at six?" I asked.

"Perfect. The shop will be closed by then. We'll have all the privacy we need." Maeve walked me to the door. "And Alexis? This is going to work. Orla has no idea what's coming."

"Good." I stepped out into the cold afternoon air. "She shouldn't have come to Larkspur Valley. Shouldn't have killed Hazel. And she definitely shouldn't have underestimated me."

I walked back to my café, my mind already planning. Tomorrow evening, spell work with Maeve. Wednesday morning, the trap. And hopefully, by Wednesday afternoon, Orla Weston would be in custody and Hazel would have justice.

The cats were waiting when I got back.

"Well?" Poppy demanded the moment I locked the door behind me.

"We have a plan." I flipped the sign back to Open. "Wednesday morning, we're going to make Orla Weston confess to murder."

"How?" Rocky asked, his tail twitching with excitement. Sage was pressed against his side, listening intently.

"Magic," I said simply. "The one thing she won't be expecting."

"What kind of magic?" Gus asked from his bed, his eyes sharp and interested.

I told them about the photograph, about the compulsion spell and the translation layer, about how Orla's own pride would be her downfall. They listened intently, and when I finished, Poppy looked satisfied.

"Hazel would approve," she said. "Using magic to catch a magical killer. It's fitting."

"It's dangerous," Millie worried. "What if something goes wrong? What if Orla realizes what's happening?"

"Then I'll deal with it." I said it with more confidence than I felt. "But it won't come to that. Orla thinks she's the only witch in Larkspur Valley now. She doesn't know about me. Doesn't know about

Maeve. Doesn't know that we're about to bring her forty years of patient planning crashing down around her."

"When does Maeve expect you tomorrow?" Gus asked.

"Six o'clock. After I close." I glanced toward my apartment stairs, thinking about the photograph upstairs in Hazel's box. "I need to practice what I'm going to say to Orla. How to make it sound urgent enough that she'll come but not so suspicious that she'll suspect a trap."

"Keep it simple," Poppy advised. "Tell her you found something in Hazel's things that has her sister's name on it. That you think she deserves to have it. Appeal to her sentimentality."

"Do you think she has sentimentality?" Rocky asked. "She killed someone."

"She killed someone for her sister. That's sentimentality, twisted as it is." Gus shifted in his bed. "Use it against her."

They were right. Orla had spent forty years hunting Hazel to avenge Moira. That kind of devotion, however dark, was rooted in love. In family. In the belief that her sister's death had to be answered.

I could use that.

The afternoon passed in a blur of customers and coffee. Every time the door opened, my heart jumped, expecting to see Orla. But she never came. She was probably at work, arranging yarn and helping customers and acting like she hadn't murdered someone two weeks ago.

By closing time, I was exhausted and wired in equal measure. Upstairs, I pulled out the photograph of Moira Weston and studied it. A strong face, proud, commanding. The kind of person who would start a coven war rather than back down.

The kind of person whose sister would kill to avenge her.

Sage jumped up beside me, peering at the photograph with curious eyes. "She looks mean."

"She was," I said quietly. "And her sister killed Hazel because of her."

"But you're going to stop the sister. Right?"

"Right." I set the photograph down carefully. "Tomorrow, this photograph will become a weapon. Will become the tool that brings Orla to justice."

"Good," Sage said with the simple certainty of a kitten who believed I could do anything.

I just had to trust in magic. Trust in Maeve. Trust in myself.

For Hazel.

Wednesday couldn't come fast enough.

Chapter Twenty-One

Wednesday morning arrived cold and clear, and I'd been awake since four.

I kept replaying Tuesday evening in my mind. Maeve's back room, candles lit, the photograph of Moira Weston spread on the desk between us. Hazel's grimoire open to the pages we needed. Maeve's hands on one side of the photo, mine on the other, our magic weaving together in ways I'd never experienced before.

The compulsion spell had been almost easy. A desire to speak, to boast, to confess. But the translation layer had been intricate, delicate work. Every magical word mapped to a mundane equivalent. Every confession translated in real-time so that what Orla said and what Iris heard would be two different things, but both would be true.

"It's done," Maeve had said finally, lifting her hands. "The moment Orla touches this photograph, she'll want to tell you everything. And anyone listening will hear a perfectly normal confession to murder."

Now, at seven-thirty Wednesday morning, I stood in my café with that photograph in an envelope behind the counter, and my hands wouldn't stop shaking.

"You can do this," Poppy said from her perch. All five cats were positioned strategically around the café, watching, waiting. Sage sat near Rocky on one of the lower cat trees, her gray fur sleek and her confidence evident. She'd come so far from the fragile kitten I'd rescued.

"I know." But my voice wavered.

"She's just a woman," Gus said. "A woman who killed our friend. You owe her nothing. No mercy. No hesitation."

He was right.

I went through my opening routine on autopilot. Brewing coffee, arranging pastries, checking supplies. At seven forty-five, Maeve texted: *Iris will be there at 7:55. Good luck.*

My stomach twisted. Fifteen minutes.

At seven-fifty, I unlocked the front door and flipped the sign to Open. A few early customers trickled in. Jasper getting coffee before opening his store. Felix looking more awake than usual. Mabel settling at her usual table even though it wasn't Tuesday.

At seven fifty-four, Sheriff Iris Scott walked through the door.

"You're early," I said, pouring her black coffee without being asked.

"Maeve mentioned I should stop by this morning. Said she had a feeling." Iris's eyes swept the café, assessing. "Thought I'd humor her."

"Her feelings are usually right."

"They are." Iris accepted the coffee and moved to a table near the window. Not too close to the counter, but close enough to hear. Close enough to see.

Perfect.

At exactly eight o'clock, the bell chimed and Orla Weston walked in.

She looked the same as always. Unremarkable clothes, graying hair pulled back, pleasant expression. Nothing about her screamed murderer. Nothing about her suggested she'd poisoned a woman and left her to die in an alley.

"Good morning, Alexis," she said, approaching the counter. "Thank you for inviting me. Your message sounded urgent."

I'd texted her last night: *Found something of your sister's in Hazel's things. Thought you should have it.*

"Morning, Orla. Just your regular coffee?"

"Please."

I made her coffee, my hands steadier than I'd expected. Behind me, the envelope with the photograph waited. In the café, Iris read something on her phone. The other customers went about their business, unaware that they were about to witness a confession.

From the viewing room, I heard a soft chirp. Sage, curious about the tension in the air but staying safely with Rocky. I caught a glimpse of her through the doorway, sitting alert beside her protector, watching everything with those intelligent eyes.

I slid Orla's coffee across the counter. "I was going through the box Hazel left me. The one her niece gave me. There were a lot of old things in there. Photos, journals, mementos."

Orla's expression didn't change, but something flickered in her eyes. Interest. Wariness. "I see."

"One of the photographs had a name on the back. Moira Weston. I thought... well, Weston is your last name. I thought maybe you were related. That maybe you'd want the photo."

"Moira." Orla's voice was carefully neutral. "That was my sister. She died a long time ago."

"I'm so sorry." I reached behind the counter and pulled out the envelope. "If this is too painful, I understand. But I thought you should have it. A piece of your sister to remember her by."

I held out the envelope, and after a moment's hesitation, Orla took it.

She opened it slowly, pulling out the photograph. For a long moment, she just stared at it. At her sister's face, frozen in time, proud and powerful and alive.

Then her fingers made contact with the image itself, and everything changed.

Orla's eyes glazed slightly. Her breathing deepened. When she spoke, her voice was distant, almost dreamlike, but filled with satisfaction.

"She was beautiful, wasn't she? My sister. So strong. So powerful." Orla stroked the photograph gently. "Hazel Blaine killed her. Did you know that?"

My heart hammered, but I kept my voice steady. "Hazel killed your sister?"

"Forty years ago. Shot her during a family dispute. A feud between our families that had been going on for years." The translation spell was working. Orla was saying coven war, but the words that came out were family dispute, feud. "Hazel murdered my sister in cold blood and ran. Changed her name. Hid for decades."

Iris's head came up sharply. I could see her hand moving to her phone, likely starting a recording.

"But you found her," I said quietly.

"I found her." Orla smiled, still staring at the photograph. "It took me forty years, but I found her. Here, in this ridiculous little town. Working in her flower shop, pretending to be a kind old lady. Pretending she hadn't destroyed my family."

"What did you do?" My voice was barely a whisper.

"I planned. I watched. I learned her routines." Orla's words came faster now, eager, proud. "I got a job three blocks away so I could see her regularly. She came into the yarn shop sometimes. We talked. She had no idea who I was. No idea that Moira's sister was standing right in front of her."

Several customers had stopped talking, tuning into our conversation. Mabel's sharp eyes were locked on Orla. Jasper had set down his coffee. Felix was openly staring.

"And then?" I prompted.

"And then I killed her." Orla said it simply, matter-of-factly. "I made a poison from plants. Herbs and flowers, things I'd learned about from our family traditions. Slipped it into tea I brought her. I told her I wanted to learn about flowers, asked if she'd share some tips. She invited me to her apartment after the shops closed."

My hands gripped the counter. Hazel had let Orla into her home. Had trusted her.

"The poison worked slowly. Made her disoriented, dizzy. I waited until she tried to go down to her shop, until she was in that alley. Then I confronted her. I told her who I was, and told her this was for Moira." Orla's smile was cold. "She said 'You're making a terrible mistake.' Those were her last words before she fell. The poison did the rest."

"And you just left her there," I said, my voice hard.

"I left her there. Went home. Waited for someone to find her." Orla finally looked up from the photograph, meeting my eyes. "It was perfect. Forty years of patience, and I finally got my revenge. Finally, I made things right for my sister."

"But you didn't stop there," I said, my heart pounding. "Did you?"

"No." Orla's voice was still distant, still under the spell's influence. "I knew she must have had some evidence in her apartment. Something that could connect me to Moira. I had to find it." Her fingers stroked the photograph again. "I broke in a few nights ago. Searched everywhere. But it was gone. And here you had it all along."

She smiled, almost admiringly. "I knew you would figure it out eventually. You needed to stop. So, I left you a note. A warning." Her expression turned cold. "That awful, selfish Trish Lawrence. She was so easy to frame. Her perfume, her rivalry with Hazel. I just sprayed some of her signature scent on the paper and slipped it under your door. If you'd kept investigating, everyone would have suspected her, not me."

"Orla Weston." Iris's voice cut through the café, sharp and authoritative. She was on her feet, hand on her gun. "You're under arrest for the murder of Hazel Blaine."

Orla blinked, the dreamy quality leaving her eyes. She looked around the café, at Iris approaching, at the customers staring, at me behind the counter.

"What?" She looked down at the photograph in her hands. "What did I... did I just..."

"You confessed to poisoning Hazel Blaine and causing her death." Iris was behind her now, pulling out handcuffs. "You have the right to remain silent. Anything you say can and will be used against you in a court of law."

"No. No, I didn't mean..." Orla tried to step back, but Iris had her wrist. "That's not... I wouldn't have said..."

"But you did say it." Iris's voice was grim. "In front of multiple witnesses. And I recorded every word."

The handcuffs clicked into place, and Orla's face went pale. "How did you... what did you do to me?"

"Nothing." I met her eyes directly. "I just gave you a photograph of your sister. That's all."

Orla stared at me, and for just a moment, I saw understanding dawn. She'd felt something when she touched the photo. Had felt the compulsion take hold. And now she knew.

"You're..." she started, but Iris was already leading her toward the door.

"Deputy Thorne is outside," Iris called over her shoulder to me. "He'll need statements from everyone who was here. Don't let anyone leave."

The door closed behind them, and the café erupted in chaos. Everyone talking at once, demanding to know what just happened, why Orla had confessed, how I'd known.

I couldn't answer. I could only stand behind my counter, staring at the empty space where Orla had been, while five cats watched me with understanding in their eyes. Sage had crept to the doorway of the viewing room, peering out with wide eyes, Rocky right beside her.

"You're safe," Rocky murmured to her. "The bad person is gone now."

It was done.

Hazel's killer was in custody.

Justice, finally, for the woman who'd given me a year of peace and protection.

"You did it," Poppy said softly.

"We did it," I corrected. "All of us. And Hazel. And Maeve."

The photograph of Moira Weston lay on the counter where Orla had dropped it. I picked it up carefully, feeling the residual magic still clinging to it. The spell had worked perfectly. Orla had confessed to everything, and thanks to the translation layer, no one had heard anything about magic or witches or coven wars.

They'd just heard a woman admit to forty years of planning and a cold-blooded murder.

Deputy Thorne came in moments later, notebook in hand, and began taking statements. Iris had heard everything. Mabel had heard everything. Jasper, Felix, the other early morning customers, they'd all heard Orla's confession.

There was no way she could take it back. No way she could claim she'd been coerced or confused. She'd spoken clearly, deliberately, in front of too many witnesses.

It was over.

When Thorne finally finished with me and left, when the last customer had given their statement and departed, I locked the door and flipped the sign to Closed.

Then I climbed the stairs to my apartment and called Maeve.

"She confessed," I said when she answered. "Everything. The poison, the confrontation, all of it. Iris arrested her."

"Good." Maeve's voice was satisfied. "The spell worked exactly as it should. Orla never knew what hit her."

"Thank you. For everything. For helping me. For keeping your promise to Hazel."

"Thank Hazel. She's the one who made sure you wouldn't be alone." Maeve paused. "How do you feel?"

How did I feel? Relieved. Exhausted. Grief-stricken that it was over, but Hazel was still gone. Grateful that justice had been served. Terrified of what I'd done, the magic I'd used, the line I'd crossed.

"I don't know," I admitted. "Ask me again tomorrow."

"Fair enough. Get some rest, Alexis. You've earned it."

I ended the call and sank onto my couch. The cats arranged themselves around me, their warm weight grounding me. Sage climbed into my lap, purring softly, and I stroked her gray fur.

"Is it really over?" Millie asked.

"It's really over."

"What happens now?" Rocky wondered, settling beside Sage protectively.

Now. What happened now? Orla would be tried for murder. Would go to prison. Would spend the rest of her life paying for what she'd done to Hazel. The investigation would close. Life in Larkspur Valley would go back to normal.

Except nothing would ever be normal again. Because I'd used magic openly, even if no one knew it. Because I'd revealed myself to Maeve, had formed an alliance with another magical person. Because I'd stopped hiding, stopped running, and had fought back.

Because I was different now. Changed. No longer the scared witch who'd arrived in Larkspur Valley a year ago.

"Now," I said finally, "we figure out how to live in a world without Hazel. And we make sure her sacrifice wasn't in vain."

Outside my window, Larkspur Valley went about its day. Shops opened, people walked down Main Street, life continued.

But for me, everything had changed.

I was no longer alone. No longer completely hidden. No longer quite so afraid.

Hazel had given me that. Had given me a year of safety, had died protecting me, and had left me the tools I needed to catch her killer and find my place in this strange, magical town.

It wasn't the ending I'd wanted. Hazel should still be alive. We should have had years to be honest with each other, to share our magic, to be friends in truth instead of in secret.

But it was the ending we had. And I would honor it.

For Hazel. For myself. For the witch I was finally becoming.

The woman who didn't run anymore.

The woman who fought back.

The woman who'd found home.

Chapter Twenty-Two

Two weeks after Orla's arrest, life in Larkspur Valley had settled into something that resembled normal.

Orla was in county jail awaiting trial. Iris had closed Hazel's case with the satisfaction of a job well done, even if she still occasionally gave me thoughtful looks like she couldn't quite figure out how I'd known to have Orla come in that morning. The town had moved on to other gossip: Cordelia's yarn shop was hiring someone new, Trish Lawrence had apparently given up on acquiring the flower shop, and Carla had returned to wherever she'd come from, still bitter about the will but no longer actively contesting it.

And I was... different. Changed in ways I was still trying to understand.

Tuesday morning, I opened the café at eight as usual. Mabel came in at her regular time, ordered her Lavender Dreams tea, and settled at her table with her crossword puzzle. Everything exactly as it had been for the past year.

Except Hazel wasn't two doors down at her flower shop. Would never be two doors down again.

"You're doing that thing again," Poppy observed from her perch near the window.

"What thing?"

"The sad face thing. Where you stare at nothing and look like you're about to cry."

"I'm not about to cry." But my throat was tight.

"You miss her," Millie said softly from behind her fern. "We all do."

I did miss her. Every day. Every time I made chamomile tea. Every time I looked down Main Street toward where her shop sat dark and empty. Every time I remembered that I'd wasted a year of potential honesty with her because I'd been too afraid to trust.

But something else had changed too. Something harder to define.

I wasn't quite as alone as I'd been before.

In the viewing room, Sage was playing with Rocky, pouncing on his twitching tail with the exuberance of a healthy kitten. She'd grown noticeably in the past two weeks, her gray coat glossy, her movements confident. No more fragile wobbles, no more uncertainty. Just a normal, happy kitten learning the world from her devoted mentor.

Thursday evening, I closed the café at six and walked three blocks to Cordelia's Yarn Haven for the crochet circle. My terrible lumpy square had grown into a slightly less terrible rectangle, and I was actually starting to understand the rhythm of the stitches.

"Alexis!" Cordelia greeted me warmly. "So glad you're still coming. After everything that happened with Orla, I worried you might stop."

"No. I like it here." And surprisingly, I meant it.

The circle had a new member, a younger woman named Vera who'd just moved to town. We made introductions, and I found myself answering her questions about the café, about Larkspur Valley, about settling into a new place.

"It takes time," I told her. "But it's a good town. Good people."

"Even with the murder?" Vera asked, then immediately looked embarrassed. "Sorry. That was tactless."

"It's okay. Yes, even with that." I picked up my crochet project. "Bad things happen everywhere. What matters is how people respond. And this town responded by catching the person responsible. By making sure justice was served."

"That's a good way to look at it." Vera settled into her chair with her own project, a simple scarf in cheerful yellow. "I'm trying to make friends, get involved. It's hard being new."

"I know." And I did. A year ago, I'd been exactly where she was. New, scared, hiding. "But it gets easier. You find your people. Find your place."

We worked in comfortable silence for a while, the only sounds the soft click of hooks and the murmur of conversation from the other women. Pearl was telling Dorothy about a new cookbook. Beatrice was helping Mabel with a tricky pattern. Cordelia moved between us all, offering tea and encouragement.

This was community. This was connection. This was what I'd been running from for so long because I thought I couldn't have it while hiding what I was.

But maybe I'd been wrong. Maybe I could have both, carefully balanced. Maybe I could be part of this town, part of these people's lives, without revealing everything. Maybe the secret was knowing which parts to share and which to protect.

After the circle, I walked home slowly, enjoying the crisp November air. The town was settling into evening routines, lights glowing warm in windows, the smell of dinner cooking wafting from houses. Families gathering. People living their ordinary, extraordinary lives.

And I was part of it now. Not just an observer, not just someone passing through. Part of the fabric of Larkspur Valley, woven in through coffee and conversation and yes, through tragedy and justice too.

Upstairs in my apartment, all five cats were waiting. Sage had claimed a spot on the couch beside Poppy, grooming her face with tiny paws. Rocky watched her with that same protective devotion he'd shown since the day she'd arrived, but there was pride there now too. Pride in how strong she'd become.

"How was the yarn circle?" Poppy asked.

"Good. There's a new woman, Vera. She just moved here. I gave her advice about settling in."

"Look at you," Gus said from his armchair. "Giving advice to newcomers. When did you become the welcoming committee?"

"When I stopped being the newcomer, I guess."

I made dinner, the cats gathering around while I cooked. Sage had graduated to eating regular meals with the others now, twice daily servings of wet and dry food mixed together. She attacked her bowl with enthusiasm, no longer needing careful monitoring or special portions.

"She's doing well," I commented to Rocky.

"She is." He watched Sage eat with obvious satisfaction. "She's strong now. Brave. Still learning but not scared anymore."

"You taught her that."

"We all taught her that." Rocky's gaze swept the room, including all of us in his assessment. "She knows she's safe here. That we're family."

Family. That word again. The one that used to terrify me, remind me of what I'd lost when I left the coven. But this family was different. This family was chosen, not assigned. This family accepted secrets and differences and the things we couldn't explain.

This family was mine.

Friday afternoon, Lionel stopped by the café during the slow period between lunch and evening rush.

"Hey," he said, that warm smile already in place. "Wanted to check in. See how you're doing after everything."

"I'm okay. Better than okay, actually."

"Yeah?" He leaned against the counter. "You seem different. More settled, maybe. You seemed to really enjoy yourself at game night last week."

"I did." The memory brought a genuine smile. "It was good to just... be normal for a few hours."

"Well, the gang's been asking if you're coming back." His smile widened. "Apparently you're better at strategy games than you let on."

"I might have gotten lucky."

"Luck doesn't win three rounds in a row." He laughed. "But seriously, tonight? We're doing a different game this time. Something about building civilizations. Very nerdy. You should come."

A month ago, I would have made an excuse. Would have protected my isolation like it was the only thing keeping me safe.

But I wasn't that person anymore.

"I'll be there," I said.

His surprise was evident. "Really?"

"Really. I might be terrible at it, but I'll be there."

"You won't be terrible. And even if you are, that's half the fun." He pushed off the counter. "I should get back to the shop. But Alexis? I'm glad you're staying. Glad you're letting yourself be part of things."

After he left, I stood behind my counter and looked around The Cozy Purrch. My café. My space. My contribution to this town.

The windows let in afternoon light. The pastry case held Flo's baked goods. The chairs and tables waited for customers who'd become familiar faces, familiar orders, familiar conversations.

And behind the counter, visible through the archway, five cats lounged in their viewing room. Poppy on her high perch, Gus in his favorite bed, Millie behind her protective fern, Rocky on the cat tree, and Sage beside him, learning to be confident from his example.

My found family.

This was what Hazel had protected. This space, this life, this chance at belonging. She'd died so I could have it, so I could stop running and start living.

And I wouldn't waste that gift.

The bell chimed. Dr. Colton Dover walked in, his jacket damp from a light drizzle that had started falling.

"Afternoon," he said. "Thought I'd stop by, check on my favorite patient. How's Sage doing?"

"See for yourself." I gestured to the viewing room, where Sage was currently wrestling with a toy mouse while Rocky watched approvingly.

Colton peered through the archway, and his expression softened. "Would you look at that. She's thriving. I had my doubts those first few days, but she's proven me wrong."

"She's a fighter."

"Like her person." He turned back to me. "You saved her life, you know. Most people wouldn't have taken that chance."

"Most people don't talk to cats."

The words slipped out before I could stop them, and I froze. But Colton just laughed.

"True enough. But even without understanding them, you knew she needed help and you provided it. That says something about who you are." He paused, a slight smile playing at his lips. "You know, you surprised everyone at game night last week. I don't think any of us expected you to be quite so ruthless at strategy."

"I wasn't ruthless."

"You absolutely were. Lionel's still trying to figure out how you managed to cut off his supply chain in round two." His smile widened. "It was impressive. And it was good to see you enjoying yourself."

"It was good to be there." And I meant it.

"Well, we're all hoping you'll come back." He ordered a chai latte. "For what it's worth, it's good to see you settling in. Becoming part of the community. This town's better with you in it."

After he left, I watched him go through the window, then turned back to my café. My life. My home.

Because I'd stopped running, even if I was still hiding.

Because I was building something here. Something real. Something worth protecting.

The day passed in its usual rhythm. Coffee and tea and conversation. Customers coming and going. The cats lounging in their various spots, the adoptable ones charming visitors while my five permanent residents watched everything with knowing eyes.

Around four o'clock, I felt it.

A chill that had nothing to do with the temperature. A shift in the air that made my skin prickle. A sense of something approaching, something familiar and dangerous and inevitable.

The cats felt it too. All five of them went still, ears forward, attention focused on the door.

"What is it?" I asked quietly, my hand gripping the counter.

"Something's coming," Poppy said, her voice tight. "Something magical."

My heart hammered. The coven. They'd found me. After all this time, after a year of safety, they'd finally tracked me down. Orla's arrival hadn't been about me at all, but now my own past was catching up.

The bell above the door chimed.

And a woman walked in.

She was my age, maybe a year or two older, with dark hair pulled back in a braid and warm brown eyes that I recognized immediately despite the years that had passed. She wore travel-worn clothes and carried a small backpack, and when her gaze found mine across the café, her entire face lit up with relief and joy.

"Alexis," she breathed. "Finally. I've found you."

The world tilted.

Because I knew that voice. Knew that face. Knew that presence.

Lily.

My best friend from the coven. The one person I'd trusted completely before I'd run. The one person I'd left behind without explanation, without goodbye, because staying meant putting her in danger.

And now she was here, standing in my café in Larkspur Valley, looking at me like I was a miracle.

"Lily," I whispered.

She crossed the café in seconds and pulled me into a hug so tightly I could barely breathe. She smelled like rain and herbs and home, and despite the fear coursing through me, despite the thousand questions screaming in my head, I hugged her back.

"I've been looking everywhere," she said into my shoulder. "For months. I followed rumors and whispers and hints of magic, and it finally led me here. To you."

THE END

Before you go: If you loved Purr-colated Poison, be sure to visit my website to sign up for my newsletter (if you haven't already) and to stay up to date on new releases and other bookish things.

When signing up, you will receive **either a prequel from my Medium with a Heart series or a recipe that goes along with my Alphabet Soup Series. Your choice!**

Also, check out my other books! You can find links on my website.

www.ejwheltonwrites.com

Author note:

This story came together really quickly in my mind. Alexis just shouted out her story to me and then the cats, oh the cats, they were so loud. I could see and hear them all as I typed out this beauty.

I hope you enjoyed it. A fun, whimsical story about being different, or at least that's how I see it. Plus, did I mention the cats?

Yes, I have become a crazy cat lady and I make no apologies about that. Currently, just two, but I would love one more. Someday.

Anyway, I hope you will stick with me as we follow Alexis and the cats in their coming adventures.

www.ejwheltonwrites.com

www.ingramcontent.com/pod-product-compliance
Lightning Source LLC
Chambersburg PA
CBHW021656070726
47591CB00017B/369